SOMETHING'S BURNING

SOMETHING'S BURNING

A collection of 22 strike anywhere short stories.

JANET TRULL

WINNIPEG

Something's Burning

This book is a work of fiction. Names, characters, businesses, organizations, places, events, andincidents either are the product of the author's imagination or are used fictitiously.

Copyright © 2022 Janet Trull

Design and layout by Matthew Stevens and M. C. Joudrey.

Published by At Bay Press November 2022.

All rights reserved. The use of any part of this publication, reproduced, transmitted in any form or by any means electronic, mechanical, photocopying, recording or otherwise, or stored in a retrieval system without prior written consent of the publisher or in the case of photocopying or other reprographic copying, license from the Canadian Copyright Licensing Agency-is an infringement of the copyright law.

No portion of this work may be reproduced without express written permission from At Bay Press.

Library and Archives Canada cataloguing in publication is available upon request.

ISBN 978-1-988168-68-5

Printed and bound in Canada.

This book is printed on acid free paper that is 100% recycled ancient forest friendly (100% post-consumer recycled).

First Edition

10 9 8 7 6 5 4 3 2 1

atbaypress.com

To Roger

my hearth and my home

CONTENTS

TINDER
Vigilance 1
Just a Farm Girl 11
Snow Day 39
Swimming Free 53
The Ark 67

SPARK
The Nook 81
Homecoming 123
Research 133
Witness 143
In The Heyday 157

INFERNO
Hope 171
Hitchhiker 193
Anna's Last Day 205
The Pastor 219
The Promise Land 227
Correctional Services 239

COALS
Thin Ice 255
A Stubborn Muscle 267
The Downer 279
The Emperor's Clothes 291
Something's Burning 301
Games of Wrath 311

TINDER

A curl of birchbark. Some dry grass. Cattail fluff. You cannot start a story without an idea, a conversation, an experience.

Vigilance

Gerda never misses a Remembrance Day ceremony. Years ago, she insisted her children come with her. But the world cannot pause on November 11th anymore. She would be alone except that her granddaughter, Storm, got herself expelled from high school and her parents decided that accompanying Oma to the cenotaph would be an appropriate punishment. Storm is a serious girl with a head full of dark thoughts. She does not smirk, as some youngsters might, as the last of the stooped veterans shuffle by with their wreaths.

Gerda is close enough to Warren Van den Berg to notice dandruff on the faded blue-grey serge of his collar. The uniform was worn by a 140-pound boy, and that boy swelled up into a man who could only look nostalgically at the jacket hanging in his cedar closet. Now it fits once again. Warren grew up in the Netherlands, not far from Gerda's home village. When she arrived in this country without knowing a word of English, Warren gave her and her husband a job on his mushroom farm and watched over them like a kindly uncle.

The years have indeed condemned him, but Warren Van den Berg never wearies of this commitment to lost brethren. He nods as he pushes his walker past her, and Gerda feels Storm's elbow nudge hers. She is gratified to think her granddaughter is touched by the service, until she realizes that the girl is just checking her phone.

In 1944, Gerda was seven years old. She lived in Nieuwlande with her parents and twelve siblings. Twelve, ranging in age from two to twenty. Her oldest sister, Lotte, lived with them, along with her own two children. Lotte's husband joined the resistance and disappeared. They all shared a small country house with a barn attached, and only God knows how they managed to fit around the dinner table, but they did, crammed together on two long benches. Her father made some deal with the Germans that no one in the family ever spoke of. Gerda believes he was supplying German officers with food. They went hungry themselves in those grey months before the liberation.

The cast iron soup pot that hung in the hearth never went cold, but it was filled with the thinnest soup. Tulip bulb soup, bitter and gritty, and served with heavy helpings of irony. The bulbs had once fetched a fortune on the export market, 2500 florins apiece back in the seventeenth century when tulips were considered exotic, and now the Dutch choked them down to keep from starving. The world-renowned bulbs, the pride of a nation, were nothing more than humble pie.

After the war was over and they had immigrated to Canada, the Dutch were sometimes accused of being unfriendly, of keeping themselves to themselves, and Gerda blamed it on the bitter soup. Her mouth was twisted forever in an angry sort of scowl.

The only thing that made the war years bearable was routine. Manners. Order. Cleanliness. Godliness. Her mother dished out the soup into delft pottery bowls as if it was a hearty stew that the children ought to be grateful for. Her father intoned long and solemn prayers before they ate. They followed their routines even though they could hardly sit up straight, they were so weak.

Routines, Gerda realizes now, probably saved them. Setting the table, washing the bowls, boiling the weed tea, making the beds, airing the bedding, beating the rugs, sweeping the floor, scrubbing the counter, fetching water, and digging the stinking tulip bulbs out of the south garden. Gerda's numb fingertips were stained with that black soil.

The winter of 1944 was endlessly bleak and cruelly cold. Gerda remembers wanting to climb into her mother's warm lap. But that place was taken by her little brother, Simon, a sickly toddler with a wracking cough that kept the household awake at all hours. She was glad when it stopped. Her mother went to bed and wept and wept. Lotte had to see to the routines, but Gerda crept under the covers with her grieving mother and the warmth returned to her hands and feet, and she did not feel sad.

Many years later, Gerda told the story in a way that

elicited much empathy from listeners. Whenever the theme of hardship arose, Gerda would tell about the family's experiences at the hands of the Nazi devils, and especially about the sweet child who died.

"He starved to death," she said. "My mother never recovered."

Gerda named her second son Simon in remembrance. A mistake, because that boy inherited the bad chest, and his health became one of her life's burdens until he ran off at eighteen to Arizona where the climate suited him. He married an American woman with different values and Gerda hasn't spoken to him in years. All her energy goes to the seven children, twelve grandchildren and four great grandchildren that have stayed nearby.

Vigilance is a good characteristic for a parent. There are a lot of things that can happen to a child when you're not paying attention. When Gerda had young children, and she raised eight of them more or less successfully, vigilance resulted in a lot of playpen time. Mothers of her generation were well aware of all the dangers lurking in the world. Stairs and electrical outlets and hot stoves. So, when Gerda needed to throw in a load of laundry or answer the phone (a device that was wired to the wall in the kitchen) she'd plunk her kids in a wooden playpen with some stacking blocks. Mommy's busy. End of story.

Now, I'm not telling you that the babies always wanted to go in the playpen. Sometimes they complained. That's when Mommy turned the radio up loud. Gerda was a student of classical music. Her children grew up listening to Bach,

Beethoven and Handel. German composers. She forgave them their nationality. The Dutch and German people share many characteristics, physical and otherwise. Gerda is a German name, in fact, she was named for a German grandmother. European borders are more fluid than people think.

Gerda married a boy from her village. His name was Dick. They left the Netherlands for Canada where they found farm work alongside other Dutch immigrants. When the babies came, Gerda brought her babies home from the hospital in a cute little woven basket in the back seat. Car seats were coming on the market, but there wasn't much regulation. The driver was always the father. Dutch mothers didn't drive much, because women drivers were likely to put the car in the ditch or bump into someone in the parking lot. The Dutch were committed patriarchs.

Things have changed. No more climbing into the front seat to sit in between Mommy and Daddy when you are poking your sister. No more lounging in the wayback seat of the station wagon with a book and a bag of corn chips.

Gerda raised her children in the strict way she was raised. Her children understood that this was just part of the deal. They wore the clothes that were given to them, patched and repaired hand-me-downs perhaps, but always clean and ironed. They did not expect anything except brisk efficiency from Gerda. They learned to amuse themselves until they could be trusted to wander about without cracking their heads open or setting the house on fire.

As children grew out of the playpen, more came along to fill it. The playpen was a godsend for Gerda. Occasionally, there would be a howl. A toddler would bonk a baby. Or maybe a toddler would fool around with the metal latch and get his finger pinched. Sometimes a toddler, in his bid for escape, would stick his head through the too-far-apart bars. Well, he only did that a few times, because he learned, didn't he, that it was not worth the pain of getting his ears almost ripped off when Mommy yanked his head back through the tight space. And if you have interrupted Mommy from an important task, like beating egg whites, which is a delicate and crucial step in making the dessert for Daddy's supper, you might even get a spank for good measure. Were children better behaved in those days? Heavens, yes! They learned their lessons.

One of Gerda's babies, she doesn't recall if it was John or Luke, chewed the nipple right off his sippy cup and choked on it. Gerda didn't even realize what had happened until she'd finished making the beds and found him in a pool of vomit with rubber fragments mixed in. That could have ended badly, but it didn't. He was fine. No spanking that day.

Gerda's children do not raise their babies the same way. First of all, her younger children and her grandchildren wait until they are old enough to be grandparents to get into the parenting game. Then, they laugh hysterically at all the ancient baby paraphernalia that Gerda has preserved in the fruit cellar.

"Take those old death traps to the dump," they tell her. The crib, the playpen, the big, beautiful Perego pram with only a little rust on the wheels. "They are antiques."

"What about all the lovely items in the cedar chest?" Gerda says. She sewed and knitted them herself.

"Forget it, Mother," they tell her. "Bumper pads and

blankets cause suffocation."

Gerda tries to argue. Won't Baby be cold? Won't Baby be uncomfortable? But it is hard to argue with scientific documentation.

"The research is clear, Mother. Incidents of crib death have decreased dramatically since babies have been bedded without all those little hand-knit covers. Nothing goes in the crib except Baby, flat on his back."

Gerda flouts these rules time and again and she is punished. She is not allowed unsupervised visits to the grandchildren, which she can't help but feel resentful about. She sees that her children are exhausting themselves over one solitary little creature. They carry the monitor around with them. It buzzes when Baby rolls over or burps, events that require immediate responses. Mommy and Daddy worked hard to get this baby and they will not let anything bad happen.

"This is impossible," Gerda tells them. "Your sleepless supervision is taking a toll on your own health. Leave Baby alone so he can learn how to soothe himself. Can't you see he is desperate to sleep on his tummy?"

"Not allowed," the middle-aged parents say. Gerda goes home and looks forward to the day when she will be trusted to babysit. Perhaps when the child is two?

Gerda wants to pick up her four-year-old granddaughter and take her to the park, but the used car seat she purchased is not safe. The son-in-law checks the make and model online.

"Yes," he says. "Just as I thought. Obsolete."

"Surely, at four years of age, the child can sit in the backseat with a seatbelt?"

"Surely, you are kidding," he says. "Who would dare to put a child at risk just to save a few hundred bucks?"

"But can't you see that all this vigilance is a scam?" Gerda asks.

"Why take the chance?" he says.

At the beach one day, long ago, Gerda was not vigilant. She was reading a magazine while her kids played in shallow water. But when she looked up, three-year-old Johnny was missing. His sisters didn't know where he was. That's when she noticed that the water was murky, so murky she couldn't see her feet when she waded in to look for him. She surveyed the waterfront in panic. Other families were oblivious, digging sandcastles, eating their picnics. Gerda ran back to the blanket. She ran up to the port-a-potty and opened the door. She should have screamed for help, but something made her delay the public scrutiny.

Then, as if pulled from the water by a guardian angel, Johnny's little head popped up. He'd been floating below the surface, not realizing that he could touch the bottom. Gerda ran and grabbed him and hugged him, showing some uncommon affection.

"I almost drowned," he said.

Nobody can be vigilant all the time. Gerda knows this. All the government safety regulations in the world can't anticipate that one minute when your attention is elsewhere. Her children are consumed with careers and extra-marital relationships while her grandchildren wallow in despair. One granddaughter does not eat. One eats too much. One never leaves the house. The boys struggle, too. One is being home-schooled because of anti-social behaviour. The oldest, her favourite, joined a cult and drinks his own urine.

"He is sick," her husband says.

"No," she says. But she isn't sure.

Gerda hosts Christmas dinner and Thanksgiving and birthdays. Her home is not big, but she knows how to prepare dinner for a crowd. What's the big deal? A turkey, a ham, a bag of potatoes. It is not that difficult. But her daughters work, and the thought of hosting a family event has them calling the caterers and pulling out their credit cards. Gerda puts her foot down. There will be no take-out for family dinners as long as she is alive. The children and grandchildren arrive and make fun of her shag carpet and her Royal Doulton collection, but no one else, not one of the daughters or daughters-in-law, will step up and say, "Come to our place, next time."

Her third-oldest granddaughter, Lisa, has beautiful teeth and she never got poked in the eye. She wore her mouthguard and goggles to play badminton, she got a scholarship to U of T, and she followed all the rules. Then she got cancer. Her parents are angry. It is unfair. But they weren't listening when Gerda told them about fair. She is the one who takes Lisa to chemotherapy and sits with her during the three hours that it takes for the cocktail to drip into her system. Poison so vile that the nurse wears a HAZMAT suit to mix the concoction. Gerda wasn't allowed to take Lisa to the park, but now she is trusted to take this thirty-year-old woman to the cancer clinic.

Together they sit and do the crossword and Gerda reads aloud from Readers Digest, a story about the healing qualities of nature. The writer recommends a walk in the woods.

Gerda worries about her great-grandchildren, a group of anxious teens and young adults who never seem to have any fun. They have their sights set on administration jobs that they have no experience or competence for. Boring positions with benefits. They will never marry. They will never have children of their own. Gerda longs for the olden days. She really believes that things were better when she grew up. Eating tulip bulbs was better than eating fentanyl. Wearing patched overalls and darned socks was better than spending good money on ripped jeans. Starving to death because there was no food was better than starving to death because of some mistaken ideal of being thin.

A war, she thinks, might be just the thing.

Just A Farm Girl

Carol lives on a farm. There were eras when farm life was romanticized. Farmers were once appreciated and admired. But it is 1972. Them times are gone, Grandpa says.

Farming is hard work. Lots of difficult things conspire to ruin your crops. Disease, bugs, weather. Animals need cleaning, feeding, breeding and tending. There are all kinds of shit on a farm. Dog shit, cat shit, horse shit, chicken shit, cow shit. You name it, Carol steps in it. The chores are seasonal. Right now, spring is the worst. Her dad is building an irrigation system for the back forty, and all day Sunday she worked alongside him digging ditches and laying pipe.

Monday morning, the bus ride will be quiet. Every student on this route has been up before dawn, mucking out stables or some such chore. They have eaten fresh eggs or hot oatmeal in silent kitchens. Farm kitchens are busy, but short on conversation.

Carol grabs her black lunch box. No pizza or fries with gravy in the cafeteria for her. She traipses down the gravel laneway to wait in a wind-tilted weather shelter by the road, walking through as many puddles as possible to get the manure off her boots so some jock in math class won't point at them and exclaim to the entire class that somebody reeks. In the weather shelter, she and her brothers take their sandwiches and apples out of their lunch pails and shove them in their backpacks. She has explained to her grandmother, who makes the lunches, that nobody in high school brings a lunch pail anymore, but it is a waste of time. They pick up the old metal relics at the end of the day and return them to the kitchen.

Her brothers board the bus ahead of her and go all the way to the back seat. Eddie the bus driver greets Carol. "Morning Sunshine," he says, without taking the cigarette out of his mouth. There is a big 'No Smoking' poster over the windshield, but Eddie doesn't pay any attention, and no one on this bus cares if he smokes. The last driver, Marnie Bull, couldn't drive worth a crap. She put them in the ditch twice. Eddie can drive. Farm kids don't care about rules in the world at large. They follow common sense.

The Dutch Line kids slump in their bus seats and enjoy the respite of simply sitting. There are no popular people on the bus. No social committee girls with plans to decorate the gym for the spring prom. No student council reps. The Zimmerman boys, the closest thing this bus route has to celebrities, are football players, not stars, but not outcasts. They won't be dating cheerleaders, let's just say that much.

Under the radar is the best this bunch can hope for. Family

and farm come first. Before fashion. Before fads. Before music or cars or pep rallies. Their expectations are mostly in line with their parents' strict codes. Parents that survived horrendous childhoods in the shadowy privations of World War II Europe. They grew up hungry and fearful and suspicious of neighbours. Their trust was limited to immediate family, and sometimes, even then, they were betrayed to authorities for hoarding something in a root cellar or hiding someone under the floorboards. These were parents who did not care if their kids had zits or crooked teeth or pigeon toes. Play the hand you were dealt, they would say if anyone dared complain, which they never did.

Carol's father wore canvas overalls and a canvas jacket and a greasy peaked cap. His face was set in a study of determination with a lipless mouth that made him seem eternally joyless. Carol's mother never sat down. There was cooking and cleaning and laundry. They had an old wringer washing machine and no dryer, so clothes were hung on the line in all weather, sheets and towels and long johns freezing solid on winter days. Tired was the only word Carol could come up with to describe her mother. She never troubled her with extra worries, like menstrual cramps or cruel comments from other girls at school or the lump in her right breast. From a young age, she addressed her problems in a pragmatic way. On Saturdays, she worked at the pharmacy in town to pay for personal items that her mother considered wasteful like tampons, deodorant and shampoo that smelled nice. She was no romantic, but she did have a crush on Carl. The older of the Zimmerman brothers. And since they started grade twelve, Carl had been sitting next to her on the bus. Carl likes the smell of Herbal Essences Shampoo. He likes the flowers she embroidered on her jeans. When she noticed the rip in his jacket, Carol offered to sew a patch on it for him.

"Oh ya? You could do that? I tore it on the barbed wire back near the crick."

"Sure. I'll bring thread and stuff tomorrow. It'll only take about ten minutes."

"Cool. Thanks."

Carol read an article in Seventeen magazine. Ten things boys like to watch girls do. Brush their hair, suntan on the beach, cook, cry over sad movies. Stuff like that. And sew. Sew on a button, the article suggested. But a patch would have to do.

It worked. Carl asked Carol to come over to his place Friday night. His parents were going out and his brothers were having a party. He would pick her up around eight.

It was chilly for May, and damp, but the boys had a big bonfire going and Carl had balanced his stereo speakers, so they were blasting Pink Floyd out his bedroom window. There were more people than Carol expected. Some football team guys and their girlfriends. Townies. A bunch of Vissers from up the road. They all looked alike. Tall. Awkwardly tall. Too tall to talk to anyone but each other. And there were some big farm boys that Carl introduced as his cousins from Tillsonburg who were drinking rye and cokes and eating potato chips out of a family-size bag.

"Tobacco farmers," Carl said with a roll of his eyes when they did not respond to the introduction. "Want a beer? Or wine? Or there's some cider in the cooler over by the barn."

"Cider sounds good," she said.

Carl opened a bottle of cider for her, using the buckle on his belt. She drank it fast. They stood by the fire for a bit, listening to a girl talking about how you cannot go straight to teachers' college after grade thirteen anymore. You have to go to university first. The girl went on and on, waving her hands. Carl soon grabbed Carol's arm and asked her; did she want a tour of his house?

She said she did.

"Man, that girl thinks a lot of herself," he said, guiding Carol straight upstairs to his bedroom where they made out on Carl's bed for a while. Carol had never kissed a boy before, and she was alarmed to find Carl's big tongue halfway down her throat and his bulging crotch rubbing up and down her thigh while all the lectures from health class were flashing before her eyes.

"Hang on," she said.

"What?"

"I could use another drink," she said.

"I'll get you one. Wait here."

"No. I'm coming too."

Carl looked at her in a way that made her feel like a cocktease. Sewing that patch on his jacket worked too well, she thought. She was saved from further explanations by a knock on the door and the oldest Zimmerman brother yelling to change the album. The crowd was getting sick of Pink Floyd. So, Carl tucked his shirt in, put a Led Zeppelin album on the turntable and Carol followed him down the back stairway, not to heaven as the song said, but to the kitchen.

It was an old house. With dark green linoleum on the kitchen floor that curled up around the edges, a stained sink, a pile of mail and newspapers on the counter and an old black phone hanging on the wall. A pot of tulips wilted on the square table under harsh overhead fluorescent lights. Carol tried to remember the last time she saw Mrs. Zimmerman, probably at church. Easter. Saggy-breasted and grim, dwarfed in the pew by four big sons and a husband with a weather map of a face. Carol might have been traumatized if she had seen into the future. All the meals she would help to prepare in this kitchen. All the criticisms she would deflect while peeling carrots or snapping peas.

Carl opened the pantry and grabbed a tin of smoked oysters and a box of Ritz crackers. "Hungry?"

"A little. Thirsty, too."

Carl poured Carol a rye and ginger. She topped it up while Carl was in the washroom and helped herself to some oysters, salty and oily and surprisingly delicious.

Outside, Carl took her hand and led her over to the picnic table where the football guys were sitting. They were listening to Jack Marshall tell some bullshit stories about breaking into the school last summer. Then Alex Bell told about some venereal disease his cousin got.

"How do you know if you got it?"

"You'll know. He says it feels like you're pissing barbed wire."

The boys laugh and cringe.

"My cousin thinks he got it from Rosie."

Carol perks up and pays attention. She knows Rosie, a teenage mother who comes to the pharmacy, shopping for formula, diaper rash cream and cigarettes. Carol likes the way Rosie saunters up and down the aisles, pushing the stroller and glaring at anyone who looks in her direction. People think it is their business to ask her why she didn't give her baby up for adoption. They call her a slut to her face. Once, Carol saw Rosie put a tube of mascara in her pocket. But she did not say anything.

Carol steps back into the shadows and Carl doesn't even notice. He is invested in the knowledgeable conversation about whores. She wanders over to the barn, gets another cider from the cooler and chats with Carl's younger brother for a while. Tom. Who tells her that Carl is an asshole. Tom seems sweet and sincere until he grabs her boob, and she screams, and Carl comes over and punches him in the face. The other brothers laugh. Carol has one more cider.

Around eleven o'clock, Carol stands up too fast from an upturned milk case at the bonfire and gets the spins. Carl watches her stumble and briefly considers following her. He worries she might be mad at him, so he stays put and doesn't think about her again until one of the Visser boys comes to get him.

"Your woman is puking."

By the time Carl comes to the rescue, Carol has puked her guts up. She is not alone. There are seven barn cats lapping up her vomit as fast as she can produce it.

"They like oysters," Carl says.

"I need a ride home," she says.

"I'm too drunk to drive. You'll have to stay over."

Carol looks at him. He seems serious. "I have to work in the morning," she says. "I have to be at the pharmacy at 8:30. Besides..."

"Besides?"

"You told my dad you'd get me home by midnight." She hates the way her voice cracks, like she is overly emotional. But Carl finds it sweet. He gives her a hug.

"It's 11:15. I'll find somebody sober to drive you."

Carol gets in the passenger seat of a Mercury Meteor. A big blue car with bench seats in the front and in the back. Like two living room sofas.

"I'm Simon," the guy says. Carol recognizes him. He goes to her church. He is older than the high school boys. His horn-rimmed glasses make him look like a businessman. Or maybe a banker. Carol feels bad for dragging him away from the party.

"I'm sorry."

"I thought you were Carol."

A lame joke. She smiles.

"If you have to get sick again, just tell me. I'll pull over."

"Okay." She feels around for a seat belt.

"No seat belts. This baby rolled off the line in 1960. You want some gum?"

"Yes, please."

"Take some aspirin and drink two glasses of water before you go to bed. You'll be fine."

"Thanks." Carol is still woozy. She is trying not to breathe in the layers of odours in the car. A pine-scented air freshener.

Gasoline. Unwashed armpits covered up with a spicy deodorant. She rolls the window down and gulps greedily.

"Carl shouldn't have served you alcohol. I don't drink the stuff myself. Devil's juice. If you were my girlfriend, I wouldn't let you drink."

Carol turns toward him and smiles, wondering if he will laugh off his comment. But apparently, he isn't joking.

"You're pretty when you smile," Simon says, patting the seat beside him. "Scooch over here," he says. "You're too far away."

"Oh. No. Not a good idea."

Simon leans sideways and puts a hand on her knee. His fingernails are long and discoloured, like an old man's toenails.

"Turn here," Carol says. "This is my road."

Simon does what she asks, cranking the wheel so hard she falls into his lap. She screams and gags.

"I'm going to be sick," she says, pushing herself upright.

He pulls the car over onto the soft shoulder and shuts off the motor. Carol's heart speeds up. She is not drunk anymore. She reaches for the door handle but Simon's long arm wraps around her shoulder.

"Hey! Relax! Simon says relax!" He chuckles low and dirty as she stops struggling. "That's better! Let's just listen to the crickets."

"They're frogs," Carol says.

"I don't think so."

Carol does not argue. No self-respecting farmer would ever mistake spring peepers for crickets. Something is seriously wrong with this guy. Her dad would say he has a screw loose.

"Carl doesn't deserve you. Why would you even waste your time with a jerk like him? You're too pretty for Carl." Simon keeps an iron grip on her shoulder. He spits a little while he talks.

No one has ever told Carol she is pretty. She is slim and blonde, and her skin is clear, and her eyes are blue. But she is plain. Just a farm girl.

"I really need to get home before midnight."

Simon checks his watch. "We got twenty minutes."

"My dad sets the alarm clock in the kitchen and when I get in, I have to turn it off, or it rings and wakes him up."

"Sounds like a good system. Your dad is strict. He wouldn't be too happy to know you've been drinking alcohol, I bet. Maybe I'll come in with you and introduce myself. Let him know there are still some honourable guys around."

Simon lowers his arm and Carol slides over quickly. She opens the door and hops out. They are parked at the back property line of her farm. She could jump the ditch and start running home if it wasn't so wet. No way could she get far in that muddy gumbo. She can feel the gravel through the thin soles of her shoes as she starts running along the shoulder of the road toward the light on the pole that marks her laneway. The car starts behind her. Carol thinks he must have a hole in his muffler, it is so loud.

Simon drives slowly along, following closely. Her door is still open. If he speeds up, it will slam into her. Instead, he pulls around her and then starts backing up. She is trapped unless she slides into the ditch. Simon throws the car in park and runs around the car laughing.

"Hey. Sorry. I'll be a gentleman. Seriously. I just want to get to know you." Carol trips and twists her ankle.

"Slow down. I got you. You alright?"

"Leave me alone. I'm fine."

"Get in the car! Simon says! Get! In the Car!"

Carol screams. He grabs her and throws her inside hard, so her head hits the metal handle on the opposite side, and then he is on her ripping her pants down and she goes still until he is done. He lies on her for a while, stroking her hair. He kisses her with chilly lips and tells her she's a good girl. The peepers sound like terrorists when he opens the door and crosses the road to piss in the ditch. A dog barks.

Carol starts taking cautious little sips of air, like she is drinking through a straw. She pulls up her pants. It is messy between her legs, and she thinks she is bleeding.

"Which house is yours?"

Carol points to the reflector tape on her mailbox. "Right here. Stop here."

Simon drives about a hundred meters past the laneway. He does not want to meet her dad after all. Not tonight. It is past midnight.

"I'll call you," Simon promises as she limps away.

There is a lamp on in the front room. Carol's dad is sitting in his chair, looking at a seed catalogue. She opens the back door and takes off her muddy jacket and hangs it on a hook. Takes off her ruined shoes. Walks to the front room to face the music.

"Goodnight, Daddy," she says, hoping that the endearment will keep him from asking questions. But he looks at her, all messed up, and he knows, and she starts bawling and she can't stop, and her dad calls up the stairs, "Cornelia? Cornelia! Get down here!"

Carl

When Simon gets back from driving Carol home, Carl is waiting for him.

"What took you so long?"

"I drove over to Cayuga. To the gas station."

"Ya? You got gas?"

Carl's brother, Al, comes up behind him. "They close at ten."

"You get my girlfriend home safe?"

"I did. Safe and sound. She's not your girlfriend though. Not anymore."

Carl winds up like he is going to punch him and Al grabs his arm.

"Relax, man. He's just being an idiot."

"I don't trust that motherfucker."

"Nobody does. You can call Carol tomorrow. If he tried anything you can kick the shit out of him another time."

John

After Cornelia got Carol cleaned up and into bed, John whispered to his wife about what they should do.

"What should we do? Nothing. Your girl goes to a party. She has some alcohol. She gets raped. You want to, what? Call the police? Make a big deal? Tell the whole town your daughter is a pig?"

"Jesus, Cornelia! Of course not! But the boy, Carl, he shouldn't get away with this."

"It wasn't Carl."

"What? Carl was her date, no?"

"Yes. But he was drunk, and she got a ride home with Simon Weilhauser."

"Gerda and Dirk's boy?"

"Not a boy. He's in his twenties."

"The one with glasses that we see in church? That shifty-looking bastard?"

"Yes."

John sits up. He pulls his pants on, over his long underwear.

"Where are you going?"

"To kill him. What else?"

"Get back in bed, John. You don't even know where he is. What? You planning to wake up Gerda and Dirk and ask to kill their son? He probably went back to the party at Zimmerman's."

"Then, that's where I'm going."

"Don't!"

"Shut up, Cornelia."

"Don't make a fool of yourself."

"Protecting my family makes me a fool?" He pulls a sweater on and digs in his drawer for socks.

Cornelia

It is four a.m. before Cornelia hears John's truck coming back up the lane. She has been in the kitchen, dressed and ready for disaster, since he left. The coffee is on. She is shaken but resolute. Her daughter is a good girl. A strong girl. This will not kill her. Cornelia knows because it did not kill her when she was fifteen. Younger than Carol is now. She was the youngest member of the choir. The choir director, Gerrit Anderson, asked her to stay behind after the others left. To help him select music for Easter. Cornelia was an obedient girl, like Carol. She trusted people.

John stomped up the porch steps. The musky barn smell of his canvas jacket preceded him into the kitchen. Cornelia pushed her chair back and smoothed her apron.

"Fried or poached?" she asks.

"I'm not hungry."

"What happened?"

John hangs up his coat. He looks old.

"Nothing."

"Nothing?"

"I drove by Zimmerman's and there were a few people sitting by the bonfire. But I didn't pull in. I thought about what you said. That maybe it could make things worse for her." He wipes at his eyes with the heel of his hand.

Cornelia is relieved. Girls get raped. They learn the hard way. Mating has a brutality to it. No more romantic than the bellowing steer in the field mounting the nearest cow. Cornelia worries more about John. Men think they can keep their families safe. No telling what they will do when they find out that is not possible.

"You want coffee?"

John nods. He sits at the table and stirs some sugar into

his cup. "I'm going to talk to the Pastor."

"What will he do?"

"Give us some guidance."

Cornelia knows what kind of advice the Pastor will give. Her sister, Glenda, went to him years ago when her marriage was troubled. Glenda's husband was having an affair with a woman from work. The pastor advised her to lose some weight and make more of an effort in the bedroom.

"I have to do something, Corrie. Maybe he will talk to the boy. I need help. I cannot just forgive and forget." He stands and retrieves his coat and goes out to the barn. It is too early to start the milking, but too late to go back to bed.

Pastor

Pastor Henrick Bakker sits behind his desk. A cross on the wall behind him catches the afternoon sunlight and reflects in Carol's eyes so she has to squint. She moves her chair until the glare is directed elsewhere. She is being judged by Jesus; she supposes. That is why she is here.

"Your father tells me you are a good student."

Carol waits.

"And you have a part time job."

Carol waits.

"He tells me you are a good obedient daughter."

There is a clock on the mantle that has a very loud tick. Tick. Tick. Carol's mother called in sick for her today. Flu, she heard her tell the manager at the pharmacy. Her mother has been very kind. Surprisingly so, as she has never been one to show much affection. Today she has been very apologetic on behalf of the world and the burden it has put on Carol's shoulders. She tried to talk Carol's father out of this meeting with the Pastor, but she was not successful. Now Carol sits and waits to be chastised. Her forehead, where it hit the door handle, is bruised. Her bottom is tender.

"Say as little as possible," her mother whispered to her before her father hustled her out to the truck.

"So," Pastor Henrick says. Finally getting down to brass tacks. "Tell me about your experience."

"I was raped by Simon Weilhauser."

This is not, apparently, what the Pastor wants to hear.

"Whoa," As if she is a runaway horse and he needs to stop her. "Let's examine the circumstances."

Carol waits.

"Were you drinking? Your father says you had some alcohol. Do you think that contributed to Simon's behaviour?"

Carol waits.

"You know. Boys sometimes…"

"He is not a boy. He is a man. And he was trusted by Carl to give me a ride home. And he. Stopped the car. I tried to run. He. Hurt. Me." Carol hears her own voice, talking like a robot in time to the mantle clock. It echos in the cold office. Cold and bereft of comfort. She hates this man. How dare he interrogate her. With her father listening in a chair just outside the office.

"Carl is your boyfriend?"

"It was our first date."

"You should know that, after your father telephoned me this morning, I called Simon. He came in right away. He sat in the chair you are sitting in now. I heard his side of the story. It is very convincing. His story."

Carol waits.

"Do you want to hear it?"

"Not if it's a lie."

The Pastor flinches a bit, as if this daughter of Eve has revealed her true nature. And it confirms his suspicions.

"He says you were in Carl's bedroom earlier in the night."

Carol waits.

"He says Carl implied that you are a girl with loose morals."

Carol waits.

"He says that Carl when he asked Simon to drive you home, indicated that you might show your appreciation. In a physical way. Do you see how that misunderstanding might have come about? A pretty girl who drinks alcohol? And goes with a boy to his bedroom?"

Carol waits.

"Simon likes you. He told me he would like to see you again. He is looking for a nice Dutch girl. His parents are after him to find a girl and get married, he said. He is willing to overlook your, you know. The fact that you have had premarital relations."

"But I haven't."

"With Carl?"

"No. I told you it was our first date. If he told Simon we did something, he lied."

"But now, you have done something."

"Something. Like being raped, you mean?"

"I think you should not say that word. Simon tells me that you consented."

Carol's throat aches. It feels as if she has to squeeze the words out, like toothpaste from an empty tube. "He threatened me. I got out of the car. He almost ran me over. He threw me in the back seat and rammed my head on the door handle and he raped me."

The Pastor peers at her over the top of his glasses, as if waiting for the Lord to give him some sign. Something to prove her guilt.

"I thought he was going to kill me!" she screams. "I thought I was going to die!"

Carol's father rushes into the room and takes his daughter by the arm. "That's enough, Pastor. I thought you would help us, but I can see I was wrong."

"Now, John. Don't do anything rash. There is a young man's future at stake here. Your daughter has made some dangerous accusations. We haven't talked yet about atonement."

Carol

Their family doctor is not like the Pastor. He doesn't blame Carol. He tells her she has the right to press charges. "But," he says, "to be honest, you are not likely to get justice. I have been to court on behalf of women who have been raped and the men are seldom convicted."

"I don't care if he is convicted. As long as I'm not pregnant."

"When is your period due?"

"Soon."

"Call me when you get it. But also, bring in a urine sample in four weeks and we'll run a test to be sure." He hands her a small plastic bottle. "And Carol? I'm sorry this happened to you. It's not your fault. Having a few drinks at a party is not a good idea, but it is not an invitation for rape."

"I know."

"Good. You'll be okay. Not all men are violent."

Carol gets a call from Simon two weeks later. He asks if she wants to go to the theatre in Hamilton. They could go for dinner first. Carol is standing in the kitchen. She starts shaking and hands the phone to her father while Simon is still talking.

"Call here again and I will come to your house and shoot you dead," John says in a dull, even voice. Then he hangs up the phone and hugs her. Carol has a vague memory of the last time her father hugged her. She was about three years old, and a bee flew up her dress and stung her on the stomach.

Carl sits beside her on the bus on the Monday of the last week of school before summer vacation.

"You still mad at me?"

"Why would I be?"

"Simon says you told him I'm an asshole."

"What?"

"He says you guys are dating now. That you're practically engaged. That you think I'm a jerk."

Carol squints at him to show she doesn't have a clue what

he is talking about.

"So? You still mad?"

"If I'm mad, it's only because you didn't take care of me at your party. I thought you liked me."

"I did. I do."

"Then why did you tell Simon that we had sex. He thought I was a slut and he… You know what? Never mind."

"I didn't. What? Did he hurt you?" Carl's brother Doug leans over the seat, sticking his head right in between them and Carl bats him with a math textbook.

"Never mind."

Carl lowers his voice. "When we get to school, we're going to skip first period and go over to the coffee shop and you're going to tell me what happened."

John

Carol seemed fine. She wasn't pregnant. Cornelia didn't want to talk about it. But he couldn't get past it. He couldn't get over the image of that Simon kid brutalizing his daughter. He drove past the Weilhauser farm almost every day with a crowbar on the passenger seat. Hoping to see Simon on his own. Hoping not to.

He felt sick. Couldn't eat. Bile rose in his throat and filled his mouth with the flavour of rage. The voice of the fucking Pastor looped through his thoughts. Atonement! As if his little girl had been asking for it.

John pulled on his hip waders and retreated to his flooded corn field. It was wasted labour. Cornelia was right when she said the field would drain on its own in a week or so.

But digging an irrigation ditch helped. His aching shoulders relieved the aching in his gut. He was making some progress when his shovel shattered something. Maybe pottery, he thought, until he dug down and unearthed a skull.

Not a human skull. It had a long snout. John turned it over and noted the gaps where the tusks had been removed. A common practice for domesticated pigs. Forty years had passed since this property was a pig farm, but John still found a few bones every year. He tossed the skull back into the ditch. Don't rake up old graves, his father used to say. Leave the past alone, in other words. Forget about it. Move on.

The skull landed with one eye socket glaring at him and John crouched down. Retrieved the thing. Turned it over in his big meaty hands. He pulled a small pearl-handled jackknife out of his back pocket. The blade was thin from frequent sharpening. He carved S.W. into the sloping forehead.

"Burn in hell, you fucking pig," he said. He dropped it and stomped on it and felt something close to satisfaction as the saturated clay sucked it up. Then he laid a length of irrigation pipe over it and kept working.

"To everything there is a season, and a time to every purpose under heaven. A time to be born, and a time to die; a time to plant, and a time to pluck up that which is planted." - Ecclesiastes.

A book of wisdom.

John's father had been a big man. Not fat, but big boned. Tall and solid. Immovable, it seemed. When he entered the house, the floors shook. He took up a lot of space in that house back home in the Netherlands. And God was a big part of his strength. But after the Nazis came and evicted them from their home, his father was not big. He was shrunken physically and mentally and spiritually.

Water gurgled through the pipes, following the slope down to the creek. John gathered up his tools and straightened up. Yanked on the peak of his cap. The wind was rising. It would dry this field in no time. He just wanted to punish himself. To tire himself out. And it worked. He went to bed after supper and slept like the dead.

Cornelia

She can see John squatting on his haunches out in the back field. He's been struggling with what happened to Carol. Men! Honestly, they are quite ignorant of the way women suffer. The crippling periods. The tender breasts. The aching heart. Guilt. Shame. Then pregnancy and breast-feeding. Every marriage is a type of prostitution. If you know what is good for you, you will put out, even when you are exhausted. Do you want extra spending money for Christmas? You will act pleased when your husband wakes you in the middle of the night.

Poor Carol. What she has gone through. What she has yet to go through. Cornelia does not think her daughter is one to keep her self-esteem between her legs. Something bad happened and now it is over. Like mumps or measles or a cancer scare. Will it affect future relationships? Her enjoyment of sex? Of course. That's life. Cornelia did not tell her parents when the choir director abused her. She could not bear the scrutiny. What do you expect, her father would have said. You wear that low-cut blouse. The man is only human, after all.

So, she quit the choir. She never liked it much anyway.

"I need to spend more time on my schoolwork," she told her parents.

The next Sunday, one of the choir members approached her. Mrs. Stamp.

"We'll miss you, Corrie," she said. "You know, if you ever want to talk about it, I am happy to listen. It did not go unnoticed that Gerrit asked you to stay late with him. Alone. That wasn't right."

Cornelia started to cry then, and Mrs. Stamp put her arm around her shoulder. She was not crying because of what happened, but because Mrs. Stamp was aware of it. People knew. The choir director was a pervert and people knew. Or at least suspected. And what? Why didn't Mrs. Stamp speak up? "Corrie is coming with me," she could have said. Instead, she got her coat and left Cornelia in the sanctuary with a man who thought a young girl would like an invitation to touch his purple cock.

Carol

She never saw Simon Weilhauser again. Even though she often looked over her shoulder when she was uptown, or out jogging. He was an invisible stalker. Maybe he made it his mission to stay away from her. Maybe he took her father's threat seriously. She dreamed about him sometimes and when she married Carl Zimmerman in 1975, she half expected him to show up at the church to interrupt the service when the Pastor asked if anyone had any reason why these two should not be joined in holy matrimony. Speak now or forever hold your peace. But he didn't show up. She did not test fate by inquiring after him, although she did hear that he finally got a job in Toronto and a place of his own. It was a casual remark overheard at a party.

Carol and Carl built a raised ranch-style home on the Zimmerman's property. It took eight years to finish it, because Carl did not believe in credit. Cash was king. He never did get around to putting interior trim around the windows or doors or installing flooring in the kids' rooms. Plywood with carpet remnants retrieved from the dump was good enough. Carol did insist on high-quality appliances. Maytag. Her washer and dryer lasted through thirty years of diapers for four babies and a thousand loads of crusty farm overalls. She only used her clothesline to air out quilts or beat rugs. So. She had it better than her mother.

When the kids started school, Carol got a job in town at the Old Folks' Home as a cleaner. She made some good women friends who sat out back at the picnic table reserved for staff, drank coffee, smoked cigarettes, complained about errant husbands and the best way to hard boil eggs and what kind of a wedding gift was appropriate for a niece's second wedding. Farming, as a family business, fell on hard times. Her children urged her to sell it when Carl died from heart disease.

"It killed him," her oldest boy said. "Nobody can be expected to work so hard for so little money."

Carol puts the property in order. Two homes, a barn, a drive shed, cows and chickens and corn. Two hundred and seventy acres in all. The value is almost exactly the same as the small bungalow she buys for herself in town two streets over from the Old Folks Home where she worked. It's called a Long-Term Care facility and it is a pit of despair compared to when it was run by the county. She hopes she doesn't ever have to live there herself.

The Dutch Line is still a rural road, but these days farmland is owned by big companies with big machinery and labourers from poor countries. Like the Mexican Mennonites who will do the hard labour that Carol's kids do not have the capacity for. Instead of roadside stands, the produce gets shipped off to Green Giant or Libby or Del Monte.

When Carol's dad died and her mom moved in with Auntie Glenda, she had another farm to get rid of. It was a huge job, and her brothers were useless. She hired an auctioneer who charged fifteen percent of the day's profits, and her brothers thought that was way too much, but they didn't want to help one bit. The auctioneer and his team came early and put everything outside on the lawn, organized by categories. Furniture, tools, antiques. Small stuff was divided into lots. You could buy a box of kitchen odds and ends for fifty cents. Carol's childhood got loaded into the trunks of cars. Funny, the things she was nostalgic about. Nothing valuable. The Mammy and Pappy salt and pepper shakers. The wall clock shaped like a daisy. Her dad's easy boy chair.

"Here's a dandy chair for your hunt camp," the auctioneer says. "Let's start the bidding at ten, gimme ten, gimme eight. Gimme five, then. Five dollars for a sturdy chair." It goes for a toonie. The auctioneer has a step ladder and a portable microphone, and he moves from one area to the next with good natured expertise. His wife sells sandwiches and coffee. Carol admits it was a mistake to let her mother come to watch. She was horrified about the pittance her china and silver and Royal Doulton figurines went for compared to the old wooden butter boxes in the barn. What was wrong with people?

"I hope you're happy! This auction took years off your mother's life," Aunt Glenda told Carol, as if she had orchestrated the event to hurry her mother to the grave. "I'm taking her home."

After everyone left, Carol walked through the empty rooms of the farmhouse. It looked desolate. The wallpaper and the carpets were dirty and dated. She knew they would be the first to go. The buyers were from the city, and they had all kinds of renovations planned. The floorboards of the barn were swept clean except for a corner with a rusty baler and a litter of barn cats. She never liked cats after the incident with the oysters. But she would miss the barn. The way the late afternoon light came through the chinks in the siding, illuminating dust and chaff. There was a cathedral quality to it all.

She wandered out past the apple trees, heavy with wormy spartans. The corn had been harvested. Only stubble remained. At the far end of the field, she turned and looked back at the stage where her younger self had performed, and she was satisfied that she had done well enough, all things considered.

Stepping over freshly turned dirt, she saw something in the black loam. She bent to retrieve it. Half buried; it required a good tug. It was a length of irrigation pipe. She stopped and swallowed hard, remembering that spring when her dad was so upset. More upset than she was. As if he'd been the one who was raped.

She pulled on the pipe and there it was. Carol felt like a midwife pulling the skull out of the mud. It came away with a soft sucking sound and she held it up and gazed into the eye sockets. She traced the initials on the forehead with blackened fingers. S.W.

Never in her memory had her father given her a gift. Not on her birthday or Christmas or when she graduated. Her mother took care of all that. Advice? Yes, he gave her advice. And money if she needed it. And this. The assurance that he would kill someone for her, if it came to that.

Carol loves living in town. She likes watching children walk to school. No bus for them. She appreciates the simple pleasure of stopping in at the corner store for a chocolate bar or a bag of chips. A small treat to enjoy while watching Wheel of Fortune. On Wednesday afternoons, she plays euchre at the Legion. The Baptist Church has exercise classes for seniors twice a week.

Carol's four children all live close by, except her youngest daughter, Brenda, who moved to Calgary and is well off, with a good job at the university. She married some big shot who wears a cowboy hat, and they have dogs instead of kids. They spend their money on cruises and such.

The three who live in town have, between them, eight children. Carol cared for all her grandchildren at one time or another, to help out during sickness or to pick them up from hockey, or to sit in the bleachers at the indoor pool while they learned to swim. They are badly behaved, for the most part, no better or no worse than the grandchildren of her friends. Mouthy. Glued to their phones.

Her favourite is Lorrie, who drops in at odd hours and makes herself a sandwich or a bowl of cereal. Sometimes she sleeps over in the guest room. Once upon a time, Lorrie would have been called a tomboy, but now there is some complex gender identification issue that takes up much of her granddaughter's inner life. What possible good can it do to complicate your life with that kind of worrisome thinking? Carol is still a farm girl at heart. She sees biology as straightforward. Male and female. Simple. Some females have masculine traits. Some males have feminine traits. Once they had a goat that was a hermaphrodite. Both sexes. It was a rare thing. Carol thought of Trixie as female because she was oddly serene and affectionate for a goat. And in the end, it didn't matter. A coyote got her.

The skull is in her mother's old cast iron pressure cooker on a shelf in Carol's linen closet behind a box of Christmas ornaments. She imagines showing Lorrie. But young people get traumatized easily. So, she keeps it to herself.

Snow Day

To be fair to the bus driver, it wasn't totally her fault. She was filling in for Abigail Duncan who was off on sick leave, getting a hysterectomy. So, Sue Kramer wasn't familiar with the route. And anybody who has driven around Blairhampton back roads can tell you that the township had no rational design in mind when they paved the old deer trails. You can go in circles out there and not even know it until you come back to some landmark and realize that you are lost. Add that factor to zero visibility, and you would not want Sue to lose her bus driver license either. Even the kids' parents said it wouldn't make them feel better.

It started to snow just before noon. The sky got real dark and the principal at the school got a call from the superintendent who said she was sending the buses out early. There was a big storm event coming up from the States. It was dumping on Buffalo right now and moving across Lake Erie. A bad combination of wind and freezing rain and snow pellets that was sure to make the commute home a disaster in the city. Up here, farther north, it would likely knock out power lines and make driving hazardous. Marj Bennett, the principal, told the secretary to start the phone tree and alert parents that their children would be arriving home about two hours earlier than usual. They should make arrangements to have someone meet them. Then she made the announcement over the P.A.

"Pack up your belongings and get your coats on and line up in the front hall."

Marj got bundled up in her fur coat and fur hat and Sorel boots and went out front to supervise bus duty. She was already thinking of stopping off at the Liquor Store on the way home to stock up. If tomorrow was a snow day, she wanted to be prepared.

Sue Kramer was throwing a load of towels into the dryer when she got the call from her supervisor to head over to Onondaga School. She wasn't happy about it. It meant she would have to wake up her two-year-old daughter from her nap and take her out, sleepy and whiny, to the cold bus. She got special permission to take her daughter on her route. Most of the drivers were women, so the request was not unusual. It saved daycare costs.

By the time she got herself organized, struggled to get the little girl into her snowsuit and completed the twelve-point safety check, she was running late. In fact, hers was the last bus to roll into the school parking lot. The principal, all bundled up like a brown bear, led the Blairhampton students to her bus. A gust of wind blew in, fierce with the mindless kind of violence that reminds you what a bully winter can be. The precipitation was accumulating on the windshield in icy sheets that the wipers couldn't clean off.

Later, during the interview at the board office, Sue says she remembers feeling scared. As the kids boarded, struck silent by the force of the storm, she wished she had dropped the baby off at her Mom's. But there'd been no time. And now she had responsibility for eighteen children, one of them more precious to her than the rest.

"Drive safe," Marj yelled as she closed the door. Sue wished she was a principal instead of a bus driver. She wished she'd finished high school instead of getting pregnant and marrying too young. She felt sorry that she missed out on college and sororities and better prospects. But mostly, she felt terrified that this big yellow lumbering vehicle would not be able to negotiate the Dover Road hill.

The radio crackled and her supervisor asked for her location. Told her to go slow.

"Oh, and Sue?" she said. "The MacArthurs called and said they can't get home in time to meet the kids, so let the boys off at the Walker's place. Katie Walker's mom says it's okay."

Sue was passing the community centre at the edge of town. The road was totally snow-covered, and the visibility was decreasing by the minute. She could barely see the entrance to the parking lot. She considered getting permission from her supervisor to pull in and get the kids into the warm safety of the community room. But the radio was crackling, cutting in and out. By the time it cut out completely, she was almost at the Irondale River bridge, and she knew that, even if she wanted to, there was no place to turn around.

"Did you hear that, Katie?" Sue called out. "The twins are going to get off at your place, okay?" She dared not turn around or even check the rear-view mirror. She was concentrating on the telephone poles, trying to stay in the middle of the road. Or at least where she thought the road should be. There were no other vehicles in sight. Even the laneways were blown in. She started to get a sick feeling in her stomach, but she didn't want the kids to see her panicking.

"Yes," Katie called back to her. There was no point arguing. The twins were not welcome at Katie's house, but since this was an emergency, she supposed her mother had made an exception. She turned and looked back at the boys. Calvin and Clayborn. They were not identical, but you could sure tell they were brothers. The same thick black hair with cowlicks at the crown. The same bruising under the eyes that made them look unhealthy. The same sour smell wafting off their clothing that marked the children of cigarette-smoking parents. Cal was the dominant twin. He was aggressive and angry and mean. Clay followed his lead without enthusiasm. There was something wrong with Clay, Katie thought. Like he'd been dropped on his head as a baby. Like he lost his memory of his own self, and in his perpetual confusion, he mimicked his brother. Both of the boys gave off the vibe that they wouldn't spit in a ditch to save your life. Nobody would invite the MacArthur twins over if they had any choice in the matter.

Katie stood up and sat beside Stella, Sue's little girl. "It's bad, ain't it?" Katie said. "Are you okay? Should we pull over?"

"We're okay, Sweetie," Sue said. "In bus driver training, we are taught to keep going. If we pull over in weather like this, somebody might come up behind and bump into us."

Sue looked at her speedometer. She was travelling thirty kilometres per hour. The speed limit on this stretch of Irondale Road was eighty. The route usually took an hour-and-a-half, but at this rate, she wouldn't get home until after dark. She was calculating her options. There was a turnaround area coming up at the Allsaw flats and she was tempted to go back to the community centre. She tried the radio to get permission. It was cutting out. She passed the flats and kept going.

Stella started to cry, and Katie sang her a little song. Away in a Manger.

"Can I give her a pudding cup?" Katie asked. "It's left over from my lunch."

"Sure, Sweetie. Thanks," Sue said. She was stepping on the gas, trying to increase her speed so they could make it up the Dover hill. The engine was revving high, and her heart was racing, and she was sweating under her winter coat. Halfway up, there was a little plateau and a slight curve, and she didn't know whether to slow down or speed up, but she held it steady like the captain of a doomed ship who hangs onto the helm long after the sea has taken control.

Except for a skid that drifted the bus dangerously close to the unforgiving granite cut on the right side of the road, they made it to the top and Sue shifted into low gear. They descended into the Blairhampton triangle all in one piece.

"Almost home," Katie said. "Almost home!" she called out, louder, to the MacArthur twins sitting six rows back.

"Hey you guys. Are you cold? You should move up closer to the front. It's warmer up here."

At thirteen, Katie was the closest thing to an adult that Sue had on the bus, and she wished she didn't have to drop her off. What would she do if Stella started crying again? What would happen if she skidded off the road? How long would it be until someone came looking for them?

The heater was noisy as it belted out warm air to the windshield at full blast, but even so, the ice was creeping in around the edges, affording Sue an increasingly smaller clear spot to see out of. The road signs were covered with the ice-snow mix, and Sue realized why those little curving arrows were important. Left? Right? Sharp? Steep? She almost missed the Hammond Road turnoff even though she'd been watching for it. Waiting for it. Hoping for it. She took it nice and slow and with the change in direction, she dared to hope that the snow would let up a bit. It was hurtling hard from the west and now, behind her, it seemed to push the bus a bit like the invisible hand of a benevolent god. The pine forest was protective here. She made her first stop at the Wendall's mailbox and then two more stops, successfully. At the Cochrane's driveway, there was a pick-up truck, running and waiting for Nolan, the only kindergarten kid on the bus. Mr. Cochrane struggled out of the cab and boarded the bus and asked Sue if she was all right. Why did she say yes? Why didn't she follow him up his laneway and hunker down for the night? Well, for one reason, he didn't offer. Instead, he mumbled that he was without power, and he was not having much luck trying to get the generator going.

When she thought about it later, it was only pride that stopped her from breaking down in tears and begging for help. If she'd anticipated the way the wind was about to pick up at the end of the Maitland Marsh, she would have unloaded the bus right there. But she kept going. As she passed the halfway point of her route, she visualized turning the bus into her driveway when this day was finally over. Then she would call the bus line and quit. She would get Stella fed and bathed and put to bed. Then she'd fill out that application for the Practical Nursing course that was sitting on the kitchen counter and get herself a job with benefits and a union.

The marsh was low and open, and the wind gusted across the road, drifting and shifting and cutting visibility to zero. She was down to ten kilometres per hour when Katie called out. "There! There's my mailbox!"

Sue stopped the bus about forty feet past the laneway. Katie waited for the MacArthur twins to pull on their backpacks and saunter to the front to show they weren't worried about a thing in the world. Sue opened the door. Katie let Calvin and Clayborn step down ahead of her.

Sue closed the door with a mixture of relief, at having accomplished the safe delivery of another three children, and dread, that Katie was no longer sitting behind her, able to help. The three children disappeared into the white void. Sue wiggled the gearshift into first and stepped on the gas pedal. There was only one more stop before she would reach a secondary highway where there was sure to be some traffic. Civilization was close at hand. She dropped off Cedar and Willow Wentworth at 4:05 p.m. It had taken her over three hours to do the route. At 4:50, she saw the sign. You are now entering Furnace Falls. She checked the rear-view mirror, caught Stella's trusting glance, and burst out crying. Another half kilometre and she pulled into her own driveway.

Sue went into the house and put Stella into her high-chair with a few Arrowroot cookies. She was grateful that the hydro was on. Heat and lights working. There were seven messages on the answering machine. Her mother called four times, worried sick. Her husband called to say he was stuck in Bobcaygeon, and he'd be staying in the Chuckwagon Motel overnight. And her supervisor left a message to call the bus lines as soon as possible.

"Hi Sue. I can see by the locator that your bus made it back to town. The Walkers and the MacArthurs called, and they are saying there's no sign of the kids. I'm praying to God they're with you. Call me back."

Sue remembers the gust of wind as she cranked the bus door open. She noticed Clayborn didn't zip his jacket up. Normally she would have said something, but she was conscious of the way the window was icing up. When she called out to thank Katie, her own voice sounded funny. Like it was coming from somewhere else. How long was Katie's laneway? What could possibly happen between the road and the Walker's house? Even in a blizzard. Even with the MacArthur twins in tow. Unless. Sue started shaking and she couldn't stop.

Katie knew as soon as she got close to the mailbox that she'd made a mistake. It wasn't hers. It looked almost the same, an aluminum model that had been bashed in by teenagers with a baseball bat a few years back. But half-covered with ice it was an honest mistake. The whole road looked as unfamiliar as a distant planet. Katie turned around to flag the bus down, but it was too late. Even though she could hear it rumbling off, the big yellow vehicle had already disappeared into the storm. The twins were shoving each other into the mailbox. They were mean little nine-year-olds with a reputation for being bullies, just like their parents. As next-door neighbours, the MacArthurs were less than ideal. They had big parties, cranked their country music up loud and lived like pigs. Rusty machinery littered the yard, they stole from the Walker's woodpile, and the twins tortured every living thing they could get their hands on. Barn cats, frogs, squirrels, deer. All creatures big and small were susceptible to firecrackers, jack knives, and bb-guns.

"Let's go," said Cal. Clay stared at Katie with bloodshot eyes. Snot was coursing down past his thin lips and accumulating on his coat. "It's fucking cold," Cal said, accusing her for his discomfort.

"We got off too soon," Katie said. "This isn't my place."

"You fucker," Cal said. "You goddamn cunt. Bitch. This is all your fault."

"Shut up!" she yelled.

The language was no surprise. Katie heard it echoing across the pond from the MacArthur's place all hours of the day and night. Their dad, Clem, taught the twins everything he knew about being a prick.

"I messed up. Stick with me or set out on your own. I think we should go up the lane here and hope somebody's home."

Katie had babysat the boys when they were wild little toddlers. Their mom had left town with the local grow-op guy, a long-hair from America who promised her a better life in Montana. Clem didn't expect his wife to come home, but he was ill-equipped to take on the responsibilities of two little boys. He paid Katie to look after them that summer. But when Katie came home with bite marks and bruises, Katie's dad told Clem he'd have to make other arrangements. That's when Lorraine moved in. Sometimes Clem introduced her as his cousin. Sometimes he said she was his girlfriend. He told the school she was a nanny he hired off the internet. Katie's mother said Lorraine was just a simple young woman with limited options. A sex slave, most likely, Katie's friend Joleen suggested.

"Jesus, Clay," Cal said. "Quit yer blubbering. You must be gay for Christ sake!"

Nice. Katie hoped they would opt to head back up the road and fall in a ditch and die. But she knew that cruel little bastards like the MacArthur twins did not perish easily. They were like boy soldiers. Resilient as hell. They were used to bad weather, locked out of their house half the winter as some kind of punishment.

"Look at those boys," Katie's mother would say. "Out in this weather without hats or mitts. I've got half a mind to call the Children's Aid."

"Don't," was all Katie's father said. "Clem'd be over here with his twelve gauge and shoot us all."

Katie did not want the responsibility she had, but she took it on anyway. "Hold onto my hand," she told Cal. "And

Clay, you hang on to your brother's hand. It's easy to get lost." She started walking up the laneway, stepping high through the crust-covered layers of snowdrifts. She thought she knew who lived here, two old bachelors. The Smeltzer brothers. Some folks passed along rumours about them, how they were perverts, but Katie's dad knew them.

"Harmless," he told her. "They don't care for the modern world. They live like pioneers. Off the grid."

Katie could smell the wood smoke as they trudged up the laneway. She saw a pale face in the small square of window glass in the door and controlled the jolt of terror that seized her bowels. It looked like a skull peering out at them. It looked like somebody long dead. The door opened before they had a chance to knock.

"Sir," Katie said. "Mr. Smeltzer. We're lost in the storm. The bus driver let us off at the wrong stop. I'm Katie Walker."

"Come in, Miss," he said. "Call me Ian. My brother is Angus." His voice surprised her, flowing out of his ruined mouth, kind and smooth like a radio announcer. She saw that there was a boot tray and hooks for coats inside the back porch, and she went ahead and started to get out of her wet things.

"Boys?" the man said.

Cal tried to barrel past the old fellow and was stopped by an arm with unexpected iron strength.

"Introduce yourself, son. Like the young lady did."

"Hah! I'm not your son," Cal said. "I don't have to tell you nothing. I'm not supposed to talk to strangers."

Katie noticed the other Mr. Smeltzer in the kitchen, filling the kettle. She went in to meet him and offered to help with the tea. The boys would have to fend for themselves. She heard the weighty silence on the porch and recognized the power of it against boys who were accustomed to verbal warfare. There were some lowered voices, as an understanding was agreed upon.

By the time Cal and Clay entered the kitchen, Katie had buttered some toast. Angus Smeltzer smiled kindly and nodded as he put a knitted wool tea cozy on an old teapot and set it carefully on an iron trivet in the middle of the table. The boys obediently went to the sink and washed their hands, looking back at Ian for acknowledgement. He nodded and they sat down. Never had Katie seen the boys so chastened. Never had she seen past their horrid meanness to the fact of them. Their dirty, unloved selves. The word "respect" occurred to her, and she used it later to describe the evening of the big storm.

"The Smeltzers demanded respect," she told her dad. "And the boys gave it to them. It seemed like they had no choice, but it also seemed like they were surprised by their own calmness. Like they didn't know it was something they were even capable of. They didn't want to leave when the police arrived at ten o'clock."

They sat in the main room, beside the wood stove, listening to the wind shout down the chimney and the ice pellets hurling themselves at the windows. They felt the generational pull of the place with the ancestors peeking out of faded portraits. Angus spoke not a word. Not one word the whole evening. He sipped his tea and he worked away at a crossword puzzle, and he listened intently as Ian talked and the children answered his queries.

At one point, when it looked like they might be sleeping overnight, Ian brought up the matter of trust. Could he trust the boys to stay in his house?

"I've seen ya both in the bush," he said. "I've seen the way ya treat animals. Quite frankly, I don't trust men who aren't kind to animals."

Cal looked at Clay. Clay started to cry. Angus rose up out of his armchair and handed Clayborn a cloth handkerchief. Clay blew his nose and wiped his eyes and then he hid his face in the handkerchief.

Sue was good to her own commitment. She quit the bus route and signed up for the nursing course. It must have been ten years that went by before she saw the MacArthur twins again. She was on duty in Emergency one night. Clayborn came running in, screaming and crying, carrying his brother, Cal, who was covered in blood. They had been driving into town and Cal had taken the curve at the bottom of the Dover hill too fast. Skidded on gravel. The car flipped a couple of times and smashed into the rock face. Granite. Unforgiving. And you know the odd part? By some ironic coincidence, it was the Smeltzer brothers that were first on the scene. They drove the boys to the hospital and stayed with Clay all night while the doctors tried to save Cal. The father never did show up, but Angus and Ian were there, and they never left the young lad's side.

"The nicest gentlemen you could ever meet," Sue told

the investigating officer after it was all over. "I don't know if Clayborn would have got through it without them," she said. "Angus? The one that don't speak? He never said a word, but he sat by that boy, and he was such a comfort. You could feel the warmth of the man. The way he shared that boy's grief. When they got the bad news that Cal didn't make it, Angus handed Clay a hankie."

Sue stopped and looked over the officer's shoulder toward the waiting room. It seemed like maybe she was done talking, so he said, "Anything else, Ms. Kramer?"

"Remember them old-fashioned hankies? My grandfather used them," Sue said. "Grandma laundered them and ironed them and put them in Grandpa's top drawer. Those were the days before Kleenex got so popular, I guess. I haven't seen anyone use them in years. But Clay took that handkerchief from Angus, and he put his face into it, and he cried his heart out. Lord. He bawled like a baby."

Swimming Free

Ollie the sea lion escaped from Springbank Park in London, Ontario one June night in 1958. He was sick of slapping his flippers together, tired of balancing a ball on his nose. That evening, after the sticky-fingered crowd had retreated, the frogs called to him from the banks of the Thames River. Back in the far corner of his enclosure, he pushed the mud around until there was a hole big enough for him to slip out. Did he turn back, expecting his female companion, Dollie, to follow? Perhaps she looked at him, with his back all scraped and bleeding from the wire fence and wished him well. More likely, she rolled her eyes and went back to sleep.

I had been observing the sea lions for years. I knew that Ollie was unhappy. Some people said he was lazy, letting Dollie perform the sea lion's share of the antics. But I recognized the symptoms of despair. I knew what it was like to live with someone who went about their daily tasks with efficiency and vitality. My mother glared at me, her disappointing son, with the same deep resentment that Dollie gave Ollie.

Just do it, my mother would say. Just make your bed. Could you brush your teeth, just once, without me asking you to? How difficult can it be to finish twenty math problems?

After a while, it wears you down. You have to get out. The first time I ran away, my mother packed me a lunch. She taunted me all the way out the door. You'll be back, she said. You'll be back in time for dinner. We're having Southern Fried Chicken.

I imagine Dollie barking at Ollie as he was halfway out of the enclosure. Too far to change his mind. He had to keep going, didn't he? It took guts.

Media reports started referring to Ollie as "Slippery, the Sea Lion". They sensationalized his escape from Springbank Park. They took pictures of Dollie, alone in the enclosure, and tagged her with the name of "Lonesome". I guess they thought it would sell newspapers if the sea lions had catchy nicknames. It worked. Everyone started calling them something other than what they were. Not me. I knew Ollie and Dollie. I would not be manipulated by the media, even as a twelve-year-old.

While every other kid in town was down at the river hoping to spot "Slippery" and collect the $200 reward, I staked out the sea lion exhibit in Springbank Park. I hoped that I would find Ollie if he was lurking around, regretting his rash behaviour. I knew from experience how hard it is to save face when you run away. I didn't regret leaving. How else to make somebody sorry they were mean to you? But I regretted my lack of planning. A map. Some cash. A good story for the suspicious neighbour who found me squatting in her tomatoes, juice dripping down my chin like blood.

People are not much different than animals. I figured Ollie was nearby, waiting for all the hoopla to die down. I brought along a sea lion catcher of my own invention, which was really a laundry sack, and I set up camp under a pine tree where I had a very good view but couldn't be seen. The staff at Springbank Park covered Slippery's escape route with mesh and chicken wire, so Dollie couldn't follow her impulsive boyfriend, but she didn't show any interest in the new high security measures. She seemed embarrassed, in fact, by the commotion. No clapping or barking or ringing the bell. Maybe, without Ollie there, she lost her ambition to prove that she was the one who did all the work. What the heck? They fed her either way.

I had binoculars, a tin of sardines and a Hardy Boys mystery to read. *The Secret of Wildcat Swamp*. I had not anticipated the difficulty of coaxing a five-hundred-pound sea lion into a sack that might hold, at best, twelve pounds of dirty clothes, but I was convinced of my imminent success. People came and went but no one noticed me back in the trees. I could hear the voices of kids echoing along the valley. They sat on bridges making sea lion noises. Without the encumbrance of life jackets or parental supervision, they waded and pushed each other in the water. Kids were responsible for their own safety in 1958. If you came home with a dog bite or a gash in the forehead, you wouldn't get any sympathy from your parents.

I was just one lieutenant in the army of children born after World War II. The bad business of genocide and greed for world superiority had been settled once and for all. Emboldened by the moral certainty that the good guys had won, North Americans got busy. They built factories to work in and schools to warehouse their progeny. They built little houses with tidy flower gardens out front, and in the back, diapers flapped on clotheslines like flags of liberation. And, just to be safe, every basement had a fruit cellar full of canned goods that could double as a bomb shelter in case the commies made good on their threat to retaliate.

After a week, I felt certain that Ollie was long gone. And indeed, he was. He had already negotiated the waters of Lake St. Clair and the Detroit River. He was crossing Lake Erie, floating in the fresh current of emancipation. Schools of perch were chasing him through that big body of warm water, no fences, no barriers. Buoyant and giddy, he must have marvelled at the ceiling of stars that had been hidden away in a dormant corner of his memory.

During that summer, I was consumed with a problem that was not featured in any Hardy Boys mystery. I would have rather been trapped in a seaside cave by an Aztec Warrior, than face the reality of my circumstances. I dared not share my dilemma with anyone. Not even my parents. Especially not my parents.

It happened at the Y. The YMCA swimming pool in London was located about four kilometres from my house in Byron. Biking distance. In 1958, parents did not chaperone their children to activities. Kids walked to hockey practice with skates slung over shoulders. They joined Scout troops in church basements. They got lifts to baseball practice from friends with brothers old enough to drive.

You couldn't count on your parents. Mothers usually had a baby to look after and a casserole in the oven. Dads worked long hours and then, after dinner, went to community service meetings. They were Lions or Kinsmen or Rotarians. Some kids had parents who were interested in their extra-curricular activities, but I wasn't one of them.

That summer, my mother paid for me to take swimming lessons at the Y. She wanted me to get my Bronze Medallion so I could be a lifeguard. She did nothing to encourage me to play sports, but she did not want a book worm for a son either. So, five days a week, I put a towel around my neck and biked downhill to the pool. Which was too bad, because it would have been nice the other way round, uphill to the pool, a refreshing swim and then glide all the way home. Instead, I had a sweaty and exhausting ride to look forward to after my lesson. In the heat of the day. Pedalling like crazy.

My lesson was at 9 a.m. so I bolted a bowl of Rice Krispies and called out that I was leaving, and away I went.

Now, here's the thing about the Y pool in 1958. No swimsuits were allowed. Due to a strict code of public hygiene, bathing costumes were forbidden. In the early years of the twentieth century, when public pools were built in urban areas, cholera and polio and other contagious diseases were rampant killers. The farm boys and the small-town kids who jumped into streams and ponds to cool off on hot days were likely to pick up some nasty water-borne illnesses. With the introduction of public pools, there was a danger that swimwear could pollute the water and endanger swimmers, so we swam naked.

There was a certain camaraderie in those times, owing to men chumming with men. World Wars and the Scouting movement encouraged this culture of bold athleticism. So even though my instinct was to cover my genitals, I imitated the other fellows and kicked off my pants. But some things are hard to fake and casual nudity is one of them for me.

What was it about me that made me a target? I was not muscular. I had no hint of body hair. I tended to slouch. No pretense of bravado could clothe my awkward self-consciousness.

Someone noticed. Now, I don't think there were any more perverts per square kilometre back in 1958 than there are today. But they operated in greater anonymity. There were no internet sites to make them feel they were part of a group. They worked in isolation. Parents and teachers did nothing to alert us to the possibility of pedophiles. Those preying on children in the 1950's were able to pose as good citizens and get away with it. Coaches and priests and Scout leaders and piano teachers. And swim instructors at the Y. They knew we wouldn't tell on them, because even though we were coerced, we were involved in something dirty.

This is difficult for me. I do not mean to accuse any of the youth organizations of the day. They offered opportunities that many boys would not have had otherwise. Also, even though I resented her at the time, it turns out my mother was right to ignore my pleas to quit swimming. I went on to star on my high school water polo team, winning provincial recognition. In university, lifeguarding financed pub nights at the Rathskeller and paid my bookstore bill. So, no. I did not suffer any long-term trauma. And somewhere in the world is a man who would have had his life cut short if I had not completed my lifesaving training.

It was the summer before my senior year and I was visiting my girlfriend, who had a job waitressing at Windermere House. Jean was cleaning up after the lunch shift, and I was lazing in a hammock strung between two hemlocks. The haze of August humidity made me tired, and I closed my eyes. I felt myself dropping into that bottomless state of an afternoon nap when I heard a woman calling a boy's name. Mark. Markie! Mark?

In that moment of waking, I turned my head. Noticed a flash of red on blue water. Tumbled out of the hammock. Ran and ran and dove and dove and dove again. Lake Rosseau is a deep basin with rocky shores, an inverted granite sculpture carved during the last ice age. Mark was a little fellow, without an ounce of fat to buoy him up and he had sunk like a stone beyond the drop-off ledge to the shadows. Red is a good colour. I grabbed the red trunks and hauled him out.

Mark responded well to CPR and recovered quickly. Quicker than his mother who accepted medical attention from a vacationing doctor. My girlfriend considered my actions heroic and was unusually passionate that evening, going so far as to initiate a skinny-dipping escapade that remains one of my loveliest memories. Swimming has endured as a lifelong passion.

But that summer, swimming was hell for me. I wanted to die.

According to the Y's history, swimming instruction became a priority for the organization in the 1920's when statistics showed that drowning was second only to disease in the death of boys and young men. Learning to swim would save thousands from untimely demise. Free, or at a nominal cost, boys signed up in huge numbers. Apparently, girls had other pastimes.

The instructor who taught the Bronze Medallion class in 1958 was called Ron Johnson. He was 19, newly graduated from high school and enrolled in the engineering program at the University of Western Ontario for the fall term. When he strolled into the pool enclosure on the first day, twelve boys sat waiting for him on the pavement at the shallow end of the pool.

"Call me Ron," he said, putting an ankle on a knee to balance his clipboard while he took roll call. Not wishing to be caught looking at the hairy nut that was peeping out of Ron Johnson's swimming trunks, I glanced around at the other boys. Some were sitting on their towels, leaning back on their hands, ankles crossed. Apparently quite at ease. Some had their towels draped around their shoulders, a little shivery in the morning shade. I sat with my arms hugging my knees, and my towel tucked up underneath to hide my shrivelled ball sack. Never, never, never in my life had I felt more vulnerable. And I must have worn that vulnerability on my face. Because after the lesson, when the other lads showered up and got dressed and headed up the hill on their bikes, I was alone in the change room. Despite a thorough search, my clothes were nowhere to be found.

Trying not to panic, I told Ron Johnson about my problem. He was kind and reassuring. He helped me check around and finally, he located my shorts and tee shirt tucked under the spinal board. He explained the way it was with boys. They liked to pull pranks. It was important to take it all in good humour so as not to make yourself a target. And he offered to let me keep my clothing in a safe place. His office. So it would not happen again. He put his arm around my shoulders and gave me a manly squeeze. Everything was going to be alright. I believed him. I trusted him. It was two weeks before he locked the office door behind him while I was changing.

I went from a kid who was teased for eating too much, to a kid who couldn't finish his lunch without running to the toilet. Gut pain is the worst kind of pain. You cannot fake it when your gut is twisted in knots. My mother thought maybe I had a tapeworm or something because I started to lose weight, and believe me, I was skin and bones to start with. I told her I was too sick to swim.

"Twenty-five dollars I spent on those lessons," she said. "You are going to get that badge, sick or not." She made an appointment at the clinic, then she called my swimming instructor.

Ron was worried about me, he told her. He knew it was a strenuous bike ride up the hill after lessons, so he started tossing my bike in the back of his pick-up and driving me home. He introduced himself to my mom. Told her I had real potential as a swimmer and, since I would pass my Bronze Medallion at the mid-August examination, she might consider signing me up for Masters swim classes so I could continue to develop my swimming strokes during the school year. Usually, they required kids to be 16 years old, but he could pull a few strings. He believed in me. The Masters classes were early in the morning. He would pick me up. He'd be happy to.

I understood, then, that my torture would not end with the Bronze Medallion. It would go on forever. I was trapped. The next morning, I left with my towel as usual. At the end of the block, I felt dizzy. Maybe I was dying, I thought. Last year a kid in my class, Greg Thompson, died of leukemia. The idea of lying in a hospital bed actually seemed safer to me than continuing on to the pool. I turned my bike around.

The gates to Springbank Park were padlocked. Open at 10 am, the sign said. But I found an opening in the hedge and pushed my way through. The dew was heavy and soaked my sneakers. No one was around.

For a long time, I leaned my forehead against the chain link fence and watched Dollie. She was lying under the slide. Her eyes had some kind of weird see-through eyelids that opened and closed from side to side. It seemed like maybe she was blind. That she couldn't see the paint flaking off the pool rim. Or the weeds sprouting out of the crumbling tarmac. Maybe, I thought, it was better not to notice those things.

Ollie would have noticed. They probably made his gut ache. I wandered down the slope, toward the river, trying to think like Ollie. And I found a deer trail through the pine needles leading to a sand bar where Ollie likely entered the water. Leaving my clothes and towel on the bank, I slipped into the water wearing only my tightie whities. The current was not as strong as it would have been earlier in the summer, but it was still moving along at a steady, muscular pace. I floated on my back, looking up at the clouds which seemed to be aiding and abetting my escape.

After about ten minutes, I bumped into a log jam. It was shallow and I found the muddy bottom with my toes. Willow trees drooped overhead, weeping as they do. Ollie would have flopped over this old tree limb and kept going. I imagined I could do that too. But the thought of getting farther away from my clothes seemed like it could make the situation worse. Exposed and chilled, I climbed the bank and found myself in the backyard of a mansion. Seriously. It was like a castle, with fountains and gardens and hedges clipped to look like swans and stuff. The grass was like a velvet carpet under my feet.

What would Joe Hardy do? Joe would not get himself in a situation like this. Maybe Frank would. He was the more impulsive brother. I didn't have much time to think on it though, because two big dogs came ripping out the back door, straight at me. They were going to tear me apart. I did not scream like a girl or turn and run. I stood as still as a statue. I was prepared to die.

There was a whistle and the dogs stopped in their tracks.

"Go on. Go lie down."

The voice was fragile and papery. I was, quite frankly, amazed that the killer dogs would obey such a weak command. But they did. The owner of the voice approached. An aged human, limping as if one leg was shorter than the other. The face hidden under the brim of a cloth hat. Loose khaki work clothes gave no hint of gender. The gardener, I assumed.

'You look like you're having a bad day, son,' he voice said. And I burst into tears.

I cried for a long time. Long enough to learn that I had happened into the backyard of a wealthy industrialist, famous in London for his philanthropy and despised by the general population for his reticence to appear in public. He declined invitations and refused awards (even when the mayor wanted to make him Citizen of the Year). He did not open his doors for anyone. The house had a ballroom and, it was rumoured, a bowling alley. But childless and widowed, Samuel Keifer kept to himself.

"I'm Sam," he said. He found me some pants and a belt to hold them up. He gave me an old football sweater that smelled like mothballs. He made tea.

I had never in my life had a cup of tea. Kids were given cocoa or Ovaltine if a hot drink was in order. All my adult life, whenever I felt troubled, I put on the kettle and thought about Sam. How methodically he filled the kettle and placed the teacups in saucers and set out the milk and the sugar and the Digestive cookies.

"Dunk them," he said. "Like this." He demonstrated. "Now. You better tell me the whole story, from the beginning. Take your time, son. I have nowhere to go."

I started with Ollie. Trapped and unhappy. The swimming lessons came out after a second cup of tea.

"Hmmm," Sam said. "Well, son. That is a problem. But every problem has a solution."

He led me to the garage and invited me to sit in the soft leather seat of his Cadillac. We drove to Springbank Park and retrieved my clothes. I changed in the public washroom. Sam helped me put my bike in the trunk. We drove to my father's work where we were ushered into his office after a few hushed words with the secretary. I sat in a chair beside Sam on the opposite side of my father's desk and listened to an outline of the problem, as Sam saw it. He captured the essence of the crisis without emotion. It sounded professional. Businesslike. My father was attentive and polite and appreciative. The men shook hands.

The world did not end.

Ron Johnson was let go from his position. If he stayed in London, I did not ever see him again, though sometimes I thought I did, and my heart would speed up and my stomach would clench. But always it was someone else.

He was a young man, after all. Only five years older than I was. My mother would have called him a charmer. Father did not confide in her the circumstances around Ron's firing. And of course, neither did I. We did not speak of the incident ever again.

Swimsuits were recommended for public bathing and the new policy took effect immediately. A woman, Mrs. Bernstein, taught the remaining classes for Bronze Medallion. She had once swum across the English Channel which did not impress me at the time. Her expectations were high, and her training sessions were punishing. All the boys complained except me.

When Samuel Kiefer died, he left his house to retired Catholic priests. There was an article in the Free Press questioning the value of that. What would retired priests do with a ballroom? A bowling alley? But Sam, I think, liked the idea of quiet, meditative men sipping tea and appreciating his garden. Men with nowhere else to go.

Somewhere near Sandusky Ohio, "Slippery" was sucked into an industrial pipe. He hurt himself trying to get out. A guy from the Toledo Zoo shot him with a tranquilizer gun and sent him home. London welcomed him back with a parade and a new, super-barricaded enclosure in the middle of Springbank Park called Storybook Gardens. I went to the grand opening. It was hard not to get caught up in the celebration. Our royal couple had their fairytale ending with flags flying and music piped in from a speaker in a fiddle-playing cat's belly. Hey Diddle Diddle. Humpty Dumpty was posed in a perpetual tilt on the edge of a golden rampart. An energetic trainer led the sea lions through a series of fun activities. Dollie tooted a horn. Ollie climbed the magic mountain and slid down the waterfall. After the performance, after the fish treats and applause, after the crowd dwindled, Ollie flopped to the back of the enclosure and poked his nose out between the bars toward the river. I waited, hoping for a sign that the sea lions were better off. In a perfect storybook world, Dollie would heave her great bulk to Ollie's side and offer him a nuzzle of understanding. It was with tremendous regret that I realized she had no such intention.

The Ark

Josephine Ball is always home. It's nice to know you can count on a person to be in one place. Sometimes you just want to visit with a friend, and you don't necessarily want to plan it in advance. Dropping in on friends has mostly gone out of style. People aren't at home. They are working or travelling or shopping. And if they are at home, you never know if you'll be welcome. You're likely to catch them in the middle of some renovation task, and they act like they're happy to see you, but really, they would just as soon finish painting the baseboards. Josephine is not like that. Her life is her farm, and her farm exists outside of time. She rises with the sun and wanders through her day in no particular order.

There's a name for it, when people don't leave their house. Agoraphobia. Agora is the Greek word for uptown. The last time Jo left the farm to go uptown was twenty years ago back in high school. It was Martha Collins' birthday, and we were all invited to her sleepover party. Martha's house had a finished rec room in the basement with a stereo, TV and shuffleboard table. There were six of us in baby doll pyjamas, playing music, eating chips and making prank phone calls to the boys we liked.

In the morning, there was no answer at Jo's house when she phoned to say she was ready to get picked up. So, my dad says, "Well, hop in Josie, we'll get you home. We go right past your place." And when we got there, up the long laneway, my dad says to us, he says, "Girls. I want you to stay in the car." He had an odd feeling, he told me later. The porch light was on, and it made him uneasy.

I park in the gravelled area over by the barn. Jo opens the back door, drying her hands on a towel and waving at me to come on in as if I am just the person she hoped to see at that minute. She clears away a pile of junk from the kitchen table where she has been working on some project. Hand painted greeting cards today. Last time it was wood burning. She is crafty and she doesn't mind a mess. The old buffet table that belonged to her grandmother is piled high with sewing and paint by numbers and jigsaw puzzles. Jo never lets any of it interrupt a conversation. She sets it aside and puts on a fresh pot of coffee.

"Now," she says. "What's this I read in the paper about a dog park in town?"

Town council is caving in to the pressure. There is an increasing population who like dogs better than people. Dogs are political now.

"Starting next week, Winston Park has gone to the dogs," I tell her.

"Right by the river?"

"Yep. Scenic. A shady place under the willows for hot days. Benches for dog owners. They installed a bunch of compostable dog shit bag dispensers and a couple of huge garbage bins to toss them in."

"So that goes to the landfill?"

"Right. Along with baby diapers, old people diapers. Disgusting."

The coffee machine beeps, and Jo gets two mugs out of the cupboard. We stir in some cream and sugar. I do not feel guilty about my sweet tooth here with Jo. She has gained weight since high school and so have I and neither one of us care. Her long brown hair is threaded with grey and hangs in one long braid down her back.

"I look like the wreck of the Hesperus," she sometimes admits.

The house is a bit of a wreck, too. An old farmhouse that was never properly updated. It is chilly in the winter, with old newspapers for insulation, and it is hot in summer, except for a big floor fan that maximizes the cross breeze when all the windows are open. There are no screens, because there are more flies hatching inside and trying to get out, than there are outside trying to get in.

While we chat, the residents come in and out of the kitchen and say hello. Wrecks, one and all, in one way or another.

Marilyn is at the sink, framed by trailing philodendrons

that sprout from crocheted plant hangers. She wears a gingham bib apron and rubber gloves. Doing the dishes is her job. She is not fast, but she is thorough. It is clear that she enjoys the process, the immersion of plates in sudsy water, the circular motion with the brush, the rinsing in hot, clear water. Finally, she places each dish carefully in the drying rack. Marilyn never, ever breaks a dish.

When she first arrived, angry with trauma and mean with pent-up rage, Marilyn broke a lot of dishes. Every dish in the cupboard went smashing onto the tiles. Jo punished her with hugs she didn't want. She cranked up her favourite CD of country music and they swept the floor together. And then Jo mixed up some cement from a bag in the shed and showed Marilyn how to turn the disaster into art. The disaster became colourful steppingstones leading to the raspberry bushes.

Jo put a request for dishes on the local buy and sell website and within a week, they had three complete sets of dishes from people in the town who support Jo. Marilyn treats the new dishes with reverence. She still has a temper, but now she uses it to mash potatoes or turn the compost pile.

Jo's kitchen has some history, like a hole in the ceiling where the old stove pipe used to be, and a souvenir spoon collection that was her mother's pride and joy. Buffalo. Niagara Falls. Port Colborne. Ottawa. Quebec City is the jewel in the crown, Jo says, because that is where her parents had their honeymoon.

There is a rocking chair with Jo's knitting bag next to it and an old Singer sewing machine, but the huge oak table anchors the entire room. One rainy night when Jo was a girl, a knock came at the back door and a woman fell inside screaming for help. They laid her out on the table, and she raised her knees and out came a baby. The whole event took about three minutes, Jo says, not even enough time for the water to boil. They scrubbed and scrubbed after the woman and the baby were gone, to get the blood stains out of the wood, but you can still see a dark spot at one end. Her dad joked that she should have gone to the barn. When the mares foal, it's easy to clean up. Just take and burn the straw out back. Jo didn't want to eat at that table the next morning, but her mother was strict and didn't put up with fussing and foolishness.

Marilyn fixes a coffee for herself and comes to sit with us. I pass her the cream and sugar. Jo thanks her for scrubbing the cast iron pan.

"Them eggs got scorched this morning. Good, job," she says. "I didn't think it would come clean."

"It took two SOS pads," Marilyn says.

Jo wasn't always this calm like she is now. In the year after both of her parents died of ptomaine poisoning, she suffered a rough patch on account of she didn't listen to my dad. She followed him into the house, and I followed her. Jo's mom was curled up on the bedroom floor in a puddle of vomit. We found her dad collapsed in the bathroom. He looked like St. Jerome, an image on a stained-glass window in our church. We are both Catholic. Were. This particular hollow-eyed saint looks heavenward, begging for death. He has a white beard, like Mr. Ball. Jo don't mind talking about her breakdown if you ask her, so I'm not telling you anything she wouldn't say herself. It was Father Pat that helped her climb out of it. Like climbing out of a deep dark well, Jo says.

The Catholic Church in our town has always been a small faction and if you see the Catholic graveyard out on the Harburn Road, you will see how few dead Catholics there are compared with the Evergreen Cemetery across the road, which is teeming with Protestants. Father Pat came by every day, hoping to coax Jo out of bed. Sometimes he just sat in the chair by the window and said nothing. He was there with her, so she wouldn't be alone. He coaxed a little soup into her, and he told her stories about when he was posted up north with the Inuit.

It took a long time. Months. But she got herself up and walking around the kitchen and then out to the barn. Her Uncle Jim had sold off the Ball's cows, but he came round every day to feed the horses and Aunt Beryl, his wife, would come in and do a bit of housework and drop off some eggs or a loaf of bread.

Uncle Jim, her mother's brother, was not a fan of Father Pat. He had some serious suspicions about the priest's intentions. Jim and Beryl wanted Josephine to move in with them, but Jo took a panic attack just thinking about leaving her property. Something bad would happen, she thought. She wouldn't make the same mistake twice. Now, if it had been me, I would have left that haunted place and got as far away as possible, but not Jo.

Father Pat helped Jo stand up against Beryl, who was a rough country woman. It was hard to say no to her and Jo was conflicted about what she should do. What was to become of her? Until Father Pat gave her a book to read about a man called Jean Vanier. I never heard tell of Jean Vanier, but he was a Canadian who started a community for people with disabilities and mental problems and called it L'Arche. The Ark. He had a tender feeling for people that society locked away, out of sight. People who had been trapped all their adult lives in insane asylums. He offered to share his little cottage with a few of them. He said, 'We must make a commitment to caring for one another in the most fragile moments of each of our lives.' Jo showed me the part in the book where it said that, and she copied it on a piece of paper and put it on the fridge with magnets.

"As soon as I read it," she said, "I got a vision about how I could turn this farm into an ark. Something to keep me from drowning."

We rinse our mugs and go outside to do the rounds. Warren is cleaning the cages in the rabbit hutch. In the barn, Gwendolyn and Marybeth are currying the manes of Bella and Boomerang. They are preparing for a trail ride with Carson Woodcock, a retired teacher, who comes around a couple times a week and teaches them all he knows about horses. Teaching and learning happen in a haphazard, seasonal way depending on the weather and nature and the whims of creativity that ebb and flow. When the sap starts running, Warren helps Roy get the buckets and spigots out to be washed. Then they load up the ATV and head out to the bush to get the tapping started. They have a sense for it, and they're rarely too early or too late.

When Jo started taking in roommates, Beryl nearly had

a fit. Warren Watson's propane heater blew up and his trailer burnt to the ground. Father Pat asked if she had anything to donate to get him back on his feet, knowing full well that there was a closet full of her father's clothes in perfectly good condition.

"He should stay here," Jo told him. She knew Warren. He had helped out with odd jobs around the farm. A gentle soul, her mother always said of him. She offered him her parents' room.

"I don't need so much space, Jo," Warren said. "You should have the big room and I'll take a smaller one." And so, they started transforming the house into something new. A sanctuary from the storm. Donations arrived. Twin beds for Gwendolyn and Marybeth, sisters in their forties with developmental delays. They couldn't manage after their mother passed so Father Pat asked if they might like farm life. And they did. Roy has a bed in the basement, by the washer and dryer. He's a recovered addict who lost all his teeth to pyorrhea. His false teeth hurt his gums, so he doesn't wear them. There have been transient guests who stayed a while and moved on. And one seasonal resident who used to arrive just before Christmas and stay until the ice went out of the river and the barrel went over the dam. Like the winter birds at the feeder, Brady showed up and accepted the charity he was offered. He slept on the couch by the wood stove and kept it stoked. Until one winter he didn't show up. Earl has the couch now.

Beryl stopped interfering after Father Pat retired from the priesthood and moved back to Moose Factory. She wasn't the only one in town who thought it strange that the Catholic priest would take such an interest in an orphaned girl. But even after all the evidence mounted up, folks did not like to accuse a man of the cloth of hanky-panky. Especially a benevolent man, so dedicated to community work.

She never said *I told you so,* to Jo. But it was clear that she was hurt. Jo had chosen Father Pat over her, and she never really forgave her for that.

"He kissed me often after Mom and Dad died," Jo told me. "Just on the forehead, as if I was a wee girl. I hardly noticed when his affections became more… intimate. Everything about his behaviour seemed to be spiritual. He was so encouraging. He started calling me Sister Josie, as if I was a nun. The odd thing is, we did build something good here. Do you believe that, Ruth?"

I told her I did. Lots of lovely things grow out of muck heaps.

The only hard and fast rule at Jo's place is that they eat meals together. Breakfast is at 8am. There are boxes of cereal on the table and a loaf of bread by the toaster. Fruit. Yogurt. Coffee. Tea. Jo insists they all hold hands, and she says a few words of gratefulness for having enough to eat and meaningful work to do and friends to share it all with. Then they take turns telling what they plan to do that day. And she will make suggestions if need be. Or give reminders. But she is not bossy. She is not their boss.

If you should find yourself at loose ends at mealtime, there is always a place at Jo's table. Jo remembers the wasted days and months after her parents died. A bunch of empty bedrooms. A cold stove. She ate cheese and crackers and apples. Now, nourishment is a big deal for her, the heart of the farm and what makes it work. Jo has three freezers full of food. Two chest freezers in the basement and an upright freezer in the garage. One freezer is full of meat. A local hunter keeps her well stocked with venison. Warren teases that the hunter is sweet on her, and she laughs it off, but she knows it's true. Her Uncle Jim is generous with beef and pork. And a turkey at Christmas. The other chest freezer is full of bargains, like when bread is on sale at Foodland? Jo will buy a dozen loaves. The owner delivers the order himself on his way home. Sometimes he won't take her money for food that is getting close to the 'sell by' date. "Your money is no good today," he tells her.

Jo knows the difference between bad behaviour and behaviour that is caused by despair. It doesn't happen often, but occasionally she has to evict people. There was the fella that smoked in bed and burnt a hole in the quilt. And the sullen guy who tried to pester Marybeth in the middle of the night. A roommate must respect the rights and boundaries of others. They can't say mean or hurtful things, or at least they can't make a habit of it. There are ups and downs, and Jo will cut some slack to anyone who occasionally slips up. In any group of people there are bound to be those who wear you down or get on your nerves once in a while. But if you push her too far, Jo's patience runs out. The long-time residents like it on the farm. They behave. They don't want to let Jo down. She has coached them carefully to deflect any rumours that she is running a business. They are friends who live together and contribute as they are able. That is all. There are different ways to be safe in the world that a safety inspector does not know anything about.

Josephine's ark floats along. She patches the leaks as needs must. It stays on course even after she hears some disturbing news about Jean Vanier, her inspiration. He was like Father Pat, it turns out. As he lay on his deathbed, venerated almost to the level of sainthood for his good deeds, six women came forward with stories of abuse. Father Mahéas, a spokesperson for the Catholic Church, gave a statement. Jo cut the article out of the Globe and Mail and highlighted this part in yellow. "The luminous part of him was so big that no one could suspect such a dark side, but the tendency to put people on a pedestal is not good for us Christians." After that, we both quit going to church.

Wednesday nights are music nights. Sometimes it's just a quiet evening watching a video. Warren likes the Eagles on Tour. Marilyn never gets sick of Sound of Music, the Julie Andrews movie. Recently, Roy has fallen in love with the Llewyn Davis soundtrack and has memorized all the words to 'Hang Me, oh Hang Me'. He sings it to the chickens, and they seem to like it. Some evenings, a real musician will pop in with a guitar or a banjo. And the drumming group from town comes once in a while with enough drums for everyone.

I'm the kind of person who needs company. I am married to a man who hasn't talked to me in over ten years. And no doubt, it is partly my fault for being a nuisance. I know I talk too much. At Jo's, there is always a listener. And a task. I can peel potatoes or throw a load of towels into the washer. I can set out by the creek and keep Earl company when he is fishing. He is hard of hearing, so he don't mind if I yak my head off.

One day I told him the whole story of how my old man almost killed me, and somehow, he knew to put his fishing pole down and hold my hand, and that made me cry. It was such a loving gesture. Then, he taught me some sign language. The signs for turtle and fish and bird.

Last week, Warren moved to Hanover to live with his sister so there was an empty bedroom and Jo invited me to take it.

"I am not homeless," I told her.

"Your heart needs a home, Ruth. You should come."

So, on Tuesday morning, after my husband left for work, I packed some clothes and got to Jo's in time for lunch. Pulled pork on a bun and a carrot salad.

Earl slid down the bench to make room for me.

SPARK

Sulphur smells like an invitation when the match is struck.
Once you start the fire, you must stay and tend it.
Without fuel, it will fizzle and die.

The Nook

Melba is lying face down on the sun-hot dock. Through a space between the boards, she can see rock bass suspended in the cool, green world below. The old aunties are dozing on lounge chairs in the shade over by the boathouse. The elder of the sisters, Kathleen, is engaged in a book. *The Heart is a Lonely Hunter*. Melba brought the book with her and is surprised that Aunt Kathleen, a brittle spinster, seems to be enjoying the story. She is a devout Anglican. High Anglican. So, the idea that she has been captivated by the story's ragged bunch of mistreated and misunderstood characters has her considering that there may be more emotional depth to Kathleen than she thought. Olive, the other auntie, has dropped her crochet hook and closed her eyes. She is the younger, kinder aunt. But fragile.

Melba is spending the summer here at The Nook, a

cottage on Gull Lake, purchased by Uncle Ted, the brother of the aunties. Uncle Ted came back from the Great War with a weak heart and damaged lungs, and he needed a refuge. A quiet place. The Nook is a simple structure with three tiny bedrooms, each with a curtain doorway. If you need to use a washroom, you go "up the hill". The outhouse has sunk into the earth, decomposing from the ground up, so the door doesn't close all the way. That's fine with Melba. She prefers to do her business with a full view of the lake and the trees and enough light to see the huge black spiders that lurk just below the rim of the hole. Yellowing catalogues and newspapers in a bucket serve as toilet paper. The aunties are close with a dime.

Melba comes prepared. She has a toiletries kit with tissues and some feminine hygiene products that the aunties consider wasteful. All their productive lives, they used cotton rags to stem the flow of their monthlies, soaking the soiled ones in cold water and reusing them indefinitely. The first time Melba came across a pail of the bloody bandages, she was sure someone had been murdered. "But no dear," Olive explained. "It's just the curse. You'll get it too, one day."

Melba has just finished her first year teaching at a two-room schoolhouse in Elmira. There were forty-five students in her classroom, from grades five to eight. The other teacher, Mrs. Franklin, taught grades one to four. There was also a principal, Mr. Atkinson, a young man of a serious nature, who sat in his office and did some kind of administrative work. For want of a caretaker (who was off fighting the war in Europe) Mr. Atkinson did the shovelling in winter, the grass cutting in warm weather, and took care of the mysterious boiler room tasks. No one knew why Mr. Atkinson had not joined the fight. He seemed fit enough. But there are other reasons why a man might be excused from service, and he didn't share any personal anecdotes with Melba, or with Mrs. Franklin.

Melba was exhausted by the teaching job, and glad to be at The Nook for a rest. She will be more efficient next year, having learned a great deal about behaviour management. The other reason she is here is to grieve. Or to get over her grief. "She's lost her beau," Kathleen whispers to her church friends.

Everyone assumes that Russell died in the war. And he did, sort of. He died, like so many boys, in a training maneuver; a crash landing due to human error, is what was reported. The planes are flimsy. Nothing to save you if a gust of wind catches you by surprise. Without ever seeing action, he died in a field of strawberries, seventy miles from home, behind the controls of a bright yellow Harvard.

Melba tries to summon up an appropriate amount of grief for Russell. He was a handsome boy. Of all the young men who have proposed marriage, he was the best looking, with erect posture and a strong chin. He had more testosterone than her other beaus, too. Athletic. Deep voice. Strong handshake. Her father didn't like him much. He was a bit too "hail fellow well met," for her strait-laced dad. Russell always had a flask in his pocket and a lie on his lips. A charmer. And he smoked. Lots of the boys smoked, of course. But most of her fellows, eager to impress her parents, would hold off on their vices until they were well away from the Dixon house. Russell? No. He drank and told off-colour jokes when and where it pleased him. And when Mrs. Dixon did not offer him an ashtray for his cigarette, he leaned back in his chair and carelessly flicked the ashes into the English bone china saucer under his teacup.

Melba was frankly embarrassed by him. Not that he cared much for her opinion. He expected all the girls to put up with his crass habits and be glad of the privilege. And they did. Russell had gone out with a few of Melba's girlfriends. He dumped them unceremoniously when the next girl took his fancy. But, oh. There was something special about that boy. Like a movie star! If you walked into a dance with Russell Walker? You were the belle of the ball.

At a cost, mind you. Russell was a man. With needs. He was not satisfied with a little petting in your mother's front parlour. Some boys were "respectful". They walked you to the door after a date and kissed you chastely on the cheek and told you to have sweet dreams. But Russell was, quite honestly, an animal. Oh, he knew how to treat a girl right. Corsage, compliments, romantic bits of poetry on a card. But after the party was over, you would find yourself in circumstances that required all the resolve of a stern schoolteacher. No! Hands off, Russell! Take me home. I mean it, Russell!

Russell was bewitched by Melba and her strict code of "hands to yourself!" He liked the challenge very much. And when he asked her to marry him, she was not fooled. Lots of girls ended up in the Salvation Army Home for Unwed Mothers because a boy had promised. PROMISED to marry her. That would not happen to Melba. She was immune to his passionate embraces, his wheedling, his desperation. There was always an edge of anger to his passion. And blame.

But Melba took no responsibility for Russell's behaviour, either in public or when they were alone. She was a self-contained person, with a wide following of friends who liked her lack of neediness. She had the knack of making you feel that life was effortless and interesting. But these characteristics also seemed to draw an unwanted crowd of doting young men to her door.

Courtship, Melba found, was banal. It ruined all the fun when you were expected to fall in love with one boy, and she participated reluctantly in the drama of phone calls and whispered confidences. She didn't want to appear ungrateful for the attention. She didn't want to be called "frigid", but she set her boundaries and they were non-negotiable. When Russell tried to undo her bra as they sat by the lake after a friend's engagement party, she pushed him off the dock in his good suit. For the five seconds it took for him to surface, she thought he would be furious. But he rose up, laughing and triumphant.

"I love you, Melba Dixon," he called. "Marry me!"

The aunties were protective of Melba. They had both lost their beaus in the Great War. The war that began with so much fanfare and optimism in 1914 with crowds waving at railway stations. The boys. Oh, the boys!

Kathleen's young man was Arthur, who left a successful dental practice to serve the Empire. He hung his white coat on the back of the office door and promised Kathleen he'd be home for Christmas.

"I told him not to go. What would make him believe he could be a soldier? He never fired a gun in his life. Lambs to the slaughter, they were."

Kathleen wore a locket with a twist of Arthur's red hair inside. She had a pile of letters from the front, tied with ribbon. Kathleen and Arthur had been secretly engaged on account of Arthur's mother who had a weak heart. Every time the couple was about to have their banns read from the pulpit, the miserable old lady retired to her bedroom, turned her face to the wall and prepared to pass away. But alas. The Lord spared her repeatedly, so that by the time Arthur left for the front, Kathleen was twenty-eight years old.

Spinsterhood was her service to the Empire. To King and country. Sacrifices had to be made. She went to Normal School and graduated as a teacher. So many women of her generation remained at home after their men died, caring for aging parents, dependent on small allowances from parsimonious relatives. Kathleen had a purpose in life. Her classroom was organized. Her students were disciplined. She was a pillar of her school, of her community, of her church.

Olive, however, never recovered from the loss of her beloved Percy. He was a sensitive soul, easily brought to tears by poetry or a beautiful sunset or a kind deed. Olive keeps a picture of him in uniform, in a polished sterling silver frame on her bedside table. Percival was shot at dawn. Shell-shocked and weary, he just walked away from the chaos. The telegram that arrived at his mother's house explained that he was sentenced to death by court's martial for casting away arms.

Olive pictures him dying without a blindfold, though it would have been offered to him.

Melba knows quite a lot about her ghost uncles, Arthur

and Percival. The aunties talk about them with great familiarity.

"Percy would love this sunset."

"Arthur always did enjoy Mother's home-made butter tarts."

Melba is quite certain she won't refer to Russell thirty years hence. She stands up, adjusts her swimsuit, and pulls her bathing cap over her brown curls. With strong, elegant strokes she swims to the far side of the point where the aunties cannot see her and hoists herself onto a granite outcropping.

Melba has turned down more marriage proposals than any of her friends. Seven. Including Russell. And she feels like, perhaps, she is tempting fate. The men who proposed were all perfectly good candidates, for different reasons. Some were stolid and reliable. One came from money. She would have had a fine house if she'd accepted. One was exceptionally good looking. That was Russell. And one was a theologian, bound for the ministry. Her mother's favourite. There was a musician. She liked him well enough, but she worried she would have to spend a great deal of time defending him to the world. She saw how other men weren't easy with him and she expected that a husband should have male friends who went to football games and took off on fishing weekends. Men who had interests beyond the domestic threshold. The musician cried bitterly when she turned him down and she felt sick with disappointing him, but, for heaven's sake! She was quite sure she was not worth all that fuss.

Up the hill on the far side of the point is the foundation of an old logger's cabin. One partial wall and an old wood stove are all that remain of the ruin. Inside the stove, Melba keeps a package of Player's cigarettes. Russell left them in her car the last night they were together. It was only six weeks ago. She smokes them one at a time, her own little ceremony for a handsome boy whose fingerprints are still on the package. Inside, the foil wrapping reveals three cigarettes. They smell like Russell. She lights a paper match, a tiny sulphur torch. Inhaling the tobacco hurts her throat and leaves the most unpleasant taste in her mouth. And yet she is starting to enjoy this interlude. She finds herself anticipating it and her heart beats a little faster. As the nicotine surges through her system, she is alarmed at the jolt she gets. Punishing but rewarding, like a slap on the ass from a tipsy soldier at a dance.

"Hello there!"

Melba whimpers a suppressed scream that turns into a cough.

"Swimmers shouldn't smoke," he says. He is tall and very thin with a bare chest that is hairless and pale. His swimming trunks are droopy and dripping.

"I don't usually… I'm not really a smoker. It's just that. My fiancé died a few weeks ago and this was his last pack of cigarettes and I've been finishing them for him. I don't know why. I think I might be crazy."

"How…"

"RCAF. Training accident down in Dunnville."

"I'm so sorry." He looks at the cigarette, burning itself out in between her fingers. "I feel like I've interrupted something intimate. I apologize."

"Not at all," Melba says, dropping the butt into the belly of the rusty stove. She sniffs her fingertips and then laughs. "It stinks. I don't know why on earth he liked them so much."

"Wes," the man says, holding out his hand to introduce himself. "My parents own the cottage across the bay. The one called Hillcliff. I watched you swimming, and I followed you over here."

"Melba," she said, letting him give her smelly hand a firm squeeze. "I suppose I should be flattered."

"No. You should be frightened half to death, a stranger climbing up from the depths like this." He smiles and looks away. A man not accustomed to joking with the opposite sex.

"You aren't very threatening," she says, glancing down at the concave curve of his chest, his vulnerable, goose-pimpled little nipples.

"I suppose not," he agrees. "But I am terribly lonely. Terribly bored. And you looked terribly friendly."

"No harm done, Wes."

"You're staying at Ted Cochrane's cottage?"

"Yes. He's my uncle. My mother's brother. I am there for the summer with my two aunts who are very staid and proper."

"Yes. I've seen them in their black bathing costumes early in the morning."

Melba smiles. "It's their routine. There's a little sliver of Pears soap under the dock that they use to freshen up. We've no running water in the cottage. It's rustic."

"As it should be. "

The rough log Melba sits on is cutting into the backs of her legs and she stands, suddenly wanting to return to The Nook. Something in the young man's demeanour lets her know that he is just about to ask her out on a date, and she wants to avoid hurting his feelings. He is not as sensitive as her musician, but he takes himself a bit too seriously. She thinks he might be a chartered accountant or a banker.

"Well," she says. "Nice to meet you, Wes. The aunties will be worried that I have drowned."

"Of course, yes. Me too. I better head back, too. My mother is, well she's not likely worrying about me at all. But still..."

A pair of crows make some comical comments overhead and the two young people laugh together, as if caught out by the kind of old crones that Wes imagines her aunts to be.

Melba snaps the dome on the chinstrap of her bathing cap in an enticing way, like a swimsuit model in the Eaton's catalogue. She slips off the granite ledge and treads water for a minute while Wes sits and watches her. Then she waves and heads off in a strong front crawl, knowing that he knows that she knows he will not take his eyes off her until she is out of sight.

Wes arrives soundlessly at The Nook at ten o'clock the next morning, silently paddling his canoe with enough expertise to surprise the aunts. He introduces himself and offers a tin of bran muffins that his mother baked. Kathleen and Olive are delighted to meet him. They remember his father as a child and ask after his grandparents. "Your people have always been good neighbours," Kathleen tells him. "No motorboats, no loud parties."

Wes does not mention that he met Melba yesterday. He is hoping she will appear. He is hoping to invite her to go for a paddle to the town dock where he can treat her to an ice cream cone. He doesn't imagine that she is watching him from the hammock, calculating his commitment by his ability to engage the aunties in conversation.

Kathleen, who is usually cautious about social intercourse with neighbours lest they become too familiar, is smitten with the young man. She has invited him to pull his canoe up on the little beach, to sit in Ted's chair. Would he have a cup of tea if she made a pot? Yes, he would enjoy that.

Left alone with Wes, Olive blushes. She knows exactly what Kathleen is up to and she does not approve. Melba will not appreciate it. But Wes soon puts her at ease, telling a story about a red fox who has started visiting the cottage in the evening, hoping for some leftover tidbits from their supper table. He senses that Olive is more comfortable listening than talking, but he does not like to dominate a conversation, so after a while he asks her about wildlife at The Nook and, though she speaks quietly, Olive puts her crochet hook down and describes the muskrat who lives under the boathouse. Then they sit silently for a time, until Kathleen appears with Melba, steps behind her, carrying the tea tray. Melba giggles a bit, an involuntary habit she has when she is nervous, and survives the introduction. The aunties pretend not to notice their niece's awkward behaviour as she refuses the chair that Wes offers. Instead, Melba spreads her towel at the edge of the dock and dangles her toes in the water.

"Watch out for the snapping turtle," Olive tells her. "The snapper," she adds for Wes's benefit, "is an old dinosaur of a creature who passes The Nook twice a day. Early in the morning on his way to the marsh, and then again around noontime." Kathleen smiles at her sister and raises her eyebrows. Well, well. Olive is besotted.

Wes graciously offers to pour the tea. He passes the muffin tin around. It is pleasant, Melba finds, sitting and listening to small talk. The conversations flow effortlessly from one topic to the next. The drought and the fire ban. The rumour of a new highway to cottage country from the city. The brilliance of the full moon the night before last. Wes does not talk about himself, or the war. When he notices Olive trying to hide a yawn, he stands and announces that he will be on his way.

"Will you join me, Melba?" he asks directly. There is no hesitation in his voice. He wants an answer, yes or no, and he will accept either with equanimity.

Melba is wearing her white short-shorts and a plaid shirt with rolled up sleeves. She washed her hair this morning under the pump in the yard and she very much wants to go to town. She is a pretty decent paddler, too, confident in a canoe. She earned her waterfront badge from CGIT. Canadian Girls in Training.

"No," she tells him. "But thank you for asking." She can't come up with a reason for her refusal, because there is nothing, absolutely nothing that she has to do today. Read. Swim. Suntan. All she knows is that she does not want to spend the next hour or so thinking of things to say.

Wes isn't upset. Or at least he does not show it. In fact, he is so good-natured that Melba walks with him to the beach and helps him launch his canoe. Encouraged, he makes another bid for her company.

"I'm going to the tennis court in Gravenhurst tomorrow. No game, I just want to practice my serve. Will you come along?"

"Yes. Okay, sure. I don't have my racket here," she says.

"I'll bring my mother's for you. It's a good one. I'll pick you up at 9:30."

Melba stands and watches as Wes solos out into the middle of the lake and negotiates the cross current to the far side. He is a competent paddler, she notes. A reliable sort of a man.

And that is the story of how they met, Melba and Wes. They married and had four kids who loved summers at The Nook and at Hillcliff. The story about their romantic dad pursuing their reticent mother became mythical in its retelling around campfires and on canoe trips. There were births and deaths and graduations and illnesses and weddings. The disappointments were tempered with moments of great joy. A grandchild learning to swim, the whole family huddled in sleeping bags under the August night sky as meteors dove and streaked and disappeared. The bay was their bay. A sanctuary in times of loss. First one auntie died and then, within a week, the other. The grandparents passed in the 1970's and Uncle Ted, who outlived them all, finally died in 1980, closing the World War I chapter of family history. Regardless of the season, the surviving family members honoured the dead on the dock with stories and scotch.

The oldest of Wes and Melba's children, Alan the dentist, bought a cottage of his own. His wife was fussy. She complained ceaselessly about the mildewy mattresses and mouse droppings at Hillcliff. And there were bloodsuckers at the beach, making it necessary to keep a shaker of salt handy. They purchased a newer cottage on a better lake and didn't visit much after that.

The next oldest, Martha, bought The Nook from Uncle Ted's estate. She was a single lady. A career girl, her mother always said when introducing her to friends. "Martha is a Unitarian Minister. She's our career girl."

Martha had a lot of friends, and they were outdoorsy types. They fished and swam, and in the winter, they snowshoed across the lake. She married a local man, a Gravenhurst businessman who was crazy about her, but the marriage lasted less than a year. No one in the family talks about it.

The youngest of Melba and Wes's children, Charlene, went to school for a long time. She got her PhD. In Gravenhurst, people joke about higher education, particularly graduate degrees. They make fun of their own progeny. "My kid has a PhD, too," they tell Charlene. "Pa has dough."

Charlene laughs along with them, secretly wondering if, indeed, it had all been a waste of time, jumping through the hoops of academia only to end up living in cottage country, working as a real estate agent. She had Hillcliff winterized, at her own expense, with new windows and a steel roof. She took all the old beds to the dump and bought good mattresses. She will inherit the cottage, but there's a catch. She also inherits the responsibility for the doddering old couple that her parents have become. And as a special bonus, she has been assigned power of attorney for Robert, the crazy brother.

"No need to worry," her lawyer tells Charlene. "It's actually more of a moral responsibility than a legal one. It's Canada after all. If he ever shows up, you can offer him the guidance he needs to access the system. Group homes, medical needs. You're not going to end up saddled with the responsibility of a…"

"Schizophrenic," Charlene says.

"A person with schizophrenia," the lawyer says.

Alan and Martha realize that it's a good deal for everyone. They both love their little sister. Charlene has done a great job maintaining Hillcliff and has taken over all the expenses like taxes and insurance. She's had a well drilled. The toilet flushes year-round. The older siblings agree that she deserves to inherit the cottage when the time comes.

Except things change. Nobody anticipates the mess that aging parents create until they are in the middle of the geriatric horror show. Melba died the easy way, during an afternoon nap. Heart. It is Wes that becomes the worrisome project. Always a quiet, private man, he is overwhelmed with unmanageable emotions after Melba dies and he goes straight to crazy town. Six months pass and he doesn't get better. When Martha finds him sobbing as he sorts through fifty years of memorabilia in the basement, she calls a family meeting, and they start researching long-term care homes. Wes flat out refuses to cooperate. He becomes mean and ornery, alienating his children and any family friends who happen to drop by with suggestions for senior social clubs or bus trips to Florida.

Martha calls Charlene. Her voice is strident and it is clear that Martha, the Minister, is running out of patience. "It's time. I dropped in this morning and found him sorting through all those magazine clippings of the monarchy, Char. Mom was quite in love with Queen Elizabeth, remember? Well Dad thinks they are worth something. He is classifying them into decades and putting them in file folders."

"That won't hurt anyone, Martha. It keeps him busy."

"Except that he is harassing people, Char. He believes he's sitting on a king's ransom of china, silver, crystal… all the heirlooms inherited from the aunties. He's had seven or eight antique dealers come over to have a look and evaluate it all. He's refused all cash offers. He runs them off and accuses them of being everything but a white man."

"Geez, Martha, you can't say that anymore."

"Those are Dad's words."

"Where would Dad even learn such a saying?"

"Probably he learned it where he's living. In 1950. Anyway, he's offended every junk dealer within a hundred kilometres. No one wants to come to look at his relics. He gave my phone number to the auctioneer from Selkirk. Glenn Somebody. Glenn told me there are warehouses full of this stuff. Nobody's trying to rip your dad off, he said. It's just that there's no market for it anymore."

"What do you want me to do, Martha?"

"I don't know, Char. I just want you to know. To be ready. He's really losing it."

It took Wes most of that first lonely winter as a widower to catalogue the family treasures. Then he set up his old slide projector and clicked through his life chronologically. Wedding, first house, birth of first baby, christening, the drive across Canada to Vancouver, other births and christenings that were hard to identify. Expo 67 in Montreal. Some hockey photos of Alan and his friends skating on the backyard rink.

Wes lost weight. He grew pale. His head drooped lower and lower, settling between his shoulders. But everyone was busy, not to mention a little pissed off at him. "Let him reap what he hath sown," Martha said. "Our mother was a saint."

He managed to get himself tidied up for Thanksgiving dinner at Alan's house and, except for some quiet weeping when they said the blessing, he didn't set off any alarms. At Christmas, when they met at Martha's church for the candlelight service, he looked diminished and delicate, but colds and flu and miserable weather had everyone looking poorly.

"What do you expect?" Martha says when Alan raises some questions of concern as they are wrapping up turkey leftovers in the church kitchen. "He's almost 90. He's on the decline."

"We should get him into a Long-Term Care facility," Alan suggests. Again.

"Of course. But he's a stubborn old bugger. He won't even go for a drive and look at the options. There's a nice place in Burlington where some of his friends are. Remember the Pattersons from the church? They're there. And so is Lenny Rosenburg. You could play bridge, I told him. There's a happy hour before dinner. It's time you got out of the basement, I said."

"He didn't like that."

"No. He didn't like that. So, I told him if he stays at his

own place, I'd be forced to call Community Care and get someone to help with the cooking and cleaning. The place stinks. They can give him a bath and prepare meals. I think he only eats cereal and toast."

"And?"

"And that went over about as well as our Meals on Wheels trial. He thought they were poisoning him."

"Death by Shepherd's Pie."

"What are we talking about?" says Charlene, approaching with a tray of gravy boats.

"Guess," Martha says.

They giggle like children when Wes chooses that exact moment to emerge from the men's room, holding up his pants with two hands.

"I need some help with this belt," he says, unapologetically.

Martha's friend Grace offers to help, understanding that the siblings might want to chat, but he will have none of it. He thinks that Grace is a social worker or some kind of hired help. Alan ushers him back into the washroom and gets him tidied up.

It was mid-January when they started getting the calls that kicked things up to the next level.

"Hi Dad. How are you feeling?"

"Is Mom over at your place?"

Pause.

"I can't seem to find your mother. Do you know where she is?"

Charlene drove down from Gravenhurst to take him to a

gerontologist's appointment, and ended up moving in. Temporarily. "He shouldn't be on his own," she was told.

Obviously. The house was a wreck. Their dad was a wreck. Her real estate career, selling cottages in a stalled economy, was a wreck. She took her dad on like an assignment she didn't want but couldn't think of how to decline. For a week, she focused on his house with the idea that she would get it ready for listing on the spring market. She left Wes to moulder down in the basement until she got the main part of the living quarters into shape. Seven trips to the Donation Centre and two bottles of Mr. Clean later, she poured herself a beer, sat on the top step of the cellar stairs and observed her father.

He was looking through Melba's childhood collection of china dolls and tea sets. Melba had been disappointed that her daughters were more interested in Barbies than the antique stuff she had played with as a kid. There was her wedding dress, spread out on a chair. Charlene tried to be objective, but this was sad. Very sad. She wished her dad could go to bed, like Mother, and pass away quietly in the night.

He was reading letters and crying. Bawling. He was sick with loss, or regret, or both. Finally, Charlene clomped down the stairs and asked what he was reading.

"Letters from your mother's new husband," he said. He passed them over to her. "She's left me. She never really loved me."

And then Charlene heard someone clomping down the cellar steps behind her. A man with long hair and a beard appeared out of the shadows. She screamed.

"It's me," he said. "For god sakes, Mother, it's me, Robert."

Charlene calls a family meeting. "It's an emergency," she says when Martha tries to decline.

Robert moves into his childhood bedroom. He apologizes to Charlene for mistaking her for Mother, but he keeps calling her Mom anyway.

"Sorry. Sorry, Char. I just can't seem to get it through my head that Mom has passed." Char tells him not to worry. No big deal. But she wonders how hard Alan really looked for Robert to inform him about Mom's death. It turns out he's been living in Fort Erie. Not far away. Not hiding or anything. He had an address. And a disability pension. And tax returns.

The unfortunate thing about Robert talking about Mom as if she were alive, is that it fits well with Wes's belief that she is now cohabiting with Russell, the good-looking boyfriend. The fact that the affair is happening beyond the grave does not factor into the conversation. Wes and Robert talk about this betrayal in low voices. They look like brothers instead of father and son. Robert has lived rough for a long time. He was a graduate student at Western University when his oddly brilliant career path as a mathematics professor was stopped in its tracks by a brain gone rogue. "Just like a short circuited computer," Alan described it then. "The motherboard is feeding messages to the screen that seem authentic, but they are disconnected from reality."

Thus started a nightmarish cycle of scaring the shit out of people that led to jail time that led to immersion in criminal culture that led to street drugs that led to hospitalization that led to heavy doses of clozapine. Medicated Robert is gentle and dull. He sleeps a lot. He smokes cigarettes and drinks coffee. Then he misses his medication for a day or two and goes on an alcoholic bender. Then he wakes up in jail. Then he gets back on his meds.

Charlene cannot even imagine the crooked road that has brought him back home after years of begging at death's doorstep. But here he is, chatting with their father and trying to get his head around their mother's betrayal.

"After fifty years of marriage," Wes says. "How could she?"

Robert nods but doesn't quite understand. "Who? Mom? She's standing right in front of you, Dad."

"That lady? That's not your mother. That's the housekeeper."

"Fuck. Seriously? It looks like Mom."

"Hello," Charlene says. "It's me. Charlene."

She makes sandwiches for them and then she watches as Robert takes the bread slices apart, checking for... what? Razorblades? Pills? Wes makes it clear he does not like tuna and orders a ham sandwich. And he wants ice cream for dessert. "This isn't a restaurant," she tells him. He looks at her suspiciously. She doesn't really give a shit if they both starve. "You always ate tuna sandwiches when Mom made them for you," she reminds him, even though she is not sure it's true. "If you get hungry enough, you'll eat them."

She puts her coat on and leaves for Tim Hortons where she can check her email. There is no WiFi in the nuthouse. Charlene's research on her father's behaviour leads her to a site on Lewy Body dementia, which includes hallucinations. Seeing people who are not really there. The website tells her to get help. The earlier the better. She calls her friend Sharon, the nurse.

"Jesus!" Sharon says. "Whatever you do, don't get him diagnosed! The price for long term care goes sky high for dementia patients. Get him on the waiting list for The Lodge pronto! Meanwhile, don't let on to anybody that he's seeing things. Once he gets settled in there, it'll be their problem, not yours. Hey. Maybe take him up to the cottage and keep him hidden away until they have a bed for him."

"How long will that be?" Charlene asks.

"Not long," Sharon tells her. "C difficile, is going around. The old folks are dropping like flies. The flag's permanently at half-mast."

The Lodge is the name of the county home. In this community, where a tannery used to be the biggest industry, there is an underground support system for locals. Wes grew up here and his parents grew up here, so he is on the list of "hometown people who deserve to jump the queue." Charlene follows Sharon's advice and gets her dad in to see old Doc Collins who is tottering on the edge of the abyss himself. He takes Wes's pulse and listens to Charlene's story about how her dad is alone and not able to wash himself or make his own meals and she is willing to take a short leave of absence to help care for him, but then he will be on his own. Doc gets Wes on the list right away.

As it happens, Charlene knows the manager at the clinic, Sue Clue who was first runner up for Prom Queen at the high school back in '82. Charlene placed third. The winner was Marcie Green, doomed to die in a car wreck on her way home in the wee hours.

Sue assures Charlene that she will put a star beside Wes's

name. She will get him a bed as soon as possible. Charlene wipes away a few tears and hugs her old rival and then she turns around to see her dad taking a People magazine with the Queen on the cover right out of the hands of a pregnant woman.

"ASAP," Sue calls after her as Charlene apologizes to the woman.

"That's mine," Wes insists. "She stole it." Charlene struggles to get her dad's arms into the sleeves of his coat.

Thank you, Charlene mouths, treating her dad with more deference than she might have if no one was watching. She knows she is a terrible person for wishing his life away, but this next phase of existence does not appear to have any benefits. Hurrying it along seems to be the kindest thing and she is determined to get going on it.

The first thing she does is get Wes to sign over power of attorney and power of care to her. She is businesslike, and her dad is convinced she is some kind of lawyer. He nods his head and signs his name on all the lines marked with a highlighter. She sneaks in the real estate agreement. He signs that too.

She lists the house herself, with Alan and Martha's blessing, but Robert is starting to get comfortable in his old boyhood bedroom. He senses that the gravy train is pulling away from the station. Knowing that he has a heightened awareness for conspiracies, Charlene offers to bring Robert along to the cottage. She doesn't want him hanging around to witness the junk man carting away the contents of the family home. Followed by the cleaners. Her ReMax colleague will stage the house and put a sign on the lawn. It is sneaky, yes. She knows all that. But Wes's dementia is getting more bizarre by the minute. Last night Wes wandered next door looking for Melba. He pounded at the front door in his pyjamas, shouting, "I know you're in there, Russ. I'll call the police! You better let my wife come home!"

Fortunately, the Nelans are in Florida, and nobody sees the demonstration except for a new neighbour across the street who looks curiously out the upstairs window. Charlene hasn't met him, but she knows he is some kind of refugee who has probably seen more bizarre events.

On the way to Gravenhurst, Charlene gives her dad a package of photos and keepsakes rescued from the boxes that will be on their way to the dump by now.

"We'll keep these at the cottage, Dad," she tells him. "Where you and Mom met. The cottage was always a special place for you guys."

Charlene turns on some classical music. In the back seat, Robert is dozing off. He sleeps a lot. Everything goes well until they get on Highway 11 and Wes screams, "Look out!"

Charlene veers onto the soft shoulder and skids to a stop. The pick-up truck that was following a bit too close, lays on the horn and makes it around her without incident.

"What?" Charlene yells in alarm. "What is it, Dad?"

"There were children on the road. Didn't you see the children? You almost hit them! Look. There they are. They're in that tree, now. Climbing in the tree." His voice gets quieter as he speaks, giving Charlene to understand that he knows that maybe that isn't possible. It isn't likely. And yet he continues. "You know who they are?"

From the back seat, Robert pipes up. "Who are they, Dad?"

"They're Melba's kids. She and Russell have kids. They have children. A boy and a girl."

"That's fucked up, Dad!" Robert says.

Charlene can't help it. She laughs. She actually cannot catch her breath from laughing so hard. And then Robert laughs and Wes, and they're all laughing. Charlene gets hold of herself and puts the car in gear and then Robert pipes up and says, "Should we ask them, do they want a ride?"

Wes says, "No. They're not our responsibility."

Robert finds a job working for a sketchy dude called Vince. Vince has a fleet of trucks that serve various purposes depending on the time of year. Plowing, sanding, logging, hauling. He does it all for cheaper than the next guy. Whatever price you get quoted by that company on the highway? Vince can undercut it. Robert gets to bring home a battered old pickup so he can get wherever Vince tells him to go. Vince calls every morning with a plan. He doesn't think it out too far ahead of time, which suits Robert pretty well. Robert doesn't keep a calendar. If it snows, Robert will be plowing driveways. Freezing rain? Sand and salt. Sometimes there are days off. Sometimes there are jobs that fly under the work permit radar. They might do some digging in a wetland area that the Ministry of the Environment doesn't really need to know about. They might tear down an old wreck of a garage and build a new one.

Vince likes the fact that Robert doesn't say much. He does what is asked of him and takes the cash Vince offers without question.

Sometimes there are stretches of days when there is no work, and Robert just stays home with Wes. They watch TV in their sweatpants and old flannel shirts. They make sandwiches and warm up tins of soup or spaghetti-os. Charlene is actually pleasantly surprised at how well they have all fallen into a routine. She is able to go into the office most days. The spring listings for cottages are coming in. She has some open houses booked for April when the ice will be going off the lakes. After she leaves the office, she picks up groceries and prescriptions and library books. She socializes a bit, accepting invitations for events at the arena or the Legion. Sometimes she gets an alarming pressure in her chest worrying about the possibility that something bad might be happening at home. She projects her thinking forward to the summer when she expects her father will be tucked away safely at The Lodge and Robert will have wandered off somewhere, following the path of least resistance.

Then she gets a call from Elmer Gordon, her father's lawyer.

"So, I've had a few calls from your dad," he says.

Charlene realizes she has become complacent. She has been leaving her dad alone too much with his broiling thoughts.

"He is concerned that your mother, and her new husband… and their children…"

Charlene groans. "Go on, Elmer."

"He says they are trying to steal the cottage out from

under him. He claims that she wants half of everything. And he thinks she might be trying to kill him."

"Oh Lord."

"My assistant didn't know that your mother has passed. She took down all the information and asked him a lot of questions about the property and the division of assets and he got confused."

"I bet."

"Unfortunately, he keeps calling. We've had three calls already today."

"Sorry, Elmer. I think he's been watching too many episodes of Law and Order. And my brother Robert is back living with us."

Elmer knows about Robert.

"So, who is this Russell that Wes is so worried about? This new husband?"

"Oh my God, Elmer. Russell was Mom's boyfriend that was killed back in World War II. Before Mom and Dad even met. But after Mom died, Dad found some of Russell's letters. You know. Love letters like a soldier would send to his sweetheart. And Dad has invented this whole story about how he has lost Mother's affections. That she's left him for her true love."

"Have you had him tested for… you know. Dementia? Alzheimer's?"

"Um." Charlene hesitates. "He's seeing a specialist. Trying to find the right balance for his medication. It's not easy. He's healthy other than this obsessive thinking. And everything we try has side effects. Like constipation. Which, believe it or not, is worse than your dead wife remarrying and having children. He sits on the can for hours."

Elmer can sympathize. He got backed up real bad after his kidney operation when the opioids he was taking for pain left him shitless for two weeks. It was awful.

"I would suggest you just ignore his calls, Elmer."

"You have power of attorney, Charlene. Am I right?"

"That's right, Elmer. Your office has copies of those papers. Don't worry. I'm looking after him."

"Of course. Let me know if there is anything I can do to help," he says. "Sorry for your troubles, Charlene. You're a good daughter."

Charlene thanks him and hangs up and wonders how good of a daughter she really is. You really don't have to be that good for people to believe you're dutiful and all. It just goes to show that people don't really expect much. Short of being a criminal, people will congratulate you on sticking around. Taking care of old people and watching out for mentally ill siblings gets you a lot of points, even if you do a barely adequate job.

March is what they call a shoulder season in cottage country. The warmer temperatures put an end to skiing and snowshoeing and snowmobiling and ice fishing. But the summer sports won't start until late May. Robert gets antsy. Other than a bit of illegal logging back on crown land, work has slowed down.

The personal hygiene of both Wes and Robert has become an issue. Charlene moves herself into the loft above the garage, which is not insulated and has no running water, but at least she can breathe. She buys a good quality heater from Home

Hardware and a down comforter, and she locks the door on crazy town. But some mornings when she does her rounds of the cottage before leaving for work, there is evidence of struggles.

"What happened here?" she will ask her father who hasn't shaved in weeks. He looks at her through red-rimmed eyes that appear to have witnessed a terrible holocaust.

"Those children were here last night," he tells her one morning.

"What children, Dad?" Charlene knows what children, of course, but she wants to hear him say it. She wants him to hear for himself how ridiculous it sounds.

"They left them here for me to look after. Your mother and her new husband. They went on a holiday, I think."

"They sure did, Dad. They went on a holiday to heaven. They are dead. Remember when we buried Mom next to your parents in St. Thomas? Remember that? We had the stone engraved with her name and that saying you chose? Too well-loved to be forgotten. Mom's been dead for almost two years, Dad."

"Well, she shouldn't have left the children here," he says. "I can't take care of them. They were running and hiding all night. I didn't get any sleep."

The house was a disaster. Wes was, indeed, always looking for something. If it wasn't children, it was lottery tickets. He had the winning ticket, but he misplaced it. He was slowly disassembling the entire house, turning things upside down, emptying drawers and closets. Searching for things he lost.

Searching for things he can never retrieve.

Robert, meanwhile, is coming out of hibernation, gearing up for spring mania. He has accumulated a bit of cash, and he is making some connections. Cigarettes from the reserve. Weed from Vince's cousin, Billy. It is interesting to observe the two of them together, Wes and Robert. They have a unique way of communicating, stepping around past differences and avoiding conflict with sign language. Like, when Wes is clutching the remote-control device for the TV, Robert doesn't say, "Pass the remote, Dad." He just reaches out his hand and wiggles his fingers, and Wes hands it over. Robert leaves a bowl of cereal on the TV table for Wes, or half a pot of pasta. Like you would for a dog. Because if he said, "You want anything to eat?" Wes would say, "No."

"You want some popcorn?"

"No."

The worrying thing is that even these tentative social conventions are breaking down as Robert gets increasingly jittery, saddling up for his yearly psychotic ride. Charlene recognizes all the signs. Long handwritten notes. Lights on all hours of the night. Pacing.

Charlene stays close to home. She jumps when the phone rings. She calls Martha and Alan hoping for advice. But they reassure her instead of offering to come and help. Or, God forbid, drop Dad on their doorstep.

On March 29, Charlene is working at her makeshift desk in the loft, posting ads for summer rentals on her website. It is lovely outside, and she has the window open to freshen up the stale winter interior. She hears a quick, sharp yelp, like that of a wolf, or a fox. An animal in trouble. She saves the description she has written about a four-bedroom lakeside retreat and opens the door onto the balcony. There is no sign of an animal in trouble. Then she sees her father running around on the deck in sock feet. "Help!"

"Dad!" she calls. "Dad, I'm up here!"

But her father steps down to the path that leads to the lake. There is still ice on the path.

"Dad! Stop!

Charlene can picture him falling and breaking his hip. But strangely he seems very agile. She never would have guessed that he could move that quickly. Her heart beats fast and hard as she pulls on the boots at the bottom of the stairs and she runs, slipping a bit on the rotting ice, cursing, calling for her father. Then she sees him down at the dock.

"Dad! Stop! What are you doing?"

Wes awkwardly drops to a sitting position on the dock and slides down onto the ice. His hair is wispy and wild, like the hair on a skull in one of those zombie movies. The Day of the Living Dead or some damn thing. And he lurches forward, lifting his knees high to walk through the mush that the ice has become.

Charlene falls. Gets up, falls again. Her palms are bleeding. She considers running back to the house to get her phone, but then she just watches as the scene plays out in front of her. There is a hole in the ice about twenty feet from shore, and Wes makes his way toward it.

"Robert? Robert!"

Robert drilled the ice-fishing hole last weekend. He

bought a pail of minnows. She dragged a chair down there to keep him company. When they were kids, he was the only one who wasn't squeamish about baiting the hooks. He had the patience to untangle lines and repair reels, and he took the fish off the line for her. Catch and release, always, except for invasive species, like rock bass, which he fed to the raccoons.

Does it make sense that Robert would have gone out there today? The temperature has been above zero for a few days in a row. Now Wes is on his hands and knees. He is lying prone, the correct way to reach for a victim who has fallen through thin ice, but he does not have an aid with him. No lifesaving ring or paddle or rope. Nothing. He is stretching his arm forward, and out of his mouth comes a sound. Not words, but terrible moans like you expect to hear in the seventh circle of hell. Charlene gets up. She is hurt. Her tailbone feels broken. She glances around for a tree limb, something. Anything. Then, when she looks back, her father is gone. The black hole has swallowed them both.

A red squirrel climbs down the trunk of the hemlock that she is leaning against, and scolds Charlene.

Then it is quiet. A tiny breeze touches her face, and she starts shivering uncontrollably. Her rear end is aching. She climbs back up to the cottage and searches for the phone. Both handsets are empty. Finally, she finds a phone in between the coach cushions and calls 911.

"Two men through the ice," she says.

Within an hour of the call, the laneway is blocked by emergency vehicles. Ambulance. Fire. Police. They think they see a shadow between the dock and the hole and attempt to chop away the ice, but the dark area is not a body. Just a log, half submerged. The paramedic wraps Charlene with a blanket and treats her for shock. Tomorrow the emergency team will return with a diver.

After everyone has left, Charlene lies on the couch. She has a small, excited feeling in her tummy like you get when you are happy about something. She is trying not to admit to herself that she is relieved. This little drama just solved all her problems in one fateful swoop. She wonders if she caused it herself, by wishing it to happen. The way the police officer looked around the cottage worries her. She tried to make the place presentable in the twenty minutes it took the police to arrive. She managed to get the beer cans into the recycle bin and wipe the kitchen counter. She swept a bag of Robert's weed into his dresser drawer. Still, it looks a mess. Clothes and shoes lying around.

Then the door opens.

"Martha?" Charlene says, her voice croaky. Martha had promised she would come, but not until tomorrow.

"Just me!" Robert says.

Charlene screams.

"What?"

"I thought you were dead!"

"Nope. Just a little drunk, Sis. Where's Dad?" Robert reaches for a cigarette from the pack in the breast pocket of his camouflage jacket. "You okay, Char? You look like you just seen a ghost!"

"Seriously, Robert. The cops just left. I saw Dad go running down to the lake, and I chased after him and he made a beeline straight for your fishing hole. I assumed he was saving you. Trying to save you. I thought he must have seen you go through. Right out where we were sitting last Sunday. He lay down and he was trying to save somebody. I thought it was you. Then the ice just gave way and down he went. Drowned. Dead. Gone."

"Fuck."

"Yeah. And I thought you were gone, too. Your truck was here."

"Ah. Vince picked me up about 7:30 this morning. We went out to Stan Anderson's to have a look at that roof he's been wanting us to fix. Then we sat around in Stan's workshop and had a few beers. Jesus!"

"Well, should I call the cops back and tell them we only have one dead body? They're coming in the morning with a diver and a hook."

"No. Jesus, Char, the cops need their rest, too. Morning is early enough for that report. Just tell them I came in when you were asleep, and you never saw me until breakfast. Here." Robert reaches in his pocket and pulls out a prescription bottle and hands her a little green oval-shaped pill. "This'll help you sleep," he tells her.

"What is it?"

"Sleeping pill."

"You take sleeping pills?"

"Hell, yes. Dad's been haunting around the house all night, ripping the beds apart, looking in closets. Emptying boxes of food in the pantry. I can't get a decent sleep unless I conk myself out with one of these beauties."

"You have a doctor?"

"No. I get 'em at people's houses. Me and Vince have been over at that millionaire's place on the next bay, putting hardwood floors in. He's got a nice stash of scrips."

Charlene looks at the pill. "How do you know it's a sleeping pill and not some kind of opioid?"

"Because it says, *Take one before bedtime as needed*, on the label. That's code for sleeping pill. Go on, Char. Take it. You look like a wreck. Believe me, I know what I'm talking about when it comes to pharmaceuticals."

Charlene looks at her brother. His skin is deeply wrinkled, especially around the eyes, but he seems perfectly sane. "Are you still on the clozapine?"

"Hell no. That stuff's poison. Gives you a lobotomy if you're on it for more than a few months."

"Well…" Charlene watches Robert light a cigarette with shaky hands. "How are you controlling the schizophrenia?"

"I'm bipolar, Char. Not schizo. That was an incorrect diagnosis."

"What's the difference?"

"Bipolar's less fucked up," he says and laughs like a maniac. "You should see your face, Char. Jesus. You were hoping I was dead, weren't you? Admit it. That woulda worked out good for you."

"Yeah, Robert. I was hoping you were down that ice hole."

"Well, it's a helluva way to die."

"Ironic, though, eh? Dad dying here at the cottage? You should have seen him, Robbie, just tearing down there. He must have been running on pure adrenaline. Shit. You wouldn't have believed it. He didn't even have shoes on. I thought…" Charlene looks out the window. There is a full moon, and the lake is lit up like midday. "I thought he must have been watching you from the window. I mean I figured you knew better than to take your chances on the ice, but maybe you wanted one last try for that lake trout that stole your bait on Sunday. He was after saving somebody. He was convinced there was somebody that went through the ice. You should have heard him wailing."

"Must have been those little fuckers. Our stepsister and stepbrother. Mother's little children. I bet he was hallucinating that they fell down the hole."

Charlene nods her head. "Maybe. Maybe Mom guided him down there. Remember how she used to tease him? Come on in, the water's fine!"

"You going to say that to the police?"

"What do you think?"

"Not sure. It's my experience that cops don't like a story they can't prove. That don't make sense."

Charlene noticed that Robert had adopted the local grammar. You'd never know he'd earned a Rhodes scholarship back in the day. You'd never guess he was brilliant, once. "Well, something fell through that hole in the ice."

"Maybe a deer. Maybe that fox who's been hanging around."

Charlene is buzzing with the kind of exhaustion that keeps you from the only thing that will help. She swallows the sleeping pill.

Charlene pours herself a coffee and steps out onto the deck. Spring is here. The sun is warm. Robert has pulled the lawn chairs out of the shed. He has shaved and showered and put on a clean shirt. He looks like the kind of guy you might hire for a construction job. You might even trust him with the key to your house. Charlene thanks him for brewing the coffee and tidying the kitchen.

"Martha's on her way up," he says.

"And Alan?"

"Alan didn't want to cancel his patients."

"Is it about money?"

"I think it's that bitch Gwen. She never liked us. And Char? Not to upset you, but if you look over the railing, you can see Dad floating around down there. The ice sunk overnight. We should probably call the cops and report…"

"That we've located the body?"

"And that I'm not dead."

"Oh shit. Yeah. I can do that."

The search and rescue team seemed a little disappointed that they weren't really needed. It was a pretty simple retrieval. They zipped the body into a dark green bag and took Wes down to Barrie. The police officer who had been enjoying his chat with Robert was side-lined when Martha arrived, all in control. She took charge of the situation. The police report would go to her. The death certificate would go to her. She insisted.

Robert walked the cop and the paramedic to their vehicles and shook their hands.

"So, Char," Martha said. "You've got some explaining to do."

"I've got to get out of here," Char said.

"Get your coat, Sweetie," she said in a big sister voice.

"Let's go to The Nook."

The Nook hadn't changed much. Martha liked a cottage to be a cottage. She liked that the walls of the bedrooms didn't go all the way to the ceiling. She liked the original windows and the flagstone fireplace and the wide plank floors. Alan showed up around eight o'clock with two large pizzas. The siblings were together. "Here we are," he said. Char was wrapped in one of Auntie Olive's quilts. Martha sat on the footstool in front of the fire, feeding the flames with chunks of hemlock that had fallen in a windstorm last summer. Robert sat in the rocking chair, going back and forth, back and forth.

"Do you think Mom really was infatuated with Russell?" Char asked.

"Of course. Did you see the picture of them together? They were a pretty good-looking couple," Martha said.

"I never really remember Mom and Dad, you know, being in love. Lovey-dovey," Alan said.

"Name one couple who you would say are lovey-dovey," said Martha.

"I don't know. You and Grace?"

"What?"

"You and Grace. You're always so engaged with each other's conversations. You enjoy each other. You have a real connection."

"Yeah. Well, we're friends, though. I'm asking about couples."

Char looks at Alan and realizes that he thinks that Martha and Grace really are a couple. Lots of people think they are. Char isn't a hundred percent sure herself.

"What?" Martha says.

"It's okay," Alan says. "Mom and Dad are both gone, now, Martha, it's safe to come out of the closet."

Char looks at Martha and shrugs.

"You think I'm a lesbian? That Grace and I are a couple?"

"Aren't you?" Alan says.

"No. I'm straight, idiot. I was married to a man."

"Lots of lesbians were married to men. Before. At one time," Alan says, stuttering as he sees the flush creeping up Martha's neck. "You two really do seem happy."

"Maybe we're happy because we're NOT a couple! Did that ever occur to you? What about your marriage? Are you and Gwendolyn happy? Do you even sleep in the same room?"

Robert rocks.

Alan gets up, opens the little cupboard over the fridge where, as long as any of them can remember, is where the whiskey is kept. Scotch, Irish, Canadian Club.

"Anybody want a cup of kindness?" he offers.

"Me."

"Me."

Robert rocks.

"Robert?" Alan says.

"Hmm?" Robert says.

"Want a whiskey?"

"Sure. Thanks, bro," Robert says.

"So, let's start at the beginning," Char suggests. "Let's go back to the question about Mom and Dad. Did they love each other?"

"How would we know?" Martha says. "My own brother thinks I'm gay."

"Really Martha, it's quite alright if…," says Alan.

"Alan! Stop it. I am a Unitarian Minister. I think I'd know if I was a lesbian. Half my congregation is LGBTQ2S. "

"What?"

"Gay! Never mind. What I'm getting at is… what would make us think, even for a minute, that we will ever know our parents' true feelings for each other?"

Char tosses back her whiskey and holds her glass out for a refill. It is the good stuff. Single malt. "I read the letters that Russell sent to Mom," she says. "But, of course, we never got to read Mom's letters to him. Auntie Olive believed he was the love of Mom's life. She told me Mom's heart was broken the summer he died. Dad showed up at the right time and he was a good husband, a good provider, but according to Auntie Olive, her heart belonged to that boy who died."

Alan passes the whiskey bottle over to Char. "Sip the next one, Sis," he says. "In answer to your question, Martha, Gwen and I don't sleep together. That doesn't mean we aren't devoted to each other. We take our commitment seriously, as Mom and Dad did. It's not a question of ardor."

"Holy smokes, Alan, you really do sound like an old fogey sometimes," Martha says. "You should have been the theologian."

"My point is, dear sister, that making a relationship work takes a different kind of love. I think Mom set her intentions to live well with the man she married. She was a happy person. A content person. Did she love our stodgy old father? Absolutely, she did."

"And yet, Dad probably always felt like he was competing

with Russell's ghost," says Char. "Poor bugger."

"It's like…" Robert starts talking and Martha totally tunes him out, turning to Alan and asking about funeral arrangements.

"Pardon Robert?" Char interrupts. "What is it like?"

Martha shuts up.

Robert looks out the window. The dying ice booms and pops and echoes around the bay, mournful and aching and primitive.

"It's like Dad crossed some threshold back to the past to reunite with that girl in the bathing suit. Maybe… maybe time left the door ajar in that vanished moment. And look at us, all together because he followed her. He was sure of her. He saw this, all of us together, his future children. He had a glimpse of the difficulties ahead, but he went anyway. He just dove in, and he swam toward it. Imperfect, but worth the trouble. Worth getting wet."

Homecoming

We were all in love with someone who wasn't in love with us. To complicate matters, we all had someone in love with us who wasn't getting the message that we were never, ever going to love them back.

The guy that I loved was called Keith, but he was taken. Lexie was his girlfriend's name. When he brought Lexie to campus during Homecoming, I sat beside her at the football game trying to make friends. Trying to figure out what it was that Keith liked about her so I could steal him. Lexie was planning on working for her dad's car dealership after she graduated from high school. She told me about Keith's sister, Beth, in the special needs class. How she volunteered with Beth's group and went bowling with them on Tuesday evenings. At half-time, Lexie brought me back some liquorice from the concession stand and gave me a little hug and thanked me for making her feel welcome. She had been so nervous about coming. It was clear I couldn't compete with someone that good-hearted.

The boy who liked me was a second-year business student named Gord. The feathery brown hair that hung soft and wispy over his high forehead predicted an early baldness that he wasn't going to be okay with. He wanted to study music, but his father wouldn't finance that. I had to change my study hall routine and my meal plan because Gord followed me around campus, trying to make it look like he just happened to bump into me.

"Just friends, okay Gord?" I said when he tried to kiss me in a study carrel.

I didn't want to kiss him, but I didn't want him to cry, either, in noisy sobs that disrupted the tomb-like silence in the library's sub-basement. I should have followed him when he stumbled away to make sure he was okay, but I was writing an essay for Seventeenth Century Literature due the next day.

The boy that my roommate, Rebecca, liked that didn't like her was Andrew. I knew this because Andrew told me.

"She wears too much make-up," he said.

Which was true, she did spend a lot of time at her desk in front of the fold down mirror. Besides, Andrew was recovering from a disastrous infatuation with a Wallingford Hall girl. He'd sworn off women for the time being.

Rebecca dragged me across the quad to a floor party at Whidden Hall the Thursday night after Thanksgiving with intentions to heal Andrew's aching heart. The common room was too dark for the men to appreciate Rebecca's carefully applied eyeliner. Billy Joel was on the stereo. A complimentary serving of Purple Jesus punch was handed to us upon arrival by a guy in a gorilla suit. The recipe is grape juice with pure alcohol in it. 94% proof. Served out of a garbage can. I don't recommend it.

Rebecca was leaning over the balcony spewing purple vomit when Andrew finally showed his face. He helped me escort her back to Brandon Hall, and we tucked her into bed. We sat and waited for her raspy breathing to quiet and then we left her to recover alone.

The October night was snapping with frost-crisped leaves. It was quiet. Well past closing time at the campus pubs. The satyr head carvings under the eaves of University Hall seemed benevolent at two in the morning. Snakes and ivy leaves and owls and other cryptic symbols of academia projected a sense of permanency. I felt I had discovered a safe haven against the coming winter. Against my imminent adulthood. Against the world's atrocities.

Andrew had a bounce to his step. A 'follow me' kind of stride that was irresistible. How to describe him? Trustworthy. Authoritative, maybe. There was something about him. I'm sure if the campus security rent-a-cops had found us wandering around that night, he would have come up with a believable story to convince them we had every right to be lurking in echoey lecture halls writing enigmatic philosophy on dusty blackboards. And yet he had a childish side. He laughed like an eight-year-old while we climbed up the trellis to the terrace of the Faculty Club. We watched the sun rising over Cootes Paradise and pretended we were professors.

The thing about relationships in university, is that our histories were levelled when we moved into residence with roommates assigned at random. We revealed the parts of our past that we wanted to reveal and left out the parts we'd just as soon forget. Creation myths based on romantic ideals of the people we intended to be, instead of the tawdry hometown narratives we'd outgrown. It didn't matter where you came from or who your Daddy was, we thought. We were interested in music and literature. The youth movement. Peaceful protests. We were goofing around. Drinking. Flirting. Wielding the sword of human rights. Blaming past generations for genocides and brutal regimes, certain there would be no more of that nonsense in the future. Our future. On we marched, toward teachers' college or medical school or graduate studies, memorizing the truth as it was taught to us.

Student residences are named after dead people. Whidden Hall was named for Howard Primrose Whidden, 1871-1952, educator, minister, Member of Parliament, and sixth Chancellor of McMaster University. His portrait, hanging in the hall's entryway with imposing jaw and stern demeanour, was not enough to keep student behaviour from degenerating far below Baptist standards of civility.

Frosh week in my women's residence was like camp, with songs and chants and matching tee shirts. The senior girls were like counsellors. They wanted everyone to fit in, get along, love their roommates. Adopt a nationalist fervour for their floor.

The men did Frosh Week differently. Like the army. Demanding dead horses and obedience. Some first-year students knew in advance about hazing. Expected it. Even looked forward to it. Others were totally blindsided when they were wakened in the middle of the night and instructed to put pillowcases over their heads. Guided into cars and driven far off campus. Dropped off in rural areas. Cemeteries. Conservation parks. Behind deserted factories.

Once abandoned, they would supposedly build relationships with other first year students. By the time they found their way back to campus, they were friends for life. Sometimes it worked. But it failed for some boys. Boys who found the culture of campus hi-jinx to be humiliating instead of fun. Terrorism, not brotherhood. And for these boys, Frosh Week never ended. There were rituals to be observed all year long.

Like Elevator, a birthday tradition.

Stripped naked, tied to a chair and covered with shaving cream, a birthday boy was carried to a nearby women's residence with shouts of Elevator! Elevator! Elevator! Once alerted, women filled cups of water and raced to the elevator on their respective floors. The birthday boy was placed in the elevator on the first floor. His friends pushed all the buttons to maximize the enjoyment of the celebration. By the third floor, there was no foam left on the poor naked creature. But the drenching continued, up, up, up, all the way to the 11th floor where I lived. One night, when the elevator doors opened on Gord, I recognized for the first time in my life the depthless suffering called trauma.

It had been months since Gord had tried to kiss me in the library. I occasionally saw him studying in a carrel nearby or selecting a meal in the cafeteria. Alone. He had a roommate, ill-suited to his personality and habits. A football player with locker room sensibilities who, most likely, was the one to initiate the elevator ride that night with jovial camaraderie and shots of whiskey. Gord would have been temporarily flattered, I suppose, to find himself illuminated in the attentive light of his popular roomie.

Rites of passage. Preparation for the dog-eat-dog reality of the adult world. That is what the Dean of Men told Gord's father when he came to pack up Gord's possessions. Gord's father agreed with the Dean that Gord was perhaps too sensitive for residence. That he should find a basement apartment off campus.

Full of outrage, I made an appointment with the Dean of Women to address the issue of the Elevator game. She took my elbow and closed her office door

"I've been trying to stop hazing for years," she said. "But some traditions are not easy to change. Boys will be boys, I am told, time and again. Every year I make a motion to restructure student residences into co-ed dorms. Every year, the motion gets tabled. But I haven't given up. This incident lends support to my proposal."

"Nobody forces us to go to the elevator and finish the guy off," I say. "Like prey. How do you explain that? Girls will be girls?"

The Dean composed herself. Clasped her hands. And sighed. "How indeed? Are you taking any Anthropology courses?"

"No. I'm an English major."

"Well. You've read Shakespeare, then. Cruelty is universal. Women have historically aligned themselves with aggressive men. Physically virile men. Powerful men. Otherwise, they put their own survival at risk, and the well-being of their children."

I shrugged.

"Take note of the boys who get sent up the elevator," she said. "Take note of the boys who do not."

"But you need to do something. You need to make a rule," I insisted.

"I'm working on a long-term solution. But you can do something in the meantime. Stop participating. Make your objections public. And tell your friend, Gord, to go to the police. He should press assault charges."

She stood and escorted me to the door; confident I would do no such thing. By the time we graduated, we'd all been screwed over in love or friendship or both. Along with undergraduate degrees, we'd also earned an education in the many ways to sabotage relationships. It was the decade between birth control pills and AIDS.

Our mothers, many of them, had saved themselves for marriage. They were chaste. They did not get drunk and pass out at frat parties. They did not fart or swear. They knew how to sit demurely with their ankles crossed, their hands clasped, and their mouths shut. We would not follow them into servitude. But, one by one, we did. We were bridesmaids, and then we looked down to find diamonds on our own fingers. Our marriages would be different, we thought. The women's movement had been successful. Equality had been achieved.

Yes. Our marriages were different. Instead of crystal and sterling silver tea sets, we received pottery and queen-sized bed sheets for wedding gifts. Instead of stay-at-home drudgery, we managed to exhaust ourselves by adding careers to the tasks of laundry, dishes, groceries and childbearing.

Don't get me wrong. It all became bearable. Even cherishable.

One day you go to a homecoming event at the university. You recognize landmarks amid the new buildings and feel once again the adrenaline rush from peaks of joyfulness, and the tender bruising from pits of despair. You feel as if you could walk into the Rathskeller and find the scarred wooden table where you drank twenty cent draft beer and listened to John Prine. Faded photographs reveal how many did not make it to this reunion. Cancer. Accident. Suicide. Cancer. Cancer.

And that boy who you loved, but who did not love you? Hello, my name is Keith, his name tag says. He does not remember you. Wearing an ill-fitting sports jacket and orthopedic shoes, he bores you with complaints about immigration policies.

"No," he tells you when you inquire. "Lexie is not here. I divorced her a long time ago."

What of that other boy? Andrew, the boy that your roommate liked, but he didn't like her. In the spring of your senior year when the magnolias were in bloom and the gym was filled with the dreadful silence of final exams, you opened a hollowed out copy of Samual Pepys' diary and found an antique diamond ring.

That boy has grey hair now, and a sloping posture from many years of leaning forward at the front of a high school classroom trying to convince teenagers that there is value in history. Andrew is standing under the portrait of Howard

Primrose Whidden. Whidden would have been our age when he sat for that portrait. In my youth, I supposed him to be an ancient and arrogant academic. But now I detect amusement in the lines around his mouth. His eyes are discerning, not stern. A man who loved this institution long after it stopped loving him.

Andrew is talking to a stout woman with tinted hair and a glittery purse. It is the Wallingford girl who he loved, but who did not love him back. And I can see, from all the way across the room, that she is thinking she may have misjudged him. She loops her arm through his and tilts her head back to look up at him. Scanning the hall, he finds me and tilts his head toward the cloak room, inviting me to rescue him. I raise my wine glass in his direction and go off to retrieve our coats.

Research

Rachel is conducting research on the best way to meet interesting people. She is tired of inane conversations. She is sick to death of listening to others talking about their children and grandchildren and aging parents. Her friends are nice. If she called them in the middle of the night and asked for help, they would come. Loyalty, she recognizes, is admirable, but it can also be boring. And, she hates to admit this, but her friends are not very smart. They don't want to know about the latest TED talk. Science makes their eyes glaze over. They can't wait for an opportunity to turn the conversation back to the cost of insurance or the problem with their neighbour's dog. Late night barking is a more popular topic than resolving the issue of non-recyclable plastic.

Her colleague, Stacy, wants to help. "I'll be your Life Coach," she says. "I took the course last summer. I have a certificate." She gets Rachel to fill out a questionnaire about skills and goals. Then they get to work on a plan.

"Decide what characteristics you admire in people and then get yourself qualified to hang out with them," Stacy says. "If you admire artists, you go to the art gallery and sign up to be a docent. Take an art history course at the university. Have your coffee at that place across from the School of Art and Design."

Stacy gives her a few more examples. Music? Sports? Bird watching? It doesn't really matter what you choose as long as you lay the groundwork before you try to make connections. A birdwatcher will know, for example, that you are a neophyte if you cannot discuss migration patterns with alacrity. You cannot go to the ornithologist convention and expect to fake it. Preparation is everything.

Rachel assumes that Stacy memorized this pitch straight from her textbook. Impressive.

"My recommendation to start your research would be a night at the opera."

Rachel pauses, waiting to see if Stacy is kidding. She is not.

"Opera fans are generally intelligent and wealthy. You might as well find a man with money," she says.

"I'm not searching for a husband."

"Of course, you are! It's a partner's world. If you meet an interesting man, you'll inherit his interesting and adventurous friends. So, even if it doesn't work out, you have an established social network. No need to start from scratch."

"I didn't have any luck with dating sites."

"You aren't seeking a date, per se. You're looking for a lifestyle. Energy! Open doors."

"And money?"

"Why not? A guy who can treat you to a trip to Turks and Caicos is preferable to a guy who wants you to share expenses on Karaoke night. See what I mean?"

Yes. Rachel sees the wisdom in that. She purchases a ticket for Tosca at the Canadian Opera Company's Four Seasons venue. She pays $250 for a seat in the Grand Ring. Stacy warned her not to be cheap. On the day of the performance, she gets her hair done, has a facial and a manicure, and picks up her best dress from the dry cleaners. It is her go-to dress for New Years and weddings, with a shimmery bodice, and it transforms her from a frumpy school administrator to an elite appreciator of culture.

Rachel arrives forty-five minutes before the performance for Opera Boot Camp, an interactive learning session with the Opera Education Coordinator that promises to enhance the experience with behind-the-scenes insights. About twenty early birds are ushered into a classroom. Looking around at the other attendees, she is embarrassed to find herself ridiculously overdressed. No one is in jeans, but plenty are wearing the same kind of outfit that Rachel favours for work. Black sweaters and black pants, with a colourful scarf. She decides to keep her coat on.

The performance, she learns, is sung in Italian. Which is preferable to the English translations. Tosca is set in Rome during the Napoleonic wars. Expect a psychological drama, the expert tells the group. Everyone nods. Rachel wishes she had done her due diligence. In fact, she did take a book out of the library to study Puccini. It is on her nightstand.

"There will be passion and betrayal. Murder most foul." Miss Opera Expert says. "Floria Tosca has good reason to kill the evil Scarpia, however she underestimates the consequences. Vissi d'arte is the aria to appreciate, with Adrianne Pieczonka. Prepare to be swept away by tenor Marcelo Puente in his role as Cavaradossi, Act 3. Breathtaking."

Rachel scans the group. Mostly retired single women. There are two men. One is slouched and uncomfortable in his seat. He seems to have restless leg syndrome, a problem she is familiar with because the gym teacher at her school has it. It is distracting and annoying during staff meetings. She can't seem to get the jiggling leg out of her peripheral vision. The other man, rumpled and unshaven, looks like he entered the wrong theatre. He was, perhaps, expecting erotic dancing. No one at Boot Camp looks the least bit interesting.

They are ushered out of the classroom as the lights flash, and Rachel finds her very expensive seat. Within a minute, the shabby-suited fellow from Boot Camp sits right beside her. He is an armrest hog, claiming it immediately and not moving his elbow one inch, even when she leans against his meaty bicep. She gives up and leans, instead, in the other direction, where she easily dislodges the bony appendage of an elderly woman whose oxygen tank is crowding the floor space between them.

At the first intermission, the rumpled man introduces himself and offers to buy her a drink. She accepts, knowing that Stacy will demand to hear the details of how she "put herself out there."

"You can't just observe everyone like you're watching Netflix, Rae," Stacy told her. "You've got to talk to people. If only to make yourself appear more interesting to the people you really want to get to know."

The man is called Archie. Which is not a good name for him. In her mind, Archie will forever be a red-headed teenager at Riverdale High who dated Betty and Veronica and never in his life attended the opera. She orders a glass of white wine. Archie surprises her. He is funny. He mocks the old lady with the oxygen tank and says he figures she must have stuffed a lavender sachet between her tits. Rachel spits out a little bit of wine when he says tits. She hasn't heard anybody use that word since grade ten. It is something, she realizes, a man named after a cartoon character would say.

"Lemme see your ticket," he says, when they seat themselves for the second act. Rachel reaches into her raincoat pocket and pulls it out.

"Wow," he says. "You really paid two fifty for this seat?"

"Of course. What? Did you sneak in?"

"Yep. I come early for Boot Camp and then I follow the instructor through the side entrance. See that door down by the stage? Unlocked. When I get in here, I look around for a free seat. There's always a decent choice. If somebody comes in late, I apologize and move. By then I've already had a chance to scope out another empty spot. The opera crowd is old. Unhealthy and wealthy. This seat I'm in right now? Probably the guy is in bed with pneumonia. Those two seats ahead of us in the Orchestra section? They've been empty every Thursday evening performance this year. Probably season ticket holders who went to Florida. I don't ever want you spending this kind of cash on a ticket again, hear me?"

"I hear you," she says as the curtain goes up on Act Two. Rachel wishes that the performance was in English, poor translation or not. She is totally lost. She can definitively say that she will never love opera. Even if it is free. She imagines seventeen better ways to spend two hundred and fifty bucks.

During the second intermission, Rachel accepts Archie's offer for another white wine and ducks into the ladies room. Examining herself in the mirror, she feels foolish for putting too much effort into her appearance. And why did she let Archie admonish her for poor judgement? A man without principle. She sneaks out the side door.

The next day, when Stacey asks, she manages to make a humorous story out of the opera debacle. Stacy shrugs. There is more research to be done.

"Maybe something active," Stacy suggests.

Over the next month, Rachel tries horseback riding, swimming and badminton. Fail, fail, fail. Sore ass, red eyes and too many rules. Stacy gets frustrated.

"Okay," Stacy says. "You're a hard case."

"Meaning what?"

"Meaning you need to try sports with alcohol."

"Say what?"

"The classiest drink-and-play sport is golf. The carts even have drink holders. Start with lessons for beginners over at the driving range before you join a club. It's going to be expensive, but the peer group level is worth it. Top tier."

Rachel likes golf. She likes the clothes. She likes the young instructor. She even gets into watching PGA tournaments on Sunday afternoons, following the pros. Jordan and Jason and Justin. And the cute Irishman, Rory. The only trouble is, she is a long way from competent. It takes years to learn the etiquette, develop a balanced swing, know what club to use from the rough with a downhill lie when you are 90 yards from the pin. This is not a game you take up to meet people. It is a whole other career. Rachel does not drop it, officially, but it becomes a long-range goal.

In the meantime, she tries the other drink and play sports. Darts, which take her into men's clubs that have opened their doors to women. But only because it's the law. It proves to be too political. As in right wing Conservative political. As in sexist and racist jokes that are really offensive.

Curling takes way too much cardio. "Sweep, sweep, sweep! Hurry HARD!" the skip yells. Rookies are encouraged, but not tolerated all that well. And even though curlers are historically drinkers, alcoholic beverages are no longer permitted on the ice. Things don't get social until after the game is over. And the game is too long.

Bowling, an attempt on her part to manage expectations, is more promising. Stacy is not a fan of the bowling idea.

"Bowling is over. Name a famous bowler."

"Fred Flintstone?"

"Exactly! And…"

"Barney Rubble?"

"Right again. And guess what? Even back in the sixties, when bowling was a thing, it was a blue-collar sport. Mr. Slate, their boss, did not bowl. He was a member of the Country

Club. He golfed." Stacy deems Rachel un-coachable and hands in her resignation as Life Coach.

Bowling is nostalgic for Rachel. The rental shoes, the smell of her hands after handling the balls, the thundering echoes as the pins drop in one alley after the next. It is League Night, and everybody is in a good mood. Friendly, helpful, fun. On her way to the bar to get another beer, she runs into Archie. Opera Archie. He is wearing a Def Leppard t-shirt and he looks good. The scruffy beard is much hotter in a bowling alley than it was at the Four Seasons Centre.

"White wine," he says.

"Sorry," she says.

"I had to drink it myself."

"I had a fainting spell in the bathroom. Vertigo."

Archie lowers his voice, so she is forced to lean toward him to hear what he is saying as bowling balls roll and pins crash. "You don't need to lie," he says, smiling.

"Okay. I was bored."

"You should have stayed around for the drama."

"The tenor?"

"No, the old lady with the oxygen tank was carted away on a stretcher."

"I don't believe you."

Archie shrugs. "Why would I make that up? It was a play within a play. Are you bored here?"

"No. This is more my style. My Life Coach made it clear she would drop me as a client if I joined a bowling league, but I am enjoying myself immensely."

"Here among the common folk."

"She wanted to elevate my status."

"Bowling is a status killer, for sure. I agree. But as a Big Lebowski fan, I urge you to embrace it."

Rachel and Archie slept together for the first time that night, their foot odour co-mingling in a haze of rental shoe pheromones. At four in the morning, Rachel learned that Tosca can be fascinating when performed by a naked man in a hot tub belonging to a neighbour who happens to be out of town.

Their next date was an axe throwing event. Archie proved to be better at life coaching than Stacy, and he didn't even have his certificate. "Eat your ice cream while it's on your plate," was his philosophy. "Thornton Wilder."

Archie took Rachel to a drum circle that left her with a vibrating urgency to go vegetarian and stop for turtles. He read to her from the Tibetan Book of the Dead. And for her birthday, Archie drove two hundred kilometres so they could enter a horseshoe tournament. Horseshoes are not as lucky as you might think. Every horseshoe pitcher Rachel met had a traumatic story to tell.

By the time Archie left for a consulting job in the Arctic, Rachel had enough evidence to complete her research. She relaxed back into her circle of friends. With great relief, she allowed conversations about granite countertops and breast enhancements to wash over her.

She was sick to death of interesting people.

Witness

Margaret refused the ongoing chemo and accepted the inevitable. Her oncologist was generous with pain management prescriptions. Patches and pills.

"Don't let the pain get ahead of you," he told her. "You don't need to worry about addiction, now."

Her son, Tristan, is twelve. She named him Tristan because she wanted him to be a sensitive, kind boy. She wishes she'd called him Jack or Ryan. Something a bit tougher. Because he is suffering now, and sad.

Margaret asks her best friend, Donna, to adopt him, but Donna refuses. Godmother is as much as Donna can handle. She doesn't do commitments. That's why she never married, though she was asked three times.

"You may as well put bars on my windows," she told all three. "I'd feel trapped."

Margaret never married either. Tristan's father was already married. Something she didn't find out until it was too late. He did not deserve to know about his son. She decided to keep Tristan to herself and avoid complications. Admittedly, child support payments would have been helpful, but she had her pride. So, Tristan will go and live with Margaret's mother in the small town where she grew up. He will be okay.

Donna knows she made the right decision, but she feels guilty. Maybe if Tristan was a baby, she would consider adopting him. Then she could raise him with more discipline. It was hard to watch Margaret spoil the boy and look how he turned out. Just as you would expect. Of course, it's possible that a child's character is built into the DNA and no amount of structure would make a difference. Also, a puppy is cuter than a dog. So there's that.

Donna picks Tristan up and takes him to see a movie while Margaret rests one Sunday afternoon. It is a violent movie. Superman died, you see, and all hope is lost in the world, but by some miracle that has to do with a nuclear reactor and the teaming up of all the superheroes in town, Superman is resurrected. He isn't the same. Coming back from the dead can mess with your mental ability. But Lois Lane sets him straight and the world makes a comeback from the brink of destruction.

"Well? What did you think of the movie?" Donna asks on the way home.

"It was boring," Tristan says.

"I picked it because I thought you were into superheroes."

"Yeah. Like five years ago."

"What kind of movies do you prefer?"

"Horror movies, I guess." He pauses. "And romantic comedies."

"Okay. Next time you choose. It's your mom's birthday next week. Is there something the three of us could do together?"

Tristan paused. "Well," he says. "There is one thing she talked about. It was a while ago. So, maybe it's too late."

"What?"

"She wanted to go to Florida, and swim with the dolphins.

Donna laughs. "Yes, you're right. She shared that with me too. She thinks it would be amazing." Donna cannot think of anything worse than latching onto a poor defenseless dolphin. It seems like a terrifying activity for the human and the fish.

"Is a dolphin a fish?"

"No. They're mammals like us. They have lungs."

"So how would you feel about swimming with them? I think the animal rights activists might be against it."

Tristan shrugs. "It would make her happy."

Donna thinks back to this moment. The moment she could have shut this idea down. Somehow, she agreed to this despite serious concerns about the ethics of the thing. Surely dolphins do not enjoy being ridden any more than mules at the Grand Canyon or elephants in Cambodia. But maybe it will make her feel better about abandoning the kid.

Tristan rides shotgun. Margaret is propped up on pillows in the back seat in a makeshift bed, high on painkillers and quite comfortable, although she mumbles incoherently once in a while.

Donna is a fast driver, but safe. She drives with two hands on the wheel. Ten o'clock and two o'clock. Always. They cross the Peace Bridge at nine-thirty and make it to Knoxville, Tennessee by suppertime. Margaret manages to walk into the Quality Inn without her wheelchair, but she looks like she just got hit by a car. Tristan glares at anyone who turns to take a second glance. At the Cracker Barrel, Margaret sips on chicken soup while Donna and Tristan have the turkey dinner special. It is American Thanksgiving. They didn't even know. Canadian Thanksgiving was in October, but Americans celebrate at the end of November.

"It seems too close to Christmas," Tristan says, and they are all a bit quiet for a while. Donna wonders if this will be Margaret's last Christmas. Or was last Christmas her last Christmas? Every year, we unknowingly pass the anniversary of our death.

Donna lies awake in the roll-away cot, listening to Tristan's muffled crying in the queen-sized bed closest to the bathroom. It is a hard thing to admit, but she doesn't like him much. His fragility makes her uncomfortable. He will require constant rescuing from bullies and gym teachers and sarcastic high school girls. Girls who are waiting inescapably in Tristan's future. They will lead him on and then laugh when he asks them to the prom. She knows she could do a better job than his grandmother, but at what cost? It's not in her to make that kind of sacrifice.

Margaret is snoring softly. Donna tries to dredge up some endearing memories that will explain why she organized this Make-a-Wish style vacation. They had almost nothing in common. Donna was a goth in high school, with black eyeliner and black lipstick and a long black trench coat. Margaret was a babysitter, a band member, and an honour student. Oil and Water, Margaret's mother called them. Donna imagined dirty, stinky motor oil and took offence.

"Isn't it possible." Margaret said when Donna dragged out this memory over gin martinis, "that she was referring to olive oil. Light and fragrant and essential."

"Nice try," Donna said. Margaret's mother was not one to spare anyone's feelings. It's a wonder that Margaret grew up to be so kind.

It isn't even ten o'clock yet. The television in the adjoining room is right behind her head. The people next door are watching The Simpsons. The Paul McCartney episode. Oh, for God's sake, it was going to be a long night. And there was a sharp rod in the middle of the damn cot, poking into her spine. Tristan should have taken it, but she insisted. She did it to punish herself. Her guilt is unquenchable.

Donna rolls one knee over the side of the little bed, then the other, and crawls on hands and knees over to the bathroom. She gets dressed and slips out the door. All day she's wanted a cigarette so bad. But you don't smoke in front of stage four lung cancer. She floats down the hall, her steps muffled by carpeting with extra thick underpadding. As she passes the front desk, she nods at the attendant, holding up her cigarette package and shrugging. The woman nods back.

It is cold outside, the grass crisp with hoarfrost. Tomorrow will be different. Warmer. She will do this last thing for her childhood friend and then she will be released from responsibility. Margaret has always assumed that their best friend status is mutual. A lifetime commitment. Donna finds it embarrassing when Margaret refers to her as her bestie. Friendships for her are fluid and sometimes they end. She has artsy friends, yoga friends, musical friends. But Margaret does not like to hear Donna talk about other friends. She has a claim on Donna. It puts a lot of pressure on a person. Still, when Margaret dies, part of her will disappear, too.

Donna read somewhere that long friendships are about bearing witness.

Margaret knows me, she thinks. She knew me when I was young. I do not have to explain to Margaret that I dislike dogs and bridal showers. She does not expect a birthday card from me, although I always get a gift from her. She has my history in her head. And yes, we have witnessed things for each other. Struggles. Drunken diatribes. Losses. Wins. Bad choices. Bad behaviour. Bad boyfriends. When Margaret dies, there will be no record of the night I climbed the lighthouse at Port Maitland, intending to hurl myself into the lightning and thunder of an August night. There will be nothing to tie me to the spray-painting incident at the Legion. The big dick on the army tank in florescent orange.

The door opens. "Come on inside-a here, girl," the woman says. "You freezing out there. Nobody gonna know."

The night desk woman is on her smoke break. They stand inside the vestibule and enjoy their tobacco.

"Yo friend sick?"

"Yeah. Cancer. Lung cancer and she didn't even smoke."

"Nah-uh-uh, that ain't right. That ain't fair."

"Her son is taking it hard."

"Daddy around?"

"Nope. I made a promise to take them to Florida. We're going to swim with the dolphins."

"God bless you," the woman says, and gives Donna a spine-crushing hug. Then she opens the outside door to air the place out and they go back inside. "You'll get your reward in heaven, girl," the woman tells her. "Old Saint Peter, he gonna say, right this way, Miss. You earned your wings."

Donna starts to cry. She wishes more than anything that she deserves the woman's faith in her goodness.

When Donna returns to the room, Margaret is in the middle of a panic attack, leaning over the toilet, vomiting salty broth and bile.

"Where were you? You shouldn't have left her!" Tristan says. He is gripping his knees at the end of his bed. Donna thinks he might bite her if she gets too close.

"Calm down, sweetie. It's all good," Margaret calls, weakly, from the bathroom. Then she lowers her voice and hisses at Donna. "You went out for a smoke? Really?"

Thinking about Saint Peter, Donna swallows the nasty comment that is on the tip of her tongue. She sticks an extra pain patch on Margaret's back and gives her another sleeping pill. She puts a cool cloth on her friend's brow, just like she learned in nursing school before she dropped out and accepted a glassblowing apprenticeship.

"Your fingers smell like cigarettes," Margaret says, just before she falls asleep.

"That is none of your business," Donna says. "Your business

is to get some rest. We got a big day tomorrow. And you, too, Mister," she tells Tristan. "I do not want to hear another peep out of either one of you." Donna sighs and returns to her cot. She shouldn't have quit nursing. One of her instructors told her she had the perfect personality for it. "Nurses are mean," she said. "But they care."

Donna woke once, around three in the morning, and listened to the hum of passing trucks on the highway and wished she was a truck driver instead of trapped in this narrative, a disaster that she authored herself.

In the morning, things looked brighter, as they tend to do. They ate waffles in the breakfast room of the hotel and filled their glasses with orange juice from a machine that made an alarming humming noise. Then they hit the road. Donna popped a copy of Lord of the Flies into the CD player that she got for free when the library had their book sale. The story was more captivating than she remembered. And maybe not appropriate for a boy who would rank near the bottom of the hierarchy on a deserted island. But it passed the time. When Margaret protested during one of her wakeful periods, Donna reminded her it was a classic.

"He has to read it in grade ten anyway. He'll be way ahead of the class."

In fact, Donna was not at all sure that Lord of the Flies was still on high school reading lists. Lots of good literature has been banned for triggering anxiety in today's youth.

"You okay with this story?" Donna asks Tristan.

"I like it," he says. "I feel sorry for Piggy."

They cross the Florida border at four and arrive in Tampa at six. It is disappointingly cool, but they bundle Margaret up in blankets and sit by the pool.

"You must be from Canada," the manager says when he comes to lock the gate at eight o'clock. "My name is Mack," he says. "I'm from Montreal. Came south for a holiday after my divorce and stayed. Twelve years I been here, tending bar, and driving a cab and managing this motel."

Donna looks over at Margaret, dozing on a lounger, and Tristan, talking to himself in the hot tub. Then she lights a cigarette and tells Mack her story. He agrees with her that dolphins probably hate people latching on to their fins. He leaves and turns the pool lights on and comes back with a couple of cans of beer.

"What about closing time?" Donna says.

Mack laughs. They flirt a bit and Donna promises to come back for another drink after she puts Margaret and Tristan to bed.

"Knock on my door," he says. "Number 1A."

Donna is drunk when she returns to the room at midnight. An unpleasant smell hits her hard as she opens the door, and she is shaken by the idea that Margaret may have died. It would be a real hassle to transport a dead body home. She pokes Margaret who snorts and coughs.

"Did you get laid?" Margaret asks.

"God, no. Go back to sleep." Donna crawls into the other bed in her t-shirt and underwear. Tristan is spread-eagle on his back on the pull-out couch. Donna lies awake listening to their breathing and wishing she had not downed four shots of tequila. Her heart is racing. She thinks of getting up and taking a baby Aspirin, so she doesn't have a stroke. She is dripping sweat. Is it menopause or is it just hot in here? Or is it the alcohol? The air conditioner is off because Margaret gets cold. Donna rolls over and slides out of bed. She gags over the toilet unsuccessfully and then rolls up a towel to use as a pillow and finally falls asleep in the bathtub. It seems like she has only slept for ten minutes when she opens her eyes and sees a bum.

"Proud of yourself?" Margaret asks as she pees.

"Kind of. Mack asked me to marry him."

"That's number four if I am not mistaken," Margaret says as she struggles to wipe herself.

"What time is it?"

"Time to rise and shine."

Swimming with the Dolphins costs fifty dollars per person and Donna clenches her teeth as she hands over her VISA to a guy with a sleeveless t-shirt and a Miami Dolphins ball cap. He has a lanyard around his neck with a photo on it that doesn't look like him. Ron, it says.

"Are you really Ron?" Donna asks.

He laughs through his nose. "Yep. Just for today."

The changeroom is a cement block building with no roof, mouldy benches and wet floors. They hang their clothes on hooks, declining Ron's recommendation that they pay two dollars for a locker.

"You can't trust anyone anymore," he tells them sadly. As if he remembers a day when you could leave your wallet on a bench in a changeroom and it would not be stolen.

Margaret needs help stepping into her bathing suit. It hangs on her emaciated frame, leaving embarrassing gaps around her crotch.

"Remember all the fad diets we tried in high school?" she says. "I choked down all that cabbage soup to lose ten pounds, and now look at me."

Donna nods and tries very hard to dispel the powerful vision she has of gas seeping out of the rusty showerheads.

They take their purses with them and enter the deck area. Tristan is waiting on a bench by the men's changeroom. He looks absolutely miserable. Donna feels like slapping his face. At least he should be able to fake some enthusiasm for this event. It was his idea, after all.

The dolphins are in tanks of cloudy water. "Pick your dolphin," Ron says.

There are three to choose from. Flipper, Otis, or The Fonz.

Flipper looks like he is sleeping, or possibly drugged, and Otis has some kind of injury or infection on his back.

Tristan says, "I want Flipper."

"Too, bad," Donna tells him. "We're taking The Fonz."

Margaret shivers and pulls the threadbare towel around her shoulders with purple hands.

Ron repeats a well-rehearsed script about swimming with dolphins.

"Don't hug them. Don't pet them above the eyes. Stay as still as possible and they will nudge you and kiss you."

Donna inquires about other staff, someone to assist them. She was expecting a woman, like the one she remembers from

Marine Land in Niagara Falls, who seemed to have a real relationship with the dolphins and could make them cooperate.

"It's Black Friday," Ron says as he lifts the latch on The Fonz's tank. "Everyone else booked the day off."

Tristan slips into the water, holding his thin arms high. Little brown nipples balance above his rib cage. Ron kneels down and feels the temperature of the water and apologizes.

"Sorry, Dude," he says. "Dolphins prefer cold water. Oceans aren't like swimming pools." Then as if he cannot bear to watch, he puts on a pair of sunglasses that look more like a blindfold and climbs into the lifeguard chair.

"You got twenty minutes," he announces.

The Fonz glides around the pool. Every time he gets near, Tristan screams and turns his back. Then, in a surprise move, The Fonz goes between Tristan's legs, lifting him up and letting him drop. Tristan disappears and then surfaces, coughing.

"Holy shit, Ron, what's wrong with this dolphin?" Donna screams.

"He's just being playful," Ron says. "Life jackets are in the red bin if you need one."

Tristan scrambles out of the pool and zips himself into some protective gear. He backs down the ladder cautiously, but The Fonz is fast. He pins Tristan against the wall at the six-foot marker. Donna grabs the assistive reaching pole and guides him back to the steps where his mother is gripping the safety bar. She looks at the clock above the changeroom door. Not even four minutes have elapsed.

"We do not have to do this," Donna says to Margaret. "Come on, let's get out of here. We can go to Busch Gardens instead."

Margaret shakes her head. So, Donna dives in and treads water, imagining ways to position herself so she can grab the dolphin's fin and cruise across the pool like the advertisement illustrated. But she is caught unaware when The Fonz swims alongside her, rubbing his huge rubbery penis up the length of her body. She recognizes this maneuver from as recently as the night before. She screams in outrage. One hundred and fifty dollars she paid, to be sexually assaulted by a dolphin.

Margaret understands the farce of the situation and comically propels herself into the water to help Donna. Ridiculous. The Fonz comes straight toward her, highly excited, and she turns away, only to be butted in the ass by his beak. The sensation is bruising and exhilarating and hilarious. Like the time Eddy Walker tried unsuccessfully to initiate anal sex under the bleachers. The ache of it all! Menstruation and intercourse and childbirth and that rapist, cancer.

Tristan is yelling. "Mom! Mom! Mom!" Margaret is underwater and his voice is muffled. She would like to reassure him, but she is experiencing an unexplainable infusion of energy. Warm! She is warm! Margaret has not been warm for a long time.

Margaret surfaces and sees Ron climbing down from his tower. Is that it? Is our twenty minutes up? She wants more time and sinks below the surface like a stone.

From the bottom of the pool, Margaret looks up. She sees the Fonz with his magnificent phallus and a struggle of limbs that is Tristan. She feels strangely detached from her son. Floating in embryonic fluid with an invisible umbilical cord pulling her, lovingly, away from the chaos, she surrenders her passport. What a surprise to understand, finally, that this border is not unlike the international border between countries. Now I am in Canada. Now I am in the United States of America. Unchanged.

In The Heyday

He was just passing through, but his timing was right. I was in a bit of a jam, you might say. Between a rock and a hard place, you might say. I asked him if he'd take a passenger.

"You need a ride somewhere?" he offered. "I'm headed east."

"Give me five minutes," I told him.

I served up an order of grilled cheese and home fries to the old cowboy at the counter, then I grabbed what was owed to me out of the cash register and slipped out the back door. Climbed up into his bus and sat in the front seat on the passenger side. Nobody else was on board.

"Thanks, Mister."

"No need to thank me. Seemed like you were ready to get out of that shit hole."

"I been ready for a while." I was tired. Been on my feet

since the breakfast shift and the whole time feeling wound up tighter than an eight-day clock. Half expecting the police to walk in any second. I mean, they probably wouldn't hang me. It was clearly self-defense.

"How far you want to go?"

"Montreal is where you're headed?"

"Yep. Montreal."

"I don't speak French very good."

"Me neither. It don't matter."

I like a guy who tells you what matters and what don't. Working at a diner, you appreciate this type. Like if the pie is three days old, or if the coffee ain't fresh, and you apologize? They just shrug their shoulders like this guy just did. Because it really don't matter in the grand scheme of things. As soon as he walked in the door, I said to myself, this is one of those guys who are good at assessing any situation. They know, don't they, that this ain't the place to expect gourmet food. Chili and toast? The farmer's breakfast? A place to pull off the highway and take a piss? Got ya covered, man. Is he a perv? Probably. Mostly all men are pervs in the right situation. But, hell, you can't rape somebody and drive a bus at the same time.

"How old are you?"

"Twenty-one." I catch his eye in the rear-view mirror as he considers this. I have been told I look older than I really am. Probably because I wear my hair in a flip instead of the long hippie style like the high school girls.

"My name's Jack."

"I'm Audrey."

"Nice to meet you, Audrey. Four hours 'til we get to Montreal. Go ahead and close your eyes if you like."

I look out the window at the fields. It's haying time, and the farmers are threshing and pitching and baling. Making hay while the sun shines, is how the saying goes. I done my share of that dirty work. When I was fourteen, my stepfather dropped me off at a farm up in Darlington County for the summer. My friends went to camp, and I went to work in the fields alongside a bunch of Mexican Mennonites. I got two hundred dollars for two months' work. I found out later that I had earned twelve hundred dollars, but my stepfather kept a grand to himself. Not only that, but when I asked for allowance to buy stuff I needed, like Kotex and Clearasil, he told me to use my own money.

"This ain't no charity," he said. "Dirty little grease monkey."

His small engine business, Woody's Garage, was seriously impacted by the Canadian Tire moving into town, and my mother worked double shifts down at the A&P to make ends meet. To pay for the basics, like beer and smokes for Woody. He took her pay packet on Fridays. There was trouble if the seal was broke.

The old bus bumps along on shock absorbers that are overdue for replacement, and the flat miles along the north shore of Lake Ontario hypnotize me. Next thing I know, I'm waking up with a bunch of midgets swarming around me.

Now, I seen midgets before at the carnival that travels through town in August. But I never seen a dozen damn midgets up close, and me half asleep wondering what the hell did I get myself into this time.

"This is Audrey," Jack tells them. They have all got sacks of gear slung over their shoulders like a bunch of dwarfs on their way to the mine. Hi ho, hi ho.

"Hi Audrey." A midget hops up onto the seat beside me. His hair is cut like an Iroquois warrior. But he don't talk Indian. "My name is Hank."

"Hi Hank," I say, moving over as close to the window as I can. It is too late to ask questions about what kind of bus this is I'm riding. I try not to be too obvious about turning my head to see what the other midgets are up to.

"Are youse all cousins or something?"

Hank laughs. "No, Audrey" he says. "We're wrestlers. Professionals."

I nod and gather my purse and my jean jacket into my lap.

"We're headed down to Sherbrooke Arena for a Battle Royale. You should come. You might bring me some luck." Hank reaches into his pack and pulls out a Kit Kat Bar and offers me half. If it was any other chocolate bar, I would have shaken my head, no. But I am hungry, and it is my favourite.

"What's a Battle Royale?"

"Twenty midgets in the ring. Last one standing is the winner."

"What do you win?"

"A belt. Some cash, depending on how many spectators show up. Might be fifty bucks. Might be five hundred."

"Is it dangerous?"

"Nah. We don't hurt each other. Not on purpose, anyways."

Jack turns to me from the driver's seat and asks me if I want a job.

"My box office girl quit on me. Getting married. Huge mistake if you ask me. I need somebody reliable to take cash at the door. Are you reliable?"

"Of course," I tell him. "You can trust me with your life."

Jack laughs and puts the bus in gear. "Just watch yourself with Hank the Handyman, there. He's got a girl at every arena."

Hank takes my hand and shakes his head to tell me not to pay any attention. "Jack is full of it," he says, but his eyes tell me something different.

The Sherbrooke arena smells like the Napanee arena. All arenas smell the same, like a urinal puck that has been frozen and thawed and frozen and thawed for many seasons with hints of mould, vomit, spilled coffee, sweaty hockey equipment and zamboni oil. Jack sets me up at the entrance to the arena in a little booth with a hole in the glass and a slot for sliding money back and forth.

The midgets are squatting in cages. Literally. Like animals at the zoo, they are rattling the bars for the paying customers as they enter. Their names are on chalkboards, wired to their cages. Short Shrift, Holy Hammerhead, Little Professor. Stage names. Hank was The Red Avenger, with a feathered headdress and some kind of a primitive scalping tool that he kept stabbing through the cage in a threatening way. Occasionally, he let out a warpath whoop that sounded like he was planning to kill the settlers in the wagon train. White women with long blonde hair and gingham dresses, clean and starched as if there was a laundry service out there on the plains.

Jack lets me out of my booth after the show starts and offers me a front row seat. Ringside. The best in the house. He gives me a coke spiked with rye and winks and tells me to enjoy myself. He'll be back in a while. This is how you treat a lady in the wrestling world, and you know what? It feels pretty fine.

There are a few "one-on-one" fights before the Battle Royale. I am surprised by the gymnastic prowess of the stars. They are not comically entertaining like I expected. This is serious. There is no doubt who to cheer for. The wrestlers stand for something. Some are good, some are evil. Some are cheats. Some are heroes. The good guys follow the rules. Listen to the referees. They fight clean. Bad guys fight dirty, and the refs cannot control them. Meanwhile, the midgets are getting mean, promising to kill each other.

The announcer sounds like any sports announcer. Maybe he does the hockey games for the local radio. His voice is professional, and he talks a lot about the holds and what is legal and what is not.

The Battle Royale begins with the introduction of all thirty midgets. There is much posing and pantomiming as they are released from their cages. Hank comes out wearing a headdress and waving a tomahawk around. George beats his chest like King Kong. Victor howls like a wolf.

A woman slides into the seat beside me and yells into my ear.

"Hi. I'm Jack's girlfriend. Squirrel."

"Shirl?"

"Squirrel. Like the animal with the fluffy tail. You must be Audrey."

"Yep. Hi."

"Where you from, Sweetie?"

Squirrel is just the kind of woman that can get away with calling me Sweetie. That big-busted, big-haired, who-gives-a-shit kind of a gal that can plow through rough times and come out the other side none the worse for wear. Her bright red lipstick seeps into the cracks around her lips and stains her cigarette filter. I recognize her perfume. Avon. Wild Rose. My grandma used to wear it. It is strong.

"Napanee."

"I been there."

"Yeah?"

"Years ago. I danced at some hotel there. If I remember right, it was called The Savoy."

I gulp some of the rye and coke and try to picture Squirrel dancing for the losers at that shitty peeler joint. One time, me and my stepfather, Woody, were walking past The Savoy and he stopped to check out the women on the posters. Their nipples were covered with stars or tassels. For decency, maybe. Woody told me if I ever wanted a job, he'd set me up. The manager was a friend of his. Then he grabbed me from behind. With any luck you'll have big boobs like your mom, he said. Don't disappoint me, he added.

I was twelve years old.

"The Savoy burned down a couple years back," I tell Squirrel and that makes her laugh.

"No great loss," she says. I notice how her front teeth are prominent. Like they could crack open an acorn, no problem. She leans over and gives my knee a little squeeze and then we turn our attention back to the show. We cheer and scream. Squirrel reaches into her big purse whenever we need our drinks freshened up.

"They are true athletes," Squirrel says when the refs call a timeout. "Short little buggers, but agile as hell. And strong. I can't speak for all of them, but Little Lord Fauntleroy there? With the lace cape? A whiz between the sheets, Sister. A goddamn whiz between the sheets."

At the end of the night, Little Hillbilly is victorious. Injured and moaning midgets litter the stage. Little Hillbilly has piled them up in the corners of the ring. He accepts his winnings while the bright florescent lights of the arena flicker back on. Everyone looks sickly pale in the greenish glow. Squirrel takes me by the hand, and we sneak out the back door through an unused dressing room. The bus is running.

I climb aboard and Jack hands me a twenty. "Good job at the box office, tonight, Audrey. Next stop is Vermont. You coming with us?"

"You want me?"

"Sure, we want you. You fit in just fine. The job's yours if it suits you."

"I'll take it. Thanks, Jack."

I look over at Squirrel, pulling a blanket around her shoulders and fluffing up a pillow to make a bed on the bench seat across from me. Behind her is the Little Professor. His real name is Malcolm. He is reading the Globe and Mail with a flashlight. Some of the guys are jostling for seats at the back and laughing about the show. They are blaming each other for errors and cursing Hank for letting the Hillbilly get the upper hand with his famous pile driver. When Hank stumbled, Hillbilly took advantage with a brain buster, followed by a backbreaker. That pretty much suitcased the win for him.

Hank rolls his eyes at me and shrugs. Without his costume or war paint he looks older and tired. He pulls himself up beside me and offers to share his blanket. I tuck my half around my lap.

"Did you like the show?"

"Yes. I liked the show." I was at a loss for how to describe it. My heart was full from the intensity of it all. But mostly I liked the conflict. How it built up and built up and then exploded. Then it was over. The air clear and clean like after a summer storm when the humidity is gone. You didn't even realize it was smothering you until you could breathe again. But how do you say that?

"It was great. You were great. I had a great time."

"It is great, isn't it? Like the Roman gladiators and the Shakespearean tragedies and the Italian operas all bundled into one big human drama."

The bus rumbles out of the parking lot, through snug Quebec villages from another era. Hank falls asleep on my shoulder. I waken as the bus crosses the border at Stanstead. An officer boards the bus and walks to the back, with a flashlight. My heart races wondering if anyone has opened the door to my bedroom yet. My guess is no. Mom is used to unannounced absences. She wouldn't think to report either one of us missing. Unless.

Maybe my boss called to see if I'm sick or something and

Mom knocked on the door. Woody busted the lock ages ago. I bought a hook and eye at the hardware store and screwed it in myself, but it just made things worse. That's when I put my dad's old hunting knife under the mattress.

I think about my mother lifting the quilt on my bed and finding my stepdad instead of me. Not asleep. Will she hate me? Will she wish she'd had the guts to do it herself and maybe even tell the police it was her? More likely she will pull the quilt up and close the door and go do her shift at the A&P.

I imagined stabbing Woody a hundred times. The knife was waiting. Waiting. I would reach down and feel for the leather haft in the dark when I heard floorboards creaking. I watched my dad slit a deer's throat once after we hit it with the truck. My dad is a big strong man, but it shook him up. Now I know why. It's a whole helluva lot harder than you expect.

I keep my eyes closed as the border guard steps past me and speaks quietly to Jack for a while, checking papers and chuckling. He steps down off the bus and walks around the vehicle, then bangs the hood a couple of times and sends us on our way. I breathe. And breathe. And breathe.

It's morning. Early. Fog hangs low and sorrowful over a church spire in a town called Frosty Hollow. High up on a hill, a graveyard looms, the stones leaning downward toward disappointed houses. Porches falling off, roofs caving in. Crumbling factories with work for nobody. Hank wakes up as we enter the next town, Sleepy Creek.

"We're in the States," I say. "I've never been out of Canada."

"Same shit. Different country. The border is just a line on a map."

We pass a junkyard. Heaps of rusty metal piled behind a sign that says Auto Repairs. Hank reaches into his knapsack and finds an apple. Takes a bite and passes it to me.

"I grew up in New York State. Buffalo," he says.

"You're American?"

"Probably. I don't know exactly where I was born. But ya. My birth certificate is more of a guess, really."

I think about my hometown. In high school we all promised we'd leave as soon as we got the chance, but not many got away. There are boyfriends and babies and parents who can't take care of themselves. But I do know, at least, where I'm from.

"Sorry."

"Some lady left me in a booth at a McDonalds and went to the toilet and disappeared without a trace. Maybe she was my mom. Maybe she wasn't. That's all I know."

My mother disappeared, too, in a way. She had a breakdown the year my dad went up to Fort McMurray to work in the oil fields. It was good money, he said. Better pay than he was getting at the lumber yard. He sent checks for a while and then a letter from Yellowknife and that was it.

When Mom took up with Woody, she tried hard to please him. She liked how he took charge and changed the oil in the car and shoveled the driveway and cut the grass and put the garbage out. She wanted somebody to tell her what to do and how to do it, I guess. Including how to raise a lazy, spoiled daughter.

The apple has a bruise, mushy and brown, but I take a bite

anyway and hand it back to Hank.

"Are you going to be a wrestler forever?"

"Hell no. I'm always on the lookout for new opportunities."

"Aren't you afraid of getting drafted? Going to Viet Nam?"

Hank laughs. That was a stupid thing to say.

"I'd rather fight for the Viet Cong than Uncle Sam. I don't believe the North Vietnamese army has a height restriction." He takes my hand. "The war is bullshit. What about you? Are you going to be a runaway forever? Go to San Francisco with flowers in your hair?"

"I'm not sure."

"Nobody's sure," he says, squeezing my hand. "Life is long. Take your time."

INFERNO

Benevolent with warmth and light.
Malevolent with a murderous heart.
A fire is unpredictable, and a story has a mind of its own

Hope

Seven dead.
Not by violence.
Or disease.
Or accident.
But by hoping.

"I hope you die," Faye said to the cop who clocked her going 92 kph in a 50 kph zone. He was waiting in his cruiser just inside the speed limit change on a stretch of the King's Highway between Hagersville and Jarvis. A straight stretch of road that used to be a little village a hundred years ago, but now there is no reason in hell it should be a slow-down zone. Except that it provides a nice little opportunity for entrapment.

Faye pulled over and apologized to the officer, a young guy with a large mole under his left eye. She is not one who finds it easy to say she's sorry, especially when she doesn't believe it's her fault. At the very least, she expected him to commiserate with her and agree that the law is not always fair. But instead, he implied that since she was local and drove this stretch of highway frequently, she should know better.

Faye humiliated herself by pretending to cry a bit. And she mentioned that it would take all her grocery money to pay the ticket. "Show a little mercy," she begged.

He kept writing.

Then Faye asked him about the reason for the change in speed.

"The road is deserted," she said. "Why is it necessary to drive more slowly through this section?"

He admitted he didn't know and handed her the citation. Three hundred and twenty dollars and three demerit points.

"Is this the maximum penalty?" She asked.

"Yes, Ma'am. It is." And then he made a mistake. He sneered at her.

In the same tone of voice you might wish someone a good day, Faye said, "I hope you die."

He squinted and scowled and then turned on his heel like a Nazi and walked back to his cruiser. Faye considered spinning a little gravel in his direction as she pulled away, but she decided not to give him the satisfaction. Anyway, she paid the ticket online and didn't give it much thought until about a week later. Faye's husband at the time was Tony. Tony was on disability for a bad back. Bad enough, he claimed, that he couldn't cut the grass or throw in a load of laundry or lift anything heavier than a can of Coors.

Faye is hustling to make dinner after a long day at work, chopping onions and frying up some hamburger, and he says "Hey, Faye! What was the name of that officer who gave you the ticket last week?"

"I forget. Why?"

"Because there's a photo of this cop who was killed on Townsend Parkway. Transport lost a wheel, and it crushed the guy. There's a photo of him, and he has a mole. You said your guy had a mole, right?"

"Under his eye, yeah. Let me see."

Of course, Tony is such a loser he can't get up off the couch to show her. Faye wipes her hands on a tea towel and looks over his shoulder.

"Yep. That's the guy. Dead, is he?"

"That's what the article says."

"He was just a young guy. A dick. But young. Probably not even thirty yet."

"What are you cooking?"

"Chili." Faye goes back to the stove and turns the heat down and pours a can of chopped tomatoes into the pot. "You want it spicy?"

"Ya, Babe. You know I like the hot sauce."

That was the fourth. The first was Faye's high school boyfriend, Donny Fitzgerald. Fitz. A bad boyfriend. She found him fascinating for a while, the way he'd throw a tantrum and shove her and accuse her of some ridiculous crime. She worked on him for a while, like a science project, trying various hypotheses to correct his bad behaviour. But in the end, she had to abandon the endeavour in favour of her own mental health. He was isolating her from friends and family. She tried to break up with him, but he had some creative strategies to keep her on a string. Like threatening to kill himself.

"I hope someone hurts you, someday, as bad as you're hurting me," he said. "So you'll know what it feels like."

For some reason, Faye agreed to see him again. And, for a while, he was sweet as pie. Took her to the prom. Bought her flowers and a promise ring. Then one night they went for a drive out in the country. Fitz had a game he wanted to play. A role-playing game where he was the king and Faye was his slave. It was funny at first. Then it wasn't. As he dropped her off at home, she cringed getting out of the car, her hands and knees were raw from crawling around on gravel. She couldn't turn her head; her neck was so sore.

"I hope you die," Faye told him.

"What?" he shouted as the car door slammed.

Faye did not repeat it. She ran-hobbled-limped to her front door and prayed her dad did not lock it, because it was after midnight and sometimes, she had to go around back and climb in the kitchen window but thank god it opened. Fitz was afraid of Faye's dad. Everyone was, after the incident with the Jehovah's Witness.

Fitz drove off, squealing his tires to make the point that Faye was in big trouble. She heard the sirens ten minutes later. Level crossing. No gates. He drove right into the side of a boxcar full of chickens. The next day, Faye walked along the tracks with her best girlfriends, and they found Fitz's shoe in a pile of feathers. Her friends helped her build a little shrine near the crossing with candles and letters and a teddy bear. Faye stood in the receiving line at the funeral home with Fitz's mother who was drunk.

"Who will take care of me now?" his mother kept sobbing until it got on Faye's nerves. As if Fitz was capable of taking care of anyone but himself. As if he didn't deserve what he got. The only sad thing was that Fitz wasn't alone. He'd picked up another girl. Sadie Wilkins. She'd been walking home from a babysitting job. He must have offered her a ride. Poor Sadie.

Who was next? A girl named Lindsay. That one was complicated, because there was alcohol involved and LSD. Faye has reimagined the events of that night a few times, in an attempt to justify what happened. Let's just say it was an unavoidable tragedy.

Then, after that, a friend of Faye's father who came over and hung out in their garage where there was a beer fridge and a bunch of old lawnmowers that the two of them planned to fix up one day. Clint liked to tease Faye.

"I notice you're wearing a bra, now. Have you got your period yet?"

Ignorant stuff. Never so her dad could hear it. Girls hadn't been trained to tell on dirty old men in those days, so she had to put up with the Clints of the world. Otherwise, you got accused of being someone who couldn't take a joke. But one Christmas, when Faye was home from college, she caught Clint looking in her bedroom window. She was fresh from the shower, just wearing a towel, when she saw something reflected in the window.

"I hope you die," she yelled at him as he skittered away through the frozen bushes.

He fell off his roof putting up holiday lights the next day. Cracked his head open on the icy patio. "A sad Christmas for his kids," Faye said when her father told her what happened.

For a long time after that, Faye didn't hope death on anyone. It seemed satisfying enough to know that she could kill people if she needed to. It was a sweet little superpower tucked in her back pocket. Then she lost her job. So. Her boss. Heart attack.

Enough, she promised herself.

Years went by before the incident in the grocery store. Over a price check on eggs. It was ridiculous. Faye had nothing against the produce manager. There was something else going on in her life that had her upset. Tony, the lazy son of a bitch, managed to haul his bad back into bed with some woman he met at the dog park. How can you meet someone at the dog park when you don't have a dog? Faye had no clue. But truthfully? She was relieved. Dog Lady could have him. Good riddance.

Tony moved a bunch of stuff out of the house while she was at work. Including his La-Z-Boy chair and the oak coffee table. Apparently, according to the neighbour, he carried all that heavy shit out to the truck by himself. So, what happened to the bad back, eh? Faye spared him his life, but her need for revenge got misdirected and she sincerely regrets the death of Billy at the IGA. A waste.

Now that the divorce is final and she is alone, Faye finds herself ruminating about the past. In particular, the whole thing with Lindsay. Faye has absolved herself of Lindsay's drowning many times, in many invented storylines. But the one she keeps returning to is the one where Lindsay is jealous of Faye. Greg McInnis wants to break up with her because he is in love with Faye, and Lindsay goes crazy because she is pregnant with Greg's baby. Lindsay tries to drown Faye, and Faye has to protect herself, and the unthinkable happens. Tragic.

Faye starts searching for Greg McInnis, increasingly certain that she and Greg were meant to be together. There is no doubt in her mind that Greg feels the same way. Faye is clever at social media stalking. She tracks down Greg McInnis via a Facebook post of a friend of hers who is friends with Greg's cousin Louise. Even with a grey ponytail and a scruffy beard, she recognizes him and her heart leaps.

He is posing at the end of a pier holding up a small shark. Longboat Key, the post says. Florida. Greg is thin, wearing jeans and a Harley t-shirt, leaning on a stainless-steel tray where you clean and gut your catch. There are gulls and pelicans nearby, hoping to get a head or a tail or better yet, the whole fish. Greg is smirking with the crooked grin of someone who is hiding bad teeth. Probably he lost a few playing hockey.

Faye downloads the photo and examines it, searching for familiar characteristics. His stance, legs slightly bowed, is the same as it was in grade 12. How many times did she follow him along the high school hallway, pretending she was going to a class, hoping he would turn around and notice her? They were the same, her and him.

Teenagers don't mind trying on the dark coat of grief

and sadness, but when something really awful happens, they back away. After her boyfriend died in a train wreck, no one asked her out. And Greg didn't date anyone after his girlfriend drowned. Both of them were living in the shadow of tragedy.

But things are different now.

Faye messaged her friend, who connected her with Greg's cousin, Louise, who didn't mind sharing everything she knew about him.

Florida is an easy destination from Windsor. Cross the border. Get on I-75. Drive south. Google maps says it will take 23 hours and 20 minutes to get to Bradenton Beach. Faye will stay in Knoxville, Tennessee overnight and arrive the next day in time for supper.

Greg looks like the kind of guy who needs taking care of. Even in high school, she longed to help him with his homework, wash his hair, make him smile. He wandered around town alone, after Lindsay died, moving in and out of different social groups. At school, he paid just enough attention to assignments and rules to get by. Smart and handsome in a rugged way, but unmotivated. Faye wants to motivate him. She feels sure she can.

Faye turns on cruise control and the car propels itself south at sixty miles per hour through Ohio. She listens to talk radio. The Doctor channel. They are discussing bowel movements. Floaters are better than sinkers, the doctor says. Faye can't ever remember having a floater. Geez. She is probably going to get colon cancer or something. She switches to country music as she crosses the bridge at Cincinnati and rolls through the hills of Kentucky. Horses graze in bluegrass fields. I-75 is a divided highway. Sometimes she cannot see the northbound lanes at all, obscured as they are by tall pines. The temperature is getting warmer. September in Ontario is a lovely month, with leaves turning colour. But here the leaves are still green. It would be a monotonous drive if not for the billboards advertising strip joints and casinos and church services.

Just past six o'clock, Faye pulls into a Marriott at the first Knoxville exit. She gets a discount for the room with her CAA card. After she unpacks her nightgown and her toiletries, she walks across the road to the Cracker Barrel and orders the soup of the day and some corn bread. While she waits, she scans the other diners looking for anyone she might want to trade places with, an old game her mother used to play with her and her sisters. It's harder than you think to find someone who looks like they have a better life than you. That was the point of the game. Her mother wanted them to be satisfied with themselves. Are there richer, more beautiful people than you in this restaurant, or bus station, or shopping mall? No. Hardly ever. Those kinds of people are on TV. They are not here.

Faye has worked hard to maintain her appearance. Botox, shaped and dyed eyebrows, manicures and pedicures, hair coloured a reddish blonde. She is amazed how many people let themselves go. She hired a personal coach after Tony moved out. Matt, a guy she chose because he was built like Michelangelo's David. She was ready for an affair. By the time she found out Matt was gay, her biceps were impressive, and her romantic focus had pivoted to Greg.

Scrolling through her Facebook posts, Faye studies the

photos of Greg again, wondering if she will recognize him. Hopeful that he will recognize her. He offered her a ride after school one day, on his motorcycle, and she hopped on the back without a helmet. Relax, he yelled back at her when she stiffened on the first curve. Lean the way I lean. They went all the way to Selkirk on the Indian Line, passing fields of corn and summer squash and ditches bursting with goldenrod. She half expected to die and did not care.

Greg's cousin Louise was happy to help out when Faye asked how to get in touch with him.

"I think I remember you," she said.

Louise left town a long time ago and moved to the city. She worked at a doctor's office, but she is retired now. She messages Faye directions to Greg's trailer park, and the name of the bar where he bartends on weekends.

L - He had a woman, but she's been gone for some time now.
F - Not looking to hook up with him. LOL.
L - Good. Because he is useless as a partner. Three wives and seven or eight girlfriends cannot be wrong.
F - Not the only guy with relationship issues.
L - Nope. He's got nothing to recommend him. Didn't help his mom out when she got sick. Didn't even come home for her funeral.

Faye is not surprised by this information. There could be all kinds of reasons for Greg's family estrangement. Maybe his mother was a psycho. Maybe she abused him. Louise was a little too happy to air her family's dirty laundry. Used to be you tried to make everyone think your family was perfect. Mind your own bees wax, you said, if they asked. Now you can hardly go downtown for groceries without learning all manner of terrible personal woes. It is like a competition for worst life ever.

Greg, she expects, is no different than most middle-aged men. The boys they once were still exist under the scars and sad mistakes. They still love the same songs, cheer for the same teams, drink the same beer, and remember the girls that got away. Faye knows in her heart that Greg was in love with her.

When you listen to those real-life murder investigations, people remember things differently. Their accounts vary widely. Maybe ten people were at a party where the dead girl was last seen, but they all have a version of their own. Faye feels a responsibility to share her narrative about Lindsay's death with Greg. She was at a loss to explain why he avoided her. Why he left town and never returned. If she can convince him that her version of events is the truth, which it is, they can rewrite the ending together. Greg and Faye. Together. Inevitable.

They were all together that night at the beach, all a little stoned. It was humid, heat lightening flashing over Lake Erie. Eerie. Faye and Lindsay had never been close friends, but Lindsay reached out after Fitz died. They were sitting by the bonfire talking seriously about nursing school, grasping for vocabulary through a haze of cheap cider and half-tabs of blotter acid. But there was something else. Something about a baby.

Lindsay was crying. Was she telling Faye she was pregnant? Lindsay had been foolish and got herself in trouble.

Faye wakes up in her hotel room and reassures herself that her dream is an accurate memory. That her unrequited crush on Greg is mutual. That her pilgrimage to Florida is preordained. She showers and checks out before six a.m. On her way through the lobby, she grabs a paper cup of coffee for the road, knowing that it will taste like dishwater. But it will have to do.

The mist-shrouded highway is already busy. RVs with shrunken octogenarian drivers pass transport trucks on the uphill, and the transports pass them on the downhill. As the sun rises, green pastures and white fences and horses with warm coats appear. Georgia is a gauntlet of billboards competing for your soul, and then slamming it with harsh judgement. Love Shack. Adult Boutique. Sexy, sexy, sexy movies. Homosexuality is an Abomination. The Wages of Sin is Death.

Faye crosses the Florida border at two o'clock and pulls into a Jack-in-the-Box. Sitting under a plastic red umbrella, she sucks hard on a vanilla milkshake and checks her messages. Nothing. No one needs her. No one even knows where she is right now. The sun is strong in Florida, and she peels off her sweatshirt. Rolls up her jeans. Gets back in the car for the final stretch. Four hours to go.

She has her choice of parking spaces when she wheels her Impala into the alley behind Chubby's Lounge. There is still some pink in the sky from the sunset, that flamingo colour you see on postcards. But a bank of purple clouds threatens just beyond the pier and the wind has picked up. Palm trees are reaching away from the beach, imploringly. When she freshened up in the bathroom of a Food Lion on the Gulf highway (casual floral print dress, a soft mauve scarf, sandals), she noticed a rush on bottled water and canned goods.

"Hurricane coming, Darlin'," the cashier told her as she paid for a pack of Marlboroughs. "You haven't heard?"

The bar is dim. Faye runs a hand through her wind-tousled hair. She adjusts the shoulder strap on her purse and pauses in front of a TV as if she is interested in the score of the ball game. Then she saunters as casually as she can to the bar. Greg! There he is.

It never occurred to Faye that he might not be here. When things are predestined, they work out. They just do. Greg is taking glasses from a tray, polishing them, and lining them up on a shelf about the sink.

"Can I get you something?" He asks it in a way that implies he couldn't care less whether she wants something or not.

"How 'bout a Dark and Stormy?" Faye hopes he will think this is clever with the hurricane coming and all.

"Sure," he says. He grabs the bottle of dark rum off the top shelf, opens the fridge to get ginger beer and lime juice, scoops a tall glass full of ice and pushes the drink in front of Faye. No flourish. Just a guy doing his job.

"Hey, you look familiar. I think I know you. Are you from Carluke, Ontario by any chance?" Faye takes a good swallow of her drink and waits for his happy acknowledgement. She expects he will come around and hug her. Oh my god, what are the chances, he will say.

Instead, he flings the mop-up rag over his shoulder and nods. "I grew up in that hick town. You?"

"You don't remember me? I'm Faye Wilson."

"Faye."

"And you're Greg McInnis."

"Guilty."

Faye wonders if Greg has some kind of early dementia.

"We hung around together back in the day. In fact, we were close. I had a crush on you. And I'm pretty sure you had a crush on me too."

"Well. That is entirely possible, I suppose. What did you say you were doing here? In Florida? You on vacation?"

"I'm down visiting my cousin. She's renting a place on Santa Maria Island. But we got our dates mixed up. Seems she won't be here until tomorrow. So, I'm on my own. I might have to sleep in the car tonight."

A guy at the table in the corner calls for a refill of his pitcher.

"Excuse me," Greg says. He is formal and distant. Like a stranger. Faye reconsiders her strategy. She is pretty talented at reading people, and she does not like the vibe Greg is giving off. He might have her confused with someone else. She chugs her Dark and Stormy and stares at the TV screen. Baseball is slow. Boring. But she likes the way the uniforms show off the players' butts.

When he comes back, Greg picks up her empty glass and replaces it with a refill without her asking. He tells her he is off in twenty minutes, or as soon as Jackie arrives to take over. "Let me buy you dinner," he says.

Okay. That's more like it! Faye takes a booth and orders the fish and chips. With gravy. Hell with it. She has gained six pounds since she quit working out with Matt and she is expecting her family's bad cholesterol count to catch up with her any time. Her dad had nine stints put in before he died. Stay away from white food, the doctor told her after taking her blood pressure. No white bread. Nothing processed or deep fried. Nothing that tastes good in other words, she said. He didn't laugh.

Faye finishes every bite, sopping up the last of the gravy with the complimentary garlic bread before Greg comes to join her.

"You were hungry," he says.

"I was. Starving. Did you eat?"

"I'm a grazer. Not really one for sit down meals." He raises his draft glass and drinks deeply.

It didn't take long to get him talking about Carluke. The school. The drinking hole where no one ever asked for I.D. The big fire at the Victoria Hotel that killed thirteen unlucky men.

"My uncle was one of them," she said.

"Who was that?"

"My uncle? I forget his name. Not an uncle really. I guess he was more of a second cousin or something. On my mother's side. He had a mental problem. I think his name was Dan. Uncle Dan."

In the gloomy humidity of hurricane season with a hard rain battering the shutters, they talked about high school teachers and local bands and car rallies. While they reminisced, games from two different conferences leading up to the World Series were flashing shadowy images from muted TVs, and an old Eagles album was echoing off the cement block walls.

"You seem to recall a lot more about those times than I do," Greg told her after a while. "They weren't exactly my glory days."

"That's hard to understand. Because you were popular. And fun."

"Hmmm. Not how I remember it." He drained his glass and caught Jackie's eye and she delivered another round.

Faye picked up the saltshaker and spun it back and forth. "We had a connection, you and me. I kind of felt we might have been closer. You know. If things had been different. I was sorry when you left town."

"What do you mean?"

"I guess I was hoping to be your girlfriend."

"But I had a girlfriend."

"I know. I was there. That night. When Lindsay died."

"Well. I was messed up."

"Of course. Who wouldn't be?"

Faye put down the saltshaker and slid her hand across the table, willing him to take it. *Hold it. Remember me! Remember what we went through together. How I got you out of your wet clothes. You were shivering. We kept each other warm under the blanket.*

Greg stood up and went to the bar. Bands of hurricane

warnings flashed continuously across the television screens. Cautious people were obeying the evacuation recommendations, paying their tabs and saying goodnight.

Greg came back with a six pack. "I told Jackie to lock up and go home. I better head on home, too," he said.

"Any idea where a girl could find some shelter for the night?"

He looked at her hard. And Faye felt afraid. But kind of thrilled too, like when you know someone might be dangerous but it's exciting. Challenging in a sexy way.

"You really don't have a place to stay?"

"No. That's dumb, I know. Never mind. I can sleep in the car."

"Tell you what. You can have my couch. How's that?"

"Thanks," she said. "For your hospitality."

"Anything for a Carluke girl," he said.

Jackie told them goodnight and warned them to take care. Faye thought she saw Jackie wink at him and felt a stab of anger. Outside, the wind was punishing in a good way. A way that pushed them together. She half expected him to grab her hand, but he adjusted the beer and increased his pace. It was hard to keep up. Faye stopped to kick her shoes off and her scarf went flying right off her neck. It caught around the trunk of a coconut palm tree. She yelled at Greg to wait but her voice was lost in the gale, and he kept walking. Didn't look back.

Faye could not help it. She felt a deep eternal love for this man. Time tilted sideways and emptied her into 1972. Onto a beach. Into a different storm. Waves crashing. Lindsay trying to claim something that didn't belong to her. Some people don't get it. Lindsay didn't get it. She interfered with the way the universe intended things to be. It had taken thirty years, but circumstances were about to get a long overdue correction.

Faye's dress was gritty with sand when they reached Greg's trailer.

"I'll be right in," he said. "Gonna take a piss out here. Washroom's on the left if you need it."

She did. While she peed, she opened the tiny cabinet under the sink and found a stash of tampons. Not good. Toilet paper, Lysol, mouthwash. She opened the cap and swigged a bit. Swished it around. Spit it into the little sink. God. Her reflection in the mirror! She was a wreck. Mascara dribbling, hair a mess. She tidied up as best she could and opened the door. Greg was at the table, pulling the tab on a beer.

Other than some dishes piled in the kitchenette, the trailer was tidy enough. Nothing to make it homey. No throw pillows or books or plants. She slid into the bench seat opposite Greg, and he pushed the beers her way.

"No thanks," she said. "Got anything stronger?"

"Whiskey above the fridge," he said. He did not make a move to retrieve it for her. The trailer shook and the windows rattled. Faye wondered aloud if the whole RV would end up in the ocean.

"There's worse ways to die," he told her. "I've considered quite a few of them." Greg put a cigarette between his lips and, squinting from the smoke, he reached around and pulled a worn wallet out of his back pocket. He placed his cigarette in the ashtray with a shaking hand. Rubbed his fingers together in preparation for something. Looked at Faye. Drew a breath in between clenched teeth as if someone was about to punch him. Pulled a photograph out of the wallet.

"Love of my life," he said, handing it to Faye.

The photograph was soft as Kleenex.

As long as we both shall live, it said on the back in girlish curlicued script.

Lindsay had black hair, parted in the middle and pulled back in a ponytail. She wasn't smiling, but she managed to look pleasant and self-assured. Like a nurse. Like the nurse she never got to be.

"I don't know why you're here," he says. "Louise told me you've been snooping around."

Faye feels herself getting hot. She scrambles for an excuse. A reason to explain her behaviour. She is usually good at this. But she has nothing.

"I always had a creepy feeling about you. Like you couldn't be trusted. And the night that Lindsay died, you were coming on to me. It made me mad. Lindsay was so nice to you after Fitz died, and you were all set to betray her if I went along with it."

"I think you must have misunderstood."

They were in bras and panties. Holding hands and wading in up to their waists and then their chests and then Faye jumped on Lindsay's back. Playfully. Waves crash against the sandbars in Lake Erie with surprising power and the water sucks along the bottom, back into the deep water, like a vacuum. Lindsay got a mouthful. Faye heard her choke and felt the girl's panicky spasms and it energized her. She kicked Lindsay's feet out from under her and flipped her on her back and pushed her shoulders down below the surface. Lindsay managed to twist around and she kneed Faye right in the crotch. A well-placed painful blow square on her pubic bone.

"I hope you die!" Faye screamed. She kicked Lindsay hard in the chest and swam off.

Faye fought the undertow as she made her way to where Greg and the boys were goofing around in the shallows. The thunder rumbled in satisfaction.

Faye stands to get the whiskey just as a gust of wind slams the trailer and sends her flying. She lands on her ass and starts to cry. Greg sits and watches as she scrambles around trying to climb back onto the bench seat. Her elbow is bleeding, and she looks around for a paper towel or a napkin but there is nothing in sight.

"Can I get a bit of help here? Have you got a washcloth? What's wrong with you?"

"What's wrong with me? I think you got that turned around. I knew there was something wrong about the way you never missed a beat after Fitz was killed. You were a cold one. And then the night Lindsay drowned, you came on to me like some crazed nymphomaniac."

"No."

"Yes. You were grinding against me. Trying to kiss me. Lindsay was still missing. They hadn't even found her body yet. I had to peel you off of me."

A panicky flutter is expanding in Faye's chest. "You think I… What? What are you saying?"

"Having Lindsay as a girlfriend was the best thing that ever happened to me. I still wake up in the middle of the night with the same nightmare. Trying to find her in that stinking green algae."

"The water was murky. The night was wild. Dark. We were drunk."

"You. You were drunk. And dangerous. You know what I think? I think you killed her."

"Or maybe she killed herself. You should consider that before you make any accusations. She was desperate. Did you know she was pregnant? Well, she was. She was up the stump with your baby, and she knew you didn't love her. You fell in love with me. She knew, didn't she, that we were meant for each other. You and me. It was meant to be. You. And me."

Greg stood up. Launched himself at her. Faye looked around for something to defend herself with. She reached for the frying pan in the drainer. He laughed and grabbed her above her sore elbow, and she turned toward him. Tried to embrace him. Passion can be like this. But he opened the door and shoved her hard into the storm. She looked back and saw him then, framed in the bright rectangle of the doorway. He was yelling at her. Words that landed on her chest like iron fists.

"I hope you die!"

The Hitchhiker

The hitchhiker was standing on the soft shoulder in the rain. He didn't look to be any older than twelve or thirteen. I'm a public health nurse. When I first took this route, it surprised me how many hitchhikers there were. I thought they'd all disappeared in the sixties after the hippies got jobs and became bureaucrats. But nope.

There are the regulars. Jonah lives in a trailer up the Smout Road, and he goes to town a couple of times a week. Tuesdays, Senior Discount Day at the drugstore, and Fridays, when they have the meat draw at the Legion. He walks to the end of his driveway and sits in a plastic white chair and sticks his thumb out.

Then there's the spunky girl, Hannah, who hitchhikes to her job at the gas station and writes a blog about the people she meets. She is feisty and foul-mouthed, and she thinks her tattoos make her rape-proof. I hope she's right.

Otherwise, it's mostly young men on their way to Cayuga where the courthouse is located. I pick them up, down on their luck, without a job and without a vehicle, on their way to plead their cases before old Judge Wilson. You can recognize them a mile away, walking on the shoulder of the road in dusty dress shoes, wearing strangling neckties that predict conviction.

But this kid is different.

"Thanks, Miss," he says politely as he tucks his wet backpack down by his feet and pulls the door closed.

"Are you headed to the courthouse?"

"Um," he hesitates. Embarrassed, I assume. "Yeah. Yes. The courthouse."

"What's up at the courthouse?" I ask.

"Custody battle," he says.

"Oh," I say. "I'm sorry. That's rough." Neither one of the parents must want him too bad if they let him hitchhike to the courthouse. But he looks cared for. His jacket is good quality. His shoes are new. Maybe there's a grandmother?

He reaches into his pocket and pulls out a phone. Finds a photo of a little baby boy. "Here," he says. "This is my son. His name is Ryder."

Bullshit. No way is this kid a dad.

"Cute little guy," I say cautiously. "How old?"

"Eighteen months. His mom and I broke up a year ago."

"Wait. How old are you?"

"Nineteen," he says. "I know. 'That's young for a dad, isn't it?'"

"Yep. Sure is. But age isn't the important thing in parenting."

"I know! That's what I'm going to tell the judge. I am the only parent that really cares about Ryder. His mother's crazy."

I crank up the heat and take another glance at my passenger. "Crazy like a serious mental illness?"

"No. Maybe. She smokes a lot of weed. I don't trust her. I don't want her raising my son."

"That makes sense," I tell him. He scrolls through a few messages and tucks his phone away."

"So," He says. Enough about me. "Tell me about you."

I laugh.

"What?'

"Just… nothing. I'm a nurse. I work for V.O.N. It's an organization…"

"I know what it is. Victorian Order of Nurses. They helped my grandmother after her stroke."

"Right. Exactly. My name is Natalie, by the way."

"I'm Carson," he says. Then he slouches down and looks out the side window. I think I offended him when I laughed but come on! We're not on a date here.

In this grim weather, the old farmhouses look bleak and unwelcoming. The barns are collapsing, one by one. Winter's over, but April isn't much better. After the snow melts everything looks bruised. We pass a laneway where someone has put a toilet with the sign 'FREE' on the raised lid. I catch Carson looking at it, too. There is no garbage service out here. You have to take your own trash to the dump. This community does not understand the new wasteful economy. They think there are people, poorer than them, who will pick up their broken old crap.

"You need a toilet?"

He murmurs. Still miffed.

"I'm stopping for coffee at Willow Corners. You want anything?"

He hesitates.

"I'm buying," I tell him.

The coffee perks him up. He orders a double double and a toasted bagel with cream cheese and tells me he wants to be a paramedic. It used to be veterinary medicine that topped the dream list for future professions, but that's changed. Young people want to drive ambulances now. They don't know about PTSD.

"What time is your court appearance?"

"Not until 11:30. I'm early. I didn't know if I'd have to walk the whole way."

It is 9:45. I'm due at Emily's house at ten. My job is visiting the sick and the elderly in isolated homes on back roads you wouldn't even know existed. I'm used to it, but I'm not going to lie, it makes me uncomfortable going to some of these places. Most of my patients are totally harmless, but some? Like the Stinsons? They have a skittish way about them that makes me wary. They've got about eight kids and a bunch of cousins and other relatives that live in shacks and trailers and structures that maybe were once animal pens. This whole clan is totally bald. No eyebrows, no eyelashes, no hair at all. When I first met the mother in the clinic, I thought she was having chemo treatments, but no. And it's not alopecia, either, which is an autoimmune disease causing hair loss. One doctor told me that the Stinsons carry some inherited gene that is very dominant. Incest, he whispered.

They are an interesting bunch, the Stinsons. Independent and resilient, they hunt and fish and heat with wood. They're resourceful, too. They come to town and shop for clothes at the thrift store, five dollars for all you can stuff into a bag. And they wear the clothes until they get dirty, and then they stuff them around the windows and into the walls for insulation. You have to admit, this is innovative thinking.

I pull the car over just before the Scotch Line at the edge of town by a row of mailboxes. The rain is coming down pretty hard, flooding the ditches on either side of the road. Looks like the culvert is blocked again.

"I go down this road. If you hop out here, it's probably about a twenty-minute walk to the Court House."

Carson hesitates. Then he pulls the hood up over his ball cap and unbuckles his seatbelt. "Thanks, Natalie."

"You're welcome. Good luck in court."

He opens the door. Steps out. Pauses. Ducks back inside to get his coffee."

"Or…"

"Ya?"

"You could come with me while I visit my client. You'd have to stay in the car, though. At least you would stay dry. I could get you to the Courthouse in plenty of time."

He hops back in. "Sounds good. Thanks."

I drive along the Scotch Line, barely touching the accelerator. I hold my breath negotiating the potholes, deep enough to disappear in. This past winter was a bugger for freezing and thaws. The whole road needs regrading. At the end of the line, there is a turnaround for the school bus, not that it comes down here anymore, and off of that is a little dirt track with no name. Emily's driveway.

Emily suffers from muscular sclerosis. Her husband took care of her for a while, but he had his own troubles. Alcohol. She is still expecting him to come home any day, but she has lost track of time. It's been over a year since he left. I am trying to talk her into moving to a long-term care facility. It is not safe for her to be way out here on her own.

As soon as we pull into Emily's lane, I notice some kind of decoration on the bush under her bathroom window. Something that wasn't there last week. I point it out to Carson. He hops out to get a closer look while I gather the things I need. I reach for my umbrella, but the rain has slackened off.

"That's toilet paper hanging in the bush," he says. "Wads of it. With shit on it."

"Oh, gross! Okay. Wait here. I won't be long."

I open the front door and announce my arrival. The house reeks. I pull my scarf up over my nose and go to the kitchen to find Emily in a state of disrepair. Her faded nightgown is hoisted up to her waist so I can see she isn't wearing underwear. Her swollen legs are propped on a dirty pillow. The place is a mess. Dishes floating in greasy water in the sink. The floor sticky. She had a cleaning lady at one time. Paid for by March of Dimes. But she quit.

"I had a bit of a disaster with the septic," Emily says. "It backed up. My daughter's got the flu, so she can't help." Emily breaks down and cries. The story about the daughter is a familiar one. There is a daughter somewhere, no doubt, but she doesn't show her face around here.

"So… you've been throwing your toilet paper out the window?"

"Sorry."

"Christ, Emily, you need to call 911."

"They'll put me in a home."

"But, Emily, you can't stay here." I lift the receiver on her phone. No dial tone. "Emily! How long has this been out of service? Stop crying. We'll get this sorted out." I pull out my mobile, hoping to catch a few bars. Internet connections are random and rare out here. But luck is with me. For the time being.

Outside, I update Carson. The ambulance is on its way. He is quite helpful. He walks up the lane to flag the paramedics down in case they miss the turn. He watches them with interest as they load Emily onto the gurney. The woman, her name is Patty, starts to lose her patience with Carson when he climbs into the back of the vehicle. She yells at him.

"Fuck off," he tells her. "I'm just trying to help."

Patty glares at me like it's my fault. And she's right. It was irresponsible of me to bring him here. I'm starting to worry. I could get reported.

"You better get in the car," I say to Carson, quietly, so as not to set him off.

I promise Emily that I'll visit her at the hospital. Then I

go back inside and lock up. Not much I can do here without a hazmat suit.

"Still want to be a paramedic?" I ask Carson when I climb back into the car.

"The guy was nice. But that lady was a bitch."

"Ya. Well, she was just doing her job. Are you okay? I didn't mean for you to see all that. It wasn't pretty. Emily was in rough shape."

"Not a problem. I seen worse."

I get Carson to the Courthouse at 11:25, with time to spare. Civilization feels good. There are daffodils on both sides of the driveway. The clouds are parting, and the sun is coming out. Carson smiles and waves, slipping his arms into his backpack straps while he walks up the imposing steps. This is an old-fashioned courthouse, built to intimidate. The courtyard, they say, is haunted by ghosts of criminals who died by hanging.

My route continues south along the river. Foggy patches hang over the fields. Next stop, Dave Wood, convalescing from kidney surgery. He will be ready for another round of painkillers and sleeping pills. I wonder if I still smell of the septic disaster at Emily's, but that can't be helped. A nice hot shower is hours away. I lean back to get my medical bag. Gone. It is hard to miss, bright orange with lots of pockets, but I try to control my panic. It's not in the back seat. It's not in the trunk. It is nowhere.

Think, think, think. Did I leave it at Emily's? Did I carry it in and put it down in the kitchen? Damn. I have been careless. I try to picture Carson climbing the steps of the courthouse.

He did not have a bulky orange bag with him. No way could he have stuffed it in his backpack. It wouldn't fit.

But he could have scooped the pills. He could have ditched the bag. Could he? Of course, in all that chaos, he could have done anything. I have no choice but to backtrack to Cayuga and make that drive down the Scotch Line again. If the orange bag isn't at Emily's house, I will be in trouble. Lost or stolen opioids are going to take some explaining. Hitchhikers. Really, Natalie? Are you kidding me? My boss is a hard-ass old battle-axe of a nurse who will never forgive me.

On the way back along the King's Highway toward Cayuga, I decide to call Muriel, my friend who works in the office at the Courthouse. I pull over alongside a sodden corn field. The ravens are helping themselves to last year's leavings as the soil thaws.

"Muriel? Natalie."

"Hey, girl."

"I'm in a bit of a pickle, Muriel. I gave a kid a ride to court this morning. A hitchhiker named Carson. I think he might have stolen a few blister packs full of painkillers. His appearance was scheduled for 11:30. Can you get a cop to check his backpack, maybe? He's just a kid. Looks like a kid. He said he's nineteen, but he looks more like, I don't know. Twelve?"

"What? Slow down, Nat. There's no kid here."

"He has to be there. I dropped him off twenty minutes ago. He had a custody hearing at 11:30."

"Natalie. That doesn't make sense. It's traffic court all week, hon."

"Crap."

"I think you gave a ride to a little thief. He's probably

down at the high school selling those pills right now. Jeez. Want me to send a cruiser over? Ken Potts is sitting here in my office right now, doing the crossword."

"Sudoku," Ken yells from the far side of the office.

"Whatever. You better talk to Natalie, Ken."

I agree to go back to Emily's and check for the orange bag, and Ken will drive by the high school. He will call me if he finds the kid. I warn him that the cell service on the Scotch Line is sketchy at best. He tells me to meet him back at the courthouse at one.

Bumping over potholes on the Scotch Line, I feel that deep cold well of dread that bubbles up when I do something stupid. Even the car heater, turned up full blast, won't get rid of the chill of failure. Bad choices litter my past like half-forgotten landfills. Bad boyfriends that took advantage, good boyfriends that I should have married. Money wasted. Unexplainable behaviour. Self-sabotage. Ruin. I have trained myself not to look in the rear-view mirror of my messed-up life, but sometimes I have to. What is wrong with me?

The orange bag shows up immediately on the grey landscape as I drive up to the house. It is under the toilet paper bush. Rifled and discarded. I know the value of a blister pack of painkillers on the street. Carson might be able to get as much as twenty dollars a pill. But he will probably take whatever he can. Carson is just the kind of shyster I fall for in adult men. Charming liars. There is something missing in them, emotionally. They do not mind hurting people. They recognize in me the kind of person who expects to get hurt. And even though it happens again and again, I never see it coming.

At the courthouse, Ken is waiting with Carson in the backseat of the cruiser. Ken picked him up at the elementary school. He is in grade eight. When I figured him for twelve years old, I was right on. There are no blister packs in his backpack. He claims he missed the bus and hitchhiked to school and he started to cry a bit when he recounted how the 'nurse lady' took him down a scary backroad. He implies that his parents will probably want to press charges. He is asking for a social worker.

I bend down and look in the cruiser. Yep. That is Carson, all right, and he glares at me, confident that he is protected from prosecution by his tender age.

"What do you think I should do?" I ask Ken.

"I think you better come with me," he says.

I lost my job. Fair enough. I was careless with medications. Careless with my actions concerning a minor. I was not found criminally responsible, however, because the principal at the school wrote a letter to corroborate my story. Carson fools a lot of people a lot of the time. Well-intentioned but naive, Judge Wilson said of my actions that day. I think that means ditzy.

I got a new job as a Personal Support Worker. It pays less than I was getting as a Public Health Nurse, but I am thankful to get it. To not be in jail. My first assignment is at Emily's house, at the end of the Scotch Line. A job that no one else wants. It takes a few trips to the laundromat and two big jugs of bleach, but the house is fresh and clean. I make the calls to have the septic fixed. Some thunderstorms get rid of the toilet paper on the bush. The bush thrives. Emily says she never remembers so many lilacs.

Every morning, as I drive down the King's Highway, and again as I drive home, I watch for hitchhikers. I might see a mailbox or a stump in the distance and my heart starts beating hard. Carson, I know, will be waiting for a ride one day, and I will pull over.

Get in, I will tell him.

And he will do as I say.

Anna's Last Day

Anna leaves the clinic and drives until she is on an unfamiliar back road somewhere near the lake. She parks on the shoulder, gets out of the car and vomits in the ditch. There. That's better. She lets the wind blow her hair away from her flushed face and looks up at the sky where the clouds move along quickly, throwing purple shadows over the field. Cornhusks rustle, clicking and clacking like skeletons. They are dying, she realizes. She is dying. How could mortality take her by surprise?

Up the road a ways, maybe forty or fifty feet, she sees a creature moving slowly out of the long grass. Slow like a turtle, but the wrong shape. She approaches it cautiously. It is a crow's head. Just the head. Moving across the road. By itself. Anna gets a stick and tips it over to reveal a dozen big black beetles. She feels like she has interrupted their giant crow head ceremony. Anna apologizes and rolls the head in the direction of the fleeing beetles, hoping they will hoist the trophy back on their armoured shoulders. She hates to ruin a party.

Anna has Huntington's Disease. After six months of genetic counselling the psychiatrist deemed she was psychologically capable of accepting the burden of knowledge. She went to the clinic, and they did the blood test. Now she knows. For sure. She has it. The defective gene. They prepare her for symptoms of depression that often present themselves after a definitive diagnosis. They encourage her to sign on for the clinical study, as they are very close to a breakthrough in the treatment of frontal lobe dementias. A nurse hands her a hefty package of information on current stem cell research.

"Call us anytime," she urges.

But Anna assures the professionals that she is okay. She is cool about it. Everybody has to die of something, right? Cancer, diabetes. Choose your poison, friend.

"I'm fine," she says out loud all the way home. Until she feels sick and takes a detour down toward the lake. The crow's head is a sign, but she can't interpret it.

Huntington's Disease (HD) is an inherited brain disorder. It was named after the doctor who first described it in 1872, George Huntington. HD causes cells in specific parts of the brain to die: the caudate and putamen, and, as the disease progresses, the cerebral cortex. The caudate and the putamen have connections to many other areas of the brain and help control movements, recall recent events, make decisions, and control emotions. The disease leads to incapacitation and, eventually, death.

Anna gets up and goes to school the next day, as usual. As if nothing has changed. She writes the date on the blackboard in chalk. She wonders if Huntington's will affect her neat primary teacher printing. She does not let herself wonder why she lied to Al about the results last night when he asked, telling him the clinic would notify her in a week or two.

"You know how the medical system is nowadays," she says, casually.

"No way do you have it," he reassures her, giving her shoulders a squeeze. She feels herself pulling away from him. Separating herself from the rest of the world that is normal and healthy.

"You're wrong," she wants to say. But she is not at all sure that he can handle the news. That he loves her enough to stick around and watch as she evolves into a horror show character like her mother did. It is almost a month before she tells him, on a Friday night when the girls are out with friends, that her test was positive. Al mixes martinis and they get drunk and make love and she feels better.

Early stage symptoms appear as slight physical changes and may also include cognitive or emotional changes. A clinical diagnosis of HD is based on the presence of involuntary movements. Individuals may notice a little clumsiness, changes in handwriting, or difficulty with daily tasks like driving. People with early Huntington's may find they have difficulty organizing routine matters or coping effectively with new situations. Difficulty recalling information may make them feel forgetful.

By December, Anna is panicking every time she drops a piece of chalk or fumbles for change in her purse. Twice this term, she has forgotten yard duty, something she has never done before. In January, she gets lost in the middle of a math lesson and can't recover. She screams at the children. "What are you looking at? Put your heads down on your desks. All of you! NOW!"

She takes the next three days off. Her doctor encourages her to fill the prescription for antidepressants.

"You'll feel better, Anna. More like yourself. And you won't be as likely to anticipate the symptoms."

"Like hell," Anna says. She is intimately familiar with the symptoms of her incurable disease. She observed its progression as it stole her mother from her. Her sweet-tempered, generous mother, sentenced to end her life in a prison of mental and physical anguish. Anna was the warden. She had the key and she used it, locking her mother away in an institution. And no one blamed her. No one questioned her motives. In fact, they praised her when she sprung her mother out one Sunday a month and brought her home for dinner. She cringed watching her mother shove food in her mouth. A woman who had been meticulous about her appearance, got her hair done weekly, ironed every article of clothing she wore, including nighties. She took special pride in her manicure.

Anna watched the slovenly stranger with flat hair and stained shirts and observed how the kids stared with disgust at their grandmother.

Work activities may become more time-consuming, and

decision-making may be impaired. Individuals at this stage may experience periods of depression, apathy, irritability, impulsiveness or perhaps changes in personality. At this stage, people with Huntington's can function quite well at work and at home.

"Julie's dad is driving, Mom! That's the third time you asked me. What? Why are you crying?"

"Anna, I have a number of complaints from parents about your temper. I've always admired your competence, so it makes me wonder… I need to ask. Are you well? Do you need to take a personal leave?"

"It's not about HD, Anna, It's about your preoccupation with it. You need to live one day at a time. I need my wife back. Take the damn antidepressants, Anna."

Anna starts taking the Zoloft. She has to admit, it helps. She can do her job. She can remember her dental appointments. She has the energy to take a shower and return phone calls to friends. Coffee tastes good again. She can rationalize that everyone has a genetic time bomb ticking within. Nearing fifty, her friends have breast cancer, bi-polar disorder, arthritis and irritable bowels. They have always envied her youthful appearance and her musical talent. She has a single-digit handicap in golf. Her daughters are beautiful and achieve high marks in high school. Her husband, as far as she knows, has been a faithful partner.

Anna remembers her mother as she was before HD. Tall

and slim, she loved the Chanel look. Classic. Chic. And always with matching gloves and hats, purses and shoes. Her posture was regal. She taught Anna the benefits of good posture like some mothers teach their daughters to sew or bake.

"If you carry yourself with confidence, Anna, you can go anywhere. Do anything." Her mother loved a party in Rosedale as much as a camping trip in Algonquin. She could paddle a canoe and build a bonfire as well as any camp counsellor. And stories? Anna's mother could tell a story under the stars very well. Lovely stories about lost Indigenous nations that are not okay to tell anymore.

"Once there was an Indian Princess," her mother would start in a soft clear voice that invited you to listen. "The Princess met a boy in the summer of her sixteenth year. But it was the wrong boy. This boy was from a rival tribe. The Princess was beside herself with grief when the Chief, her father, forbade her to see the boy. The Chief was not interested in how handsome the boy was. How gentle. How unlike the rough and teasing boys in her own tribe. The Chief was deaf to his daughter's desperate pleas. And then one morning, his beautiful daughter was gone. Never seen nor heard from again. The only clue to her possible whereabouts was an overturned canoe bobbing on the morning waves. If you stay up until midnight when the moon is full, you might see her tortured wraith-like spirit paddling to White Pine Point."

Did Anna stay awake, huddled in her sleeping bag? Yes, of course. Did she see the Princess? Yes. A figure of trailing mist quivering in the moonlight. And Anna heard her weeping, too. A mournful sound.

Drowning is Anna's preferred method of suicide. Not only because of the Indian Princess. Consider Ophelia, elegant and romantic. Virginia Wolfe, artistic and lonesome. Drowning is civilized. Water is cool and smooth and welcoming. Flipping the calendar to August, Anna sees that the full moon falls on the fifth this year. She circles it.

As the disease progresses, the symptoms become worse. The initial motor symptoms will gradually develop into more obvious involuntary movements such as jerking and twitching of the head, neck, arms and legs. These movements may interfere with walking, speaking and swallowing. People at this stage of Huntingtons often look as if they're drunk. They have increasing difficulty with working or managing a household, but can still deal with most activities of daily living.

During the June field trip to the zoo, Anna's legs give way beneath her as she stands with twenty-seven students in front of the polar bear exhibit. She reaches for the fence as her twitching knees collapse and, unbalanced, falls down three stony steps. She hears some giggling from her students, and then voices of alarm from the parent volunteers. The St. John's Ambulance attendant gently wraps her sprained wrist, and his kind concern brings her to admit her secret. "I have Huntington's Disease." Other than her family, she has told no one. She follows the confession with an outburst of undignified tears.

On the way home while the class is singing ninety-nine bottles of beer on the wall at the back of the bus, Anna has flashes of her mother in the throes of Huntington's.

"Mom," Laura calls. "You need to come and see what Nana's doing. In the kitchen. Come quick."

Surrounded by Halloween candy wrappers, Anna's mother gorges on chocolate. It dribbles down her chin, staining her dreadful pink polyester blouse. She is licking her fingers, eyes glazed over. Lunacy lives behind those eyes.

Then there was the day at work when her principal interrupted her science lesson. "I'll cover your class, Anna. The nursing home called. Some trouble, I think. You'd better go over there."

Trouble indeed. But it is not her mother she finds in the parking lot of the church next door to Extendicare. It is a madwoman swinging a broom wildly. Her face is purple with rage. Her eyes are exploding out of bruised sockets. "That bitch stole my shoes!" she screams. Over and over and over.

"What do you expect me to do?" Anna wants to know. They give her papers to sign. Her mother goes to the Yellow Wing. On the third floor. She gets a bracelet that sets off an alarm if she attempts to get into an elevator. Lock-up.

Everything Anna needs for her last day is in the black backpack under the basement steps. She showers and dresses carefully, even though she does not expect to be found. Her favourite capris and softest tee shirt and a light zippered vest. Nike running shoes. Her only jewelry is her wedding band, and the gold watch Al gave her on their 20th anniversary. She pauses and considers, slips the watch off and leaves it on her bedside table. Laura or Dana may like to have it.

She makes her bed and glances at the morning paper. A

little girl's face looks back at her from underneath the headline. Where is Darla?

Black eyes, black pigtails. Anna wonders about Darla. Nine times out of ten these stories end badly, but this time she won't be around to read the concluding episode. Will they find her in a field? A forest? A car trunk? A freezer? Regret creeps into the periphery of her consciousness.

Not knowing what's to become of Darla.

Not knowing her grandchildren.

Not being around to see the leaves turn in October.

Not being.

Anna leaves the house and swings the backpack over her shoulders. No one will start looking for her until Tuesday when Al returns from his fishing trip. The girls are away at camp. She hops on the bike she bought at a garage sale yesterday.

It is a perfect day. Last week's heat wave has lifted, and the humidity is gone. Crickets hide in the tall grass along the roadway and scream madly. Anna feels good. Strong. She wants to be strong, always. Strong of mind. Strong of body. She will never go to the Yellow Wing.

Anna ditches the bike under the bridge by the dam. She hikes to the lake under a leafy canopy that shades the footpath. This is the northern tip of the Carolinian forest. There are tree communities here that are unique in Canada. Tulip trees and birch and ash and hickory and chestnut and oak. Last year's oak leaves are still on the ground, tough and leathery with no sign of decomposing. The Druids knew what they were doing when they chose oak groves for their ceremonies. Strong and dependable. Eternal. She stops and stretches and looks up to where the branches criss-cross. There are dead branches that have been rescued from falling to the ground by other living branches. Vigilant against the elements they stand with the dead in their arms like statues of World War veterans who refuse to leave their comrades on the field. Anna caresses the smooth skin of a beech tree. She loves the forest so.

Ancient cedars surround this secret little meromictic lake, small but deep. Prehistoric bones wait for her at the bottom. Anna pictures it, silent and cool and green, her hair floating like seaweed. Her father grew up on this property. It was part of his grandparents' farm. Now it is protected by a conservation authority. Not open to the public. But Anna remembers the path, the markings on the trees. The granite ridge. Caves. There is a strange vibration in the rocks here that is calming and curative. She presses her cheek into an outcropping of quartz and limestone and listens to the heartbeat of the last ice age.

Anna opens her backpack and takes out the four things she needs: a mickey of single malt scotch, an inflatable rubber tube, a little foot pump, and a Swiss army knife. Then she collects rocks of a certain heft, half-filling the backpack. It weighs about thirty pounds when she is satisfied. About the weight of her dog, Roxy. She feels a twinge of anxiety thinking about Roxy at home alone, but then she remembers Roxy died years ago.

The late afternoon sun warms her. Burns her. She doesn't need sunscreen anymore. In fact, she hasn't used any since her diagnosis. Skin cancer is not an issue. A big bumble bee maneuvers among the goldenrod. The sun drops behind the trees. Anna sits lakeside with her feet in the water. Drinking. The scotch slips smoothly down her throat and she remembers her first taste of the stuff out on the broken pier in the shadow of the old lighthouse. That damp cold of November with snow promised. Her boyfriend had suffered some disappointment. What was it? He was turned down for a job he had counted on, maybe. She was consoling him, but it was the alcohol that took the edge off the loss of the thing, whatever it was.

The evening star appears. Make a wish, Anna, the memory of her mother's voice says. Anna's mother found a boyfriend in the Yellow Wing. She was heavily medicated, and she had put on a lot of weight. Her personal hygiene was poor. But she fell in love with another inmate named Herman. Shaky with Parkinson's and forgetful with Alzheimers, he was head over heels in love with Anna's mom. He held her hand and listened to her stories about how everyone was stealing from her. They watched old movies together. According to the gossipy night nurse they made out like jack rabbits every chance they got.

Anna starts to blow the tube up. It takes a bit longer than she counted on but, with darkness gathering, it is full and firm. She steps in. The backpack weighs heavy on her shoulders. She clips the metal hook to her belt. Extra insurance. After a little struggle, she wades into the lake, bracing herself against the cold as the water reaches her thighs, her waist, her chest. The tube finally supports her as she kicks her feet and finds the middle of the lake.

The moon rises huge and familiar, lighting up Anna's skin. She examines the fine hairs on her forearms. Her freckles. Her fingernails. A family of ducks emerges from the swampy cove. They appear to glide effortlessly across the water, even though Anna knows that their little webbed feet are pumping like crazy below the surface.

Anna is at the end of her story. Anna's Last Day, beautifully written, meticulously orchestrated. Everything has gone according to plan. Her daughters will remember the last time they saw her. It was a pleasant drive to camp with the usual stop for ice cream at Dorset. They will be spared the terror of a mother who forgets their names.

Al will be proud of her, taking care of her situation so graciously. So efficiently. The lawyer was discreet as she transferred signing privileges and arranged a cash settlement with the teachers' pension plan. All her passwords are accessible in a folder on her desktop. It is evident that she is going to get away with the perfect crime and she smiles with the pleasure of her accomplishment.

Anna takes out the knife. Red with a little white cross on it. She flips open the blades. There is a corkscrew and tiny scissors and even a screwdriver. But she selects the longest, sturdiest blade, the most substantial one, to do the job. She is shivering a little. A worm of terror crawls through her gut. She looks up at the moon. She looks down at the knife. She picks a place on the tube where the label says River Rat, with a picture of a beady-eyed green rodent. She will stab the rat.

The frogs are making a racket that beats to the tune of her heart. Her strong, healthy heart. Her doomed heart.

What is she waiting for? She scans the horizon, hoping that the tormented Indian Princess will make an appearance.

Instead, a shooting star rips across the night sky, fearless and eternal.

Make a wish Anna.

Anna wishes that Darla, the little girl with the haunting black eyes that looked out at her from the front page of the morning paper, will be found safe and sound, sleeping at a friend's house.

The Pastor

Margarethe answered the ad for an organist. It was a small ad in the local free paper, and she would have overlooked it entirely except for the name. Pastor Leonard Watkins. Lenny Watkins. He had been her camp counsellor at Bible Camp many years ago. Charismatic and kind, he drew her out of her shell. She had been a big-boned Dutch girl in homemade dresses. An outcast among the girls her age who wore denim cut-offs and halter tops. But Lenny saw the potential in her. The Christian in her.

Pastor Lenny did not recognize her voice when she called about an interview. That was to be expected. It was thirty years ago. Or more. But he sounded the same on the phone. Pleasant and businesslike, he invited her to meet him at the funeral home for an interview. Bring some music, he suggested.

She selected the traditional hymns that she knew the

Pastor would expect. Rock of Ages. Amazing Grace. Abide With Me. She showered and shaved her legs, something she was not allowed to do as a teenager because, well, only prostitutes shaved their legs. She braided her hair and coiled it carefully and put on the necklace. The one with the cross that Lenny had given her at the end of the summer. A secret gift. Because the other girls would have been envious, he said.

Lenny was seated at his desk in the alcove near the doors to the funeral home's chapel. He rose when she came in and shook her hand and introduced himself, and also introduced his wife, Leslie, who poked her head out of the kitchen pass-through window where she was chopping chives and celery to go in the egg salad sandwiches for tomorrow's funeral.

"Bob Talbot," she said. "He was only 51. Did you know him, dear?"

Margarethe said "No, sorry."

"He was the fire chief," Leslie said.

Margarethe shook her head. Her circle of acquaintances was surprisingly small, especially since she quit the Calvinist Church out on the highway. They preached original sin, making out that babies were born with black souls who had to spend their whole entire lives seeking redemption. Margarethe saw through that lie and, and one day she decided she had had enough of all that bullshit, and she quit. Never darkened those mean doors again. And no one ever called her up and said, are you okay, Margarethe? We miss you at church. No, they did not care a bit for her eternal soul. They were all out to save themselves. Well, good luck and good riddance, she said. But she did find the week dragged a bit without Sunday services. Two of them, morning and evening. And Wednesday Bible Study. And choir practice on Thursday. They had been her only social outings, she realized. A bit late. But she stuck by her principles. Aside from the people she saw in her part time job doing accounting work for a local real estate firm, she kept to herself.

She had not expected that Pastor Lenny would be married. But, of course, he would. A handsome man like him. She often overlooked the obvious. It made sense that Lenny would pretend he did not recognize her. She knew he did. He looked right at the cross hanging above her cleavage. It was a cheap thing, she knew that. But he had just been a young man at the time, still going to school. It would have been all he could afford.

Margarethe was a statuesque six-footer, and the crucifix was right at eye level for the Pastor. She blushed a bit under his gaze and looked over at Leslie who seemed flustered and turned away to finish her task in the kitchen.

Leslie did not even want to be there. She'd sooner be home working in her own kitchen. But her presence was a given since Lenny had suffered some addiction issues in the past. Sex addict is what he was diagnosed with. An illness like alcoholism. Staying clear of temptation was an important part of his recovery, and she was vigilant about supporting him, just as Hillary had been with Bill. God bless her. Margarethe, about as sexy as a telephone pole, was an acceptable candidate for an organist as far as she was concerned.

As soon as Lenny heard Leslie's chopping resume, he took a deep breath and invited the woman to be seated at the organ in the chapel. It was quite a comedown for him, this job. He had to leave his assignment at the Presbyterian Church in Effingham after his indiscretions were discovered. And before that, he had ministered to some of the biggest congregations in the Niagara Peninsula. Now this. A penance, more than a job, but still it was something.

Lenny sat in the first pew and listened as Margarethe played. She played reasonably well, not with gusto, but with a plodding sort of determination that matched her appearance. He studied her face. Oddly familiar. Wide brow. Wide set hazel eyes. Nice skin. Very nice. It was hard to determine what her age might be. She paused after playing three hymns and put her hands in her lap and turned to him, expectantly, for his response.

"Very nice," he said. "You play well. Do you know Bringing in the Sheaves?"

Margarethe opened her mouth as if to reply and then bowed her head. She was overcome. Bringing in the Sheaves had been their favourite song back at camp. They played and sang it together.

Lenny felt terrible. He should not have made a request. Organists hated that. They were professionals, not nightclub pianists who took requests. He had embarrassed himself. He stood and went to the organ and indicated that she should slide over and then he sat and played the song himself. He sang along to lighten the mood. To let Margarethe know that he was an easy-going guy. A good guy. But, as he got to the third verse, preparing to play to a crescendo, he noticed the woman rubbing herself. Hard. Masturbating, as if she was quite alone in her bedroom. He played on. He did not know what else to do. And when he came to the end, he started over at verse one. And on he played until the woman appeared to have satisfied herself and folded her hands demurely in her lap and only then did he end the piece.

"There," he said, turning toward her.

The woman was flushed but did not acknowledge what had just occurred. He searched her face for a clue. Maybe she had a yeast infection? But her face! Her wide, childlike face looked back at him with a level gaze of pure intimacy.

"Lenny," she whispered. "I've waited so long."

Lenny knew what he was. What he had been. He had a weakness for needy women. But this gal? He searched his mental hard drive for a memory but came up with nothing. Still.

"How long? Has it been?" he asked.

"Thirty-two years," she said. "I was thirteen." Her hand rose from her lap and fingered the cheap little crucifix. "You gave this to me. As a promise."

Lenny was disgusted with himself. Oh man. He did remember. She was one of those inbreds from the Inman Road. There were lots of rumours about the place. Something bad happened and all the kids were eventually scooped up and put into foster care.

This girl had been thirteen? A child in a woman's body and willing, as they all were, those simple country girls. Willing to be loved. No one else loved them, that was for sure. The devil surely knew how to tempt him. She wore calico hippie dresses that stuck to her breasts in the humidity.

Lenny had a flashback of the furnace room in the basement of the church. His twelve step strategies were useless. He felt the erection before he could turn away from Margarethe on the bench and she saw it. Reached for it. He stood abruptly and coughed and dug around in his pocket for a Fisherman's Friend. And then he blew his nose. All the while, Margarethe sat placidly on the organ bench awaiting instruction.

Lenny needed an organist badly, but he did not need this organist. Still, Bob Talbot deserved some organ music at his funeral, dammit. There would be two hundred at the funeral.

"I hate to impose, Margarethe," Lenny said, and Margarethe opened her arms, begging him to impose. "Could you play at Bob Talbot's funeral tomorrow?"

"Of course, Lenny," she said. "Pastor, I mean." So controlled and quiet that the room seemed hollow all of a sudden. Shadowy. Like she was sucking the oxygen out of it by her sheer devotion to him.

He hustled her out the side door maintaining as much distance between them as he could. She lumbered toward the bus stop. What if the only joy in her life had been those days at Bible Camp? What if the memory of his physical attentions sustained her in a bleak world? What if everyone was wrong about lust, as Lenny long suspected? Lust is a gift. A pleasure, not a sin.

"Lenny? Where are you? Come in here!"

Leslie handed Lenny a chopped egg sandwich. The ultimate funeral food. Dozens and dozens of them were piled on platters and wrapped tightly in cellophane. Lenny took a bite and nodded. "Good," he told her. "Best yet."

"Did you hire her?"

"Well, we'll give her a chance. She'll do the service tomorrow, but after that. We'll have to wait and see. She's an odd duck."

"Not that you have much choice. Organists are not knocking the door down."

"No. That's true. I can't disagree with you there."

"Well, she sounded okay to me. But what was with your little concert there? Bringing in the Sheaves? What was that all about?"

"I don't know, Leslie. I was just moved to play a bit and the woman seemed nervous. I was trying to set her at ease." Lenny took one last bite of his sandwich and threw the crust in the garbage. He leaned against the counter and watched Leslie peel a carrot with long methodical strokes. When it was smooth, she pointed it at him.

"It's not your job to put women at ease, Lenny." Then she picked up the chef's knife and chopped the tip off the carrot with professional flourish. "You finished Bob's eulogy yet?"

"No. I'll go do that now."

"Wait!"

Lenny took a deep breath and turned to face his wife. Leslie handed him a small dish of carrot sticks. He thanked her and walked back to his office.

The Promise Land

Sandra is feeling edgy when she returns to school after her leave of absence. She has taught English for twenty-five years and she has five to go. Five years until she can start collecting her pension.

Let's get it over with, she thinks. That was her dad's philosophy, and it applied to everything. Family wedding? Christmas concert? Camping trip to Algonquin? Hop in the car, kids. Let's get this over with.

She grits her teeth and greets the girls in the office. Picks up the pile of papers in her mailbox. Stops in the staff room and says good morning to Don, head of the English Department, who thinks she came back too soon. Asshole. How are the try-outs for the play going? Asshole. When will you have those midterm marks? Asshole. Alrighty then, we'll see you at the team meeting this afternoon. Asshole.

She walks purposefully through halls crowded with the urgency of adolescence. A quieter urgency than when she started teaching, because much of the angst is communicated electronically. The undercurrents are devious and dangerous as rip tides. Some kids are swimming way over their heads, but there's no way to tell who needs to be rescued.

Sandra sits at her desk and struggles to orient herself. The branches of the oak tree outside her classroom window are strung with little brown bats, curled and rattling in the wind.

"All the leaves are brown, and the sky is grey. I went for a walk on a winter's day." She is singing out loud. I am pretty much fucked, she thinks, and these kids don't even notice. Fortunately, this job requires less teaching than it used to. She is the guide on the side, rather than the sage on the stage. So, it is less obvious when she gets one of her pressure-headaches or loses track of an idea.

The class is working through some collaborative processes in groups that range from very effective to totally useless. The walls are festooned with chart paper and sticky notes. When Fran stops by to drop off a memo, she is pleased to see that Sandra seems to be getting her shit back together. Fran has been assigned to shadow Sandra for a while. Offer peer support. Fran took Grief Counselling Part 1 last summer and volunteered eagerly for this role.

Conversations stop when Sandra enters the staffroom during lunch hour. She knows they are saying in their heads, please don't sit with me. Please don't sit here. Women who have been Sandra's colleagues for years have certain expectations for the trajectory of Sandra's grief and she feels she is letting them down. They start conversations about their teenage kids and then hesitate and change the subject. They ask how she is doing, but they don't really want to know.

Thankfully Sandra found a lifeline in Tony, the caretaker, whose daughter died by suicide on Christmas Day five years ago. It doesn't get better, he says. It doesn't go away. It just changes.

Tony's the kind of guy who makes you feel like everything's going to be okay. He takes care of his people, and they seek him out in the boiler room. The very best cast-off chairs from the faculty lounge end up there.

Other denizens of the boiler room include the young artsy teachers who vape and talk about music and juried shows at the galleries downtown. Their defining dysfunctions have given them a shared dislike of the staffroom on the second floor where judgmental teachers criticize welfare parents who spend money on beer and tattoos. It's always open season on teen moms and other social outcasts.

Tony's people know that Sandra has suffered a tragedy, that her daughter was killed, but they do not expect her to wear her grief like a nasty rash. It is not contagious. But, upstairs in the staff room, it marks her as a flawed parent. Her vigilance must have lapsed.

The boiler room people understand that bad things can, and do, occur. Cursed with dark and ragged coats of shitty luck, they surround Sandra with a buffer zone of longing and philosophical ideas and low-grade depression. If they see each other in the parking lot or in the photocopy room, they do not interrupt with small talk, or let on to the general school population that they are friends. Only in the underbelly of the school do they share the terrible knowledge that makes them all vulnerable. And a little dangerous.

Sandra gets panicky every night after supper as winter approaches and the long evenings stretch before her with only the promise of more sleepless nights to look forward to. When her husband Doug retreats to the couch, Sandra slips outside and wanders through the neighbourhood using her dog as a disguise. She is nothing more than a shadow with a pooper-scooper, watching people watch Jeopardy.

Slinking soundlessly across empty soccer fields, Sandra develops a certain intimacy with her neighbours. She names them. There is a hyper little boy she calls Nolan who lives in chaos. His house has two black labs and baby paraphernalia all over the place. One night, Nolan is jumping up and down on the couch. He falls on top of Baby, and the mother just about yanks the kid's arm out of its socket. She seems more concerned with disciplining Nolan than checking to see if Baby is okay. The dogs go mental. *Hark, hark the dogs do bark, the beggars are coming to town.*

The only house that looks like it could have something criminal going on is the house where the brown siding is peeling off. The curtains are always drawn. Passing by, she feels like someone could be watching her instead of the other way around. The motion sensor light catches her in its beam, and she hurries away as if she has been accused of cruel intentions.

The biggest sin Sandra observes is gluttony. Mindlessly, people shovel chips and cereal and noodles into their mouths while they watch storage lockers being unloaded. This is sad, but not the saddest. The saddest is the white back-split that occasionally features an older woman who sits, ramrod straight, at the organ. She plays songs from a tattered old hymnal for an invisible congregation. Not even Lady wants to stop and listen to the muffled strains of "Holy, Holy, Holy."

Next, they come to the green bungalow that backs onto the school playground. The young mother who lives here is competent and organized. She looks like a Jennifer. Jennifer supervises the children as they all pitch in to wipe counters and dry dishes the old-fashioned way, by hand. Then they put the chairs up on the kitchen table and wash the floor. There is no television that Sandra can see. They look like the perfect family.

It is uncomfortable, sometimes, standing out in the raw wind, but that is the hard part of being an anthropologist. Lady is a good assistant, never questioning the validity of the project. A rescue dog that doesn't expect much.

As Christmas looms closer and closer, Sandra is filled with dread. She and Lady escape from the garish lights and tawdry decorations and cross the bridge to the tasteful end of town. Holly was a December baby, born on Boxing Day and forever resentful that no one had the energy for birthday celebrations. She was a miserable little kid, actually, bursting with regrets and struggles.

"You don't always have to do things the hard way, Holly," Sandra told her and told her. Holly was as prickly as her namesake. At least toward Sandra.

The homes that back onto the golf course are as big as

hotels. Sandra leaves footprints in the crunchy layer of frost on the fairways. From the cart path on number seven, Sandra watches a family pissing away the evening in much the same way as the people in her own neighbourhood. A soirée would be a nice scene to come upon. Music, dancing. Or a dinner party with interesting guests like the characters in Clue. More wine Miss Scarlet? Why yes, Professor, that would be lovely. Pass the lead pipe when you're finished with it, won't you?

But here in wealthy town, they are watching Storage Wars and Porn Stars and Entertainment Tonight. Just on nicer couches.

There is a rain shelter halfway up the hill on the twelfth hole, a little par three with a creek and a row of cedars that warrant Lady's close inspection. No one knows Sandra is here, hugging her knees and hiding from the world. Lost and frozen like an arctic explorer from the last century, she slips her mittens off and tucks her bare hands inside her coat, under her armpits.

Holly died on Labour Day weekend in the lake she loved. It was an accident. While she was getting ripped to pieces by a giant propeller, Sandra was cleaning out the fridge like a mad dervish, tossing limp lettuce into the compost, loading the cooler with half-filled bottles of ketchup and barbeque sauce and jam. She was pulling out the crisper drawer to wipe behind it when Wendy, from the cottage next door, came screaming in.

"There's been an accident, Sandra. Holly's canoe was hit by a powerboat. Oh my God. Where's your phone?"

When Sandra didn't react, Wendy ran out, looking for Doug.

Sandra dipped the J-cloth in the bucket of bleach one last time and wiped out the bottom shelf where some syrup had dripped. Then she pushed the drawer back in place and closed the fridge door. It seemed important to complete this task before running down to the dock.

The day after the funeral, Sandra read Holly's high school yearbook from cover to cover. She read it again, the next day and the next. Holly's pictures were everywhere: athletics, social committee, theatre club, auto mechanics club. It was a mystery to Sandra that Holly could have been so popular. Fifty or sixty friends had signed the yearbook.

U R Kewl, Holly.

Remember Mr. B.'s science experiment?

Congrats getting into UBC.

Doug kept himself busy suing the marina and the driver of the boat. He gave speeches at three high schools about water safety. He planted a tree. He worked overtime. He volunteered at a soup kitchen. He adopted Lady and brought her home.

Lady lay at the end of the bed and asked no questions. She didn't whine for attention or beg to go outside. She just looked at Sandra looking at the yearbook until Sandra couldn't ignore her any longer.

"Listen to this," she said to the dog.

"I wish I was a diamond

Upon a ladies hand

And every time she wiped her ass

I'd see the Promise Land!"

Her instinct as an English teacher was to make corrections. Lady's instead of ladies. Promised Land instead of Promise Land. For crying out loud. This generation was hopeless with biblical references. And that was the beginning of the end of the yearbook obsession. She got up and put her coat on.

Sandra hadn't really wanted Holly. She had been forty and her older daughters were independent. Kelly was ten and Christine was twelve. They could stay home by themselves while Sandra went to buy groceries or go to the gym. She had arranged for an abortion, but Doug had talked her out of it.

Sandra cuts across the eighteenth fairway to the clubhouse on feet that feel like blocks of ice. She puts Lady back on the leash and makes her way to the carnival of Christmas lights on her own street. Once home, she pauses to look at Doug through the window. Beyond her ghostly reflection, her husband lies on the couch watching the sports channel with a bowl of microwave popcorn on his chest. His grey hair is messy. Still, she likes the look of him, cozy under his favourite quilt. She thinks how good it would feel to snuggle up beside him, but she lets herself in through the garage and creeps up the back stairs to bed.

Kelly and Christine suggest a family cruise. It solves the problem of an unwanted Christmas tree and a stocking that will never need filling again. Doug accepts the idea with enthusiasm. His research is thorough: the flights, the cabins, the excursions. Sandra believes that cruises are bad for the environment, but without the will to argue she allows herself to be led up the gangplank. The stateroom is designed with a spare elegance that cocoons and protects her. On Christmas Day, the turkey is prepared and tidied up without her help. Kelly and Christine and Doug float in and out of conversations and meals and games of cribbage and evening concerts. Sandra observes them. Imitates them. She laughs when they laugh and accepts their suggestions of what to do next.

On Holly's birthday, Sandra doesn't want to get out of bed.

"Try the hot tub on the Serenity Deck, Mom," Kelly tells her. Christine helps her find her bathing suit and she puts it on, obediently. In the hot tub, she meets a Christian woman from Florida who tells her Holly is with Jesus with so much sincerity that Sandra allows her to pray for her.

"How was the cruise?" Fran asks after the holidays.

"Not as awful as I expected," Sandra says.

"I knew you'd like it," says Fran, in a voice that warns Sandra that she is still under scrutiny.

In February, Sandra gets pneumonia and takes a week off school. Doug is on a golf holiday in Florida with three friends, so she stays in bed. She reads and sleeps and watches romantic comedies on Netflix and sleeps some more. She luxuriates in her illness. By Thursday evening, she feels as if she has turned a corner. As soon as she starts pulling on her boots, she hears the metallic shake of Lady's collar. They follow their route past Nolan and the organ player. At Jennifer's bungalow, a Valentine heart hangs in the window, but something different is going on.

Here is the husband, who she has never met. His pose

as he reads aloud is domineering and wrathful. The terror of subjugation strips the children's faces of expression. Jennifer carries a basin of water from the sink to the table. The children bow their heads. Jennifer kneels before the Lord of her household and takes off his socks and shoes. She bathes his feet in the basin while he intones some dour sermon above her. One at a time, the children take turns kneeling to kiss their father's feet. Sandra is sickened by it but riveted just the same. It is Lady that insists they walk away.

Sandra cannot sit still at home. She knows she won't be able to sleep. All she has done for a week is sleep, and she is all slept out. Doug won't be back for three days, but she leaves a note on the kitchen counter anyway, in case one of the girls drops by and worries. She grabs some dog food, gets Lady settled on a blanket in the back seat of the Jeep, and drives the two hours up Highway 35 to the cottage.

It is almost midnight when Sandra turns onto the cottage road. The driveway is not plowed so the trudge to the back door is exhausting. She hip checks the frozen door to open it and flips the power switch on. While the electric blanket warms up on the couch, Sandra builds a fire in the woodstove and then falls asleep with Lady snuggled at her feet. When she awakens, it is bright. She pulls the covers up around her head and sleeps some more until Lady whimpers to go out.

Sandra takes a Muskoka chair out of the boathouse and sets it on the ice-covered lake about ten feet past the end of the dock. Eventually, she walks over the ice to the bay and locates the approximate spot of the accident. The winter silence is profound. Holly is all around her in glints of frozen sunshine.

"I'm here, Sweetie," she whispers.

"Here I am, in the Promise Land," she says, a little louder. The white pine on the point responds by dropping some snow from a low branch.

I'm going out for a last paddle, Mom.
Have you cleaned the fridge like I asked you to an hour ago, Holly?
Daddy wants to leave for home as soon as he gets back from the dump. You don't have time for a paddle.
The porch door bangs loudly in response. Bang. The end.

Lady is shivering. Back at the cottage Sandra opens a can of soup and dumps it into a battered pot. While it warms up, she stands in the doorway of Holly's room. There is a lopsided clay bowl on the dresser full of beads and coins. Swimming badges and regatta ribbons are pinned around the mirror. A book about vampires is on the bedside table. The greying mattress cover will need to be replaced this summer.

Sandra pours a cup of soup and sits in silence at the yellow formica table. Across the kitchen, the fridge is unplugged, and the door propped open. It still smells faintly of bleach. It is so white and clean. So empty.

Correctional Services

Declan and Brett are in the same class at school. A special class. It doesn't really have a name. Most people call it Mrs. Hannah's class. As in, "Oh! You guys are in Mrs. Hannah's class." Which means nobody is surprised if they are flooding the sink in the boys' washroom or writing graffiti in permanent marker on the gym wall. It is kind of a free pass to do stupid stuff. But it does not get them off the hook when they mess up out in the real world.

As they get older, they think of more profitable ways to get in trouble, like B and E's. Break and enters. They try it on their own street first, which is a mistake, because everyone knows them. They are hard to miss. Declan is super tall and super skinny. He has a condition called curvature of the spine. And, just because the world is cruel, he also has the worst case of acne you've ever seen. Seriously. It is raw and painful. Brett is little. He has some kind of syndrome that makes him walk on his toes. So, when they start their lives of crime, it is hard for him to run away.

The easiest way to steal from people is just to walk in the front door and take the purse that is usually hanging right there on the hook or grab the wallet from the front hall table. Declan learned this from a TV show called Forensic Files. The tricky part is, when the purse or wallet is home, the owners are usually home too. So, you hope they're in the kitchen or watching TV in the family room. It is just bad luck when they pick Gladys Laverty's house. She is sitting on the couch in the front room, and she watches them come up the walk and open her door.

"What can I do for you boys?" she says as they struggle to orient themselves in the dim light of the vestibule.

They run. Which is not the best choice.

Mrs. Laverty tries not to laugh as she stands in her doorway and watches them stumble down her driveway. She calls Mrs. Hannah.

"I didn't want to call the police," she says. "Those boys have enough challenges."

"I think you better report it, Gladys," Mrs. Hannah says. "Brett and Declan need a bit of a scare. They are getting away with all kinds of petty crimes and everyone feels sorry for them, so they don't have any serious consequences for their actions. Ask for Safety Officer Stan. He'll pick them up and give them a stern warning."

Declan and Brett are not actually friends. They hate each other. But since kindergarten, they have been thrown together whether they liked it or not. Speech therapy. Reading recovery. Exercises class for fine motor coordination. They get used to hearing their names called together by the special teachers. Declan and Brett. Brett and Declan. As if they come as a package. Even out on the playground at recess, the other kids act like there is some invisible fence around them, preventing them from joining in on soccer games or using the climbing equipment. No one is mean to them, exactly. But no one invites them to play.

So, when Officer Stan picks them up and puts them in the back seat of the cruiser and tells them about jail, it does not have the effect he expected.

"There are a lot of rough characters in jail, boys," he says. "And you won't be roommates in there. They will separate you guys and give you a cellmate that you won't like too much. Like a drug addict or a murderer."

He drops the boys off on George Street, where, coincidentally, they both live in a public housing project where the townhouses all have blue siding. It is known as Smurf Village.

"Smarten up, boys," Officer Stan warns them. They climb out of the cruiser and watch it disappear around the end of the court. They look at each other and shrug. Jail doesn't sound any worse than high school.

"We got to smarten up all right," Declan says. "That's good advice."

Brett laughs, even though he isn't sure it is funny.

Brett likes a girl in Mrs. Hannah's class called Daisy. She is a farm girl, and she is not a good match, physically, for little

Brett because she is big. Not fat. Big. She has muscles like a man. Brett likes her because she protects him in the locker bay. Back in elementary school, the dangerous place for special kids was the yard. You could get pushed in the mud or slammed against a brick wall or have your jacket torn off behind the garbage bins. Things like that always happened when the teacher on duty was busy elsewhere, tending to a scraped knee or a bee sting. Recess was hell.

In high school, the danger zone is the locker bay. Daisy strolls to her locker with all the confidence of a 4H champion. She can bale hay and round up cattle and shear sheep without breaking a sweat. And she can beat the shit out of anybody who has something to say about her buck teeth, which she proved on the very first day of grade nine. So even the bullies on the football team give her a wide berth. Brett likes the way Daisy puts her big arm around his shoulders and tells him to stick with her. He feels safe with Daisy. Safer than he felt with his own mother who was unpredictable, or his foster mom who tells him to man up. He wishes Daisy lived in town.

Declan has tried and tried to tell Brett that Daisy is bad news. As far as he is concerned, you shouldn't pick a girlfriend who can beat you at arm wrestling. He wants a girlfriend that is more like Kelly on his favourite TV show, Saved by the Bell. A girl who wears makeup and doesn't swear. He would be willing to go to jail for a girl like Kelly.

Breaking into the Liquor Store is Daisy's idea.

"My cousin works there on weekends," Daisy says. They are huddled behind the machine shop where a doorway used to be. It is sheltered from the wind and there are no windows so teachers can't see them. Daisy digs around in her overalls pocket until she finds her Export A's. She gives the pack a good tap and a cigarette slides out. Then, as if that isn't impressive enough, she strikes a safety match on the sole of her work boot, and it lights in one try. Between drags, Daisy holds the cigarette between thumb and forefinger, with the ash end cupped in her palm. She notices Brett staring at it and passes it over.

"Don't get the filter wet, you amateur," she warns him. Brett curls his lips in like an old toothless guy and she laughs. He takes a self-conscious haul and passes the cigarette to Declan.

"Anyway, my cousin. Gilbert. You know him? Gilbert Smith?"

Declan is coughing up a lung, but Brett says, "Ya. Everybody knows Smitty. The pyromaniac."

"Smitty. That's right. He doesn't set fire to stuff anymore. That was just a phase. He told me the code to get in the delivery entrance of the Liquor Store." She took back her cigarette and checked the filter.

"Bullshit," said Declan.

"Maybe," said Daisy.

But Saturday night rolls around and Declan and Brett have nothing better to do. Everyone else is at parties or at the show or bowling. Lame, boring stuff. They talk about how much fun they will have when they get their driver's licenses. They will blow this pop stand, for sure. In the meantime, Declan admits he wouldn't mind trying some Southern Comfort, a potent drink he's heard tell of. They are only a block away from the Liquor Store.

"So, what the hell, it's worth a try," Brett says.

"We punch the code in, and if it don't work we just go home," Declan says. "We got nothing to lose."

Brett has the code on his hand. Daisy wrote it in permanent marker yesterday afternoon. It is a bit faded, but he can still read it. He calls out the numbers and Brett punches them in.

"Now press star."

Click.

"Pull."

It opens.

Inside, it is dark except for the red EXIT signs. Declan finds a light switch. Somebody once told him that he was about as bright as a two-watt bulb. And he did agree, later, that turning the lights on wasn't the brightest thing he'd ever done.

Bob Green is driving home from the Legion and sees the store all lit up and calls his buddy, the Liquor Store manager who calls the cops. Officer Stan is off duty, so it is Officer Emily who blocks their getaway with the cruiser. Brett pisses himself when he hears the siren and sees the flashing lights. He throws his hands up and screams, "Don't shoot!"

"Well god dammit!" Emily says when she notices the stain on his sweatpants. She digs around in the trunk for a towel he can sit on, so the back seat won't smell like urine. Declan, who towers over her by a good ten inches, is sobbing like a baby and doing some spastic thing with his hands so she cuffs him. By the time the store manager arrives to secure the premises, they have calmed down considerably.

Back at the station, Emily leaves them to suffer on the hard bench in the holding cell while she tries to contact their parents. Or anybody that will claim them and get them the hell out of there. No answer at Declan's. The number Brett gave her is not in service. After a few more dead ends, she drives them home and tells them not to leave town.

So now, at fifteen, Brett and Declan are known to the police. They are on record at Correctional Services. And they enjoy the little bit of notoriety that criminality affords them in the locker bay. Knocking over a Liquor Store takes guts. Some of the cool people call out their orders. "Get me a forty pounder of Canadian Club next time," says the captain of the football team. Girls giggle and smile at them. A few greasers in their auto mechanics class invite them to hang out. "We got a clubhouse up on Mountain Street," they say. "You should drop by."

The clubhouse is a garage behind the home of Wade Spittel who left high school when he turned sixteen. Wade is handsome in a rough sort of way. He has black hair and high cheekbones, and he tells people he has Chippewa blood in him. He likes to go shirtless, showing off the stab wound from a knife fight at The Rex Hotel in Welland. "A dive," he tells them. "I'm banned for life. As if I'd go back there! Not for a million bucks!"

Wade's grandmother lives in the house, and she is deaf, so they can crank up the music. The property backs onto the woods, which makes it ideal for shooting crossbows and pellet guns. Inside the garage, there are Christmas lights strung across the ceiling that give the place a festive air. There is a poker table and six folding chairs. There are two old couches that Wade rescued from the dump. And back in the corner there is a home-fashioned urinal for bad weather days. It is made of a metal syphon with a hose that is shoved through a hole in the wall. The piss drips into a dry well outside.

Wade is good at inventing things. And he is a good teacher, too. Better than Mrs. Hannah. He makes Declan and Brett feel smart.

"You guys have been trying to learn things from the wrong curriculum," he tells them. "Everybody has different learning styles. Those nerds who do good in high school are book smart. But you guys? You guys are gonna be street smart. I'm your teacher now."

They catch on quick to Wade's training methods, which include demonstrations and helpful tutorials. How to hotwire a car. How to shoplift nudie magazines and bring them back to the clubhouse. Wade's feedback is sometimes encouraging. He pats them on the back and gives them cigarettes. They like to please him. But sometimes Wade makes them nervous. Like, for example, the afternoon he threw a dart and it whizzed by Brett's head and stuck in the wall behind him. He laughed when Brett screamed.

"What'd you do that for, Wade?" Brett asked in a trembling voice.

"I just wanted your attention, Pal. I need some information. You know that friend of yours? Lily?"

"You mean Daisy?"

"Whatever. Your flower girl. See if she can find out if the Liquor Store changed the entry code. Because. If it didn't, it deserves to get broken into for real this time. We could seriously compensate somebody who brought us some information like that, know what I mean?"

"Sure, Wade," Brett says, although he doesn't really know what Wade means at all. Compensate could be good or bad. It's not like a quiz in Mrs. Hannah's room where nothing happens if you get most of the questions wrong. You don't want to mess up when Wade asks you to do stuff.

Daisy, however, doesn't require any motivation to help her friends. She is more than happy to get some insider information from her cousin.

"Yes," Daisy tells them. "The code has changed. Want to know what it is? Take me to your leader." Daisy says she is not comfortable giving the code to Brett and Declan again, seeing how they screwed up the first time. She wants to meet Wade. She will give him the code herself. Daisy says she is trying to protect them. Her friends. But Daisy understands how hierarchies work in the underworld. She wants to meet the kingpin. She wants in on the organization and she is willing to miss her 4H meeting to make it happen.

Wade likes Daisy. He sees how she is not just a girl. She is a player. She is not afraid of nobody. He takes her information and turns it into twenty sweet cases of whiskey. The heist hits the local paper. The Liquor Store puts a dead bolt on the service entrance door. Wade loans Daisy his grandmother's car so she can come to town whenever she wants.

Seems that Brett and Declan have been replaced as star pupils. They decide to rob the convenience store out on the Diltz Road and prove to Wade that they are worthy. They case the joint. They find out when Vera Feroze is working, an old lady with a walker who cannot possibly chase them. They put on ski masks, rolled up to look like toques, and ride their bikes to the store. At the store, they cover their faces and tell Vera to fill their backpacks with cigarettes. Declan pretends to have a gun in his pocket. It is really a permanent marker.

But Vera is not afraid of these two losers. She knows exactly who they are. She can't stop laughing as she clears the cigarette shelf.

"Shut up!" Declan yells. One thing he hates is being laughed at.

"Have a good day, boys," she tells them as they trip over each other going out the door.

"I think she recognized us," Declan says. Brett pulls his mask off. He can't breathe. He thinks he might be having an asthma attack, but Declan takes off without him, so he picks up his bike and starts pushing it out of the parking lot. It is a rusty piece of crap with monkey handlebars and a banana seat. And of all the bad luck, it has started snowing. Big heavy flakes that make it hard to pedal uphill toward the clubhouse. Declan is waiting for him at the corner of Wade's street, and they pull into the driveway just ahead of the cops who followed their tire tracks.

"It's hard to make a clean getaway in the snow, fellas," Officer Stan says as he relieves Brett of his backpack. "Let's go inside, shall we?"

"Not a good idea," Declan says.

"Don't worry. Wade and I go way back," he says.

Wade is sleeping on the long couch. Officer Stan puts a

finger to his lips and closes the door quietly. Wade wakens to find Stan kneeling down next to the ping pong table, taking stock of nineteen and a half cases of the good stuff.

All in all, a productive day for Officer Stan. A bad day for Wade. A worse day for Declan and Brett who take Wade's threat to kill them seriously. The deaf grandmother waves them all goodbye and says good riddance to bad rubbish.

Jail is not so awful as people make it out to be. Declan and Brett end up at Sprucedale, a teaching facility run by Correctional Services for minors who have not graduated from high school yet. They each get their own room. It is not like the movies where you have to bunk in with serial killers and sex perverts. The meals are good. Declan especially looks forward to Wednesdays when they get cordon bleu for supper. Brett likes the desserts. Puddings and ice cream and Jello. They take a class called Careers 101, to help them figure out what they want to work at in the future. Retail. Hospitality. A trade. Anything is possible.

Their parole officer is called Julie White. She is trying to set them on the path to righteousness. Julie is religious and she can't help mentioning how Jesus will be their guiding light, helping them make good choices when they get out of Sprucedale.

The last thing the boys want is to get out. They are safe here. Wade got two years less a day in the Milton penitentiary. He has called a few times, promising to kill them. He has mailed them letters with crude drawings of two guys hanging by ropes or getting their heads severed in guillotines.

"No," they beg Julie. "Please. We beg you. We don't want early release."

Meanwhile, they decide to sign up for Hospitality Training. Brett becomes an expert at Jello. Mixing the powder with boiling water and pouring it into a shallow pan. When it sets, he cuts it carefully into cubes. Perfect jewels of red and green and yellow. Declan likes dishwashing duty. His report card praises him for efficiency.

Their parents and guardians are pleased with the government support. They like the sound of Correctional Services. They are hopeful that the boys will come home corrected.

"Dumb asses run in the family though," says Declan's mother. Her cautious optimism was warranted, as it turned out.

Brett turned out okay. He works a steady job at Walmart in the footwear section. He lives uptown above a barber shop called The Clipper Ship. Fred Wilson, the barber, cuts his hair for free in exchange for occasional window-washing and snow shovelling. Brett goes to his mother's apartment Friday nights for movies and popcorn. His real mother who got sober. At Christmas and Thanksgiving, he makes a wicked big Jello as his contribution to the family celebrations at his sister's place.

Declan did not fare so well. Deck, he called himself and signed his name like he was a wooden platform in a backyard. Wade did find him, and he did smack him around a bit. Just a black eye and a broken collarbone. Could have been worse. Deck worked for him for a year or so, dealing Special K to a bunch of down and outers. Ketamine. A drug that messes with your brain big time. Poor Deck. He lived in a rooming house in Hamilton near Jackson Square and froze to death on a January night in a Corktown alley.

For a while, it looked like Wade might turn his life around. After his second stint in jail, he got a real job, driving for an Airport Limo service. But he got hit by a bus crossing King Street on his 40th birthday. He was drunk. He has a scooter, now, to get around. You wouldn't recognize him. He's gained seventy or eighty pounds. He's back living with his grandmother.

That leaves Daisy. She sold the family farm in Mount Hope to a housing developer for millions. Bought an RV and moved out West somewhere. Brett still holds a candle for her. He expects she may pull up in front of the Clipper Ship one day and offer to take him on a road trip. He wouldn't go. But he likes to think about it nonetheless.

COALS

You may think you have doused the fire, but as you sleep, the heat creeps through the ashes and ignites against all odds. Like the story that scorched your tender heart and insists on being told.

Thin Ice

I am in the studio, applying a topcoat of varnish to an acrylic landscape painting. It is the end of April, and the lake is bracing itself for tourist season. Soon there will be fireworks and campfires and ski boats and barking dogs and children screaming as they jump off rafts. All good. The sound of having fun is good. Not everyone agrees, of course. There are plenty of complainers. There is always some way to detract from the beauty of it all.

Today is sunny, but the wind is fresh. Cold. The studio is an old boathouse with double doors that open to Lake Kashagawigamog. I have several layers of clothing over my nightgown. I am wearing thick wool socks inside my ex-husband's rubber boots, fingerless gloves hardened with old paint, and a home-knit toque. This is the wardrobe you adopt when you are sure you won't see another human being in the course of the day.

The loon has returned from an inland waterway somewhere south of here. Probably the Carolinas. His maniacal mating call echoes across to Chapel Rock and back again. The loons usually nest in the marsh behind the island, but they have been childless for the past two years. Those of us with cottages nearby have posted signs, asking boats to slow down. The new wakeboard boats, which carry thousands of pounds of extra ballast to create huge waves for their sport, are responsible for drowning baby loons in their nests. They also disrupt fish habitats and swamp canoes and topple swimmers at the beach. I have seen toddlers and old people caught off guard. But the kids on the wakeboards are having fun, and the wakeboard business is good for the economy in this little tourist town, so getting mad about it doesn't get you any converts to environmentalism. I try to be on good terms with all my neighbours. Even the assholes.

Clouds are scudding by the sun, throwing patches of light and shadow onto my canvas. I am quite content with it all. And then I see a woman standing on my dock. She looks lost, like she took a wrong turn at Yonge and Bloor and ended up here. I stick my paintbrush into a can of turps and peek my head out of the studio.

"Hi," I say. "Can I help you?"

"Hi," she says. "I am looking for a place. I am trying… It looked different in the winter. My son died here. I think it was here. Or close by at least. Last December. In a snowmobile accident."

"I'm sorry," I tell her. "I remember hearing about it, but I'm not around in the winter."

I read about it in the paper. It was just a few days after Christmas. The ice was slushy because it had snowed and snowed. Still, some people do not pay attention to the warnings. The police and the rescue service workers have little patience when riders disobey the notices to stay off the ice. Rescue workers have families, too. So, when a snow machine goes through the ice and they are not from around here, they are pissed off that our local workers and volunteers are put in dangerous situations by stupid people from the city. Idiots. City-ots.

When is the ice thick enough for snowmobiles?

When the tourists stop falling through.

That is the local wisdom.

"He was close to shore. The police officer said he could have stood up, if he'd wanted to. If he had tried. It was that shallow. But he panicked and drowned."

"I really am, so sorry," I said. And I did feel sorry for what I had said last week at my knitting circle when the topic came up about snowmobilers and stupidity. Of course, we are all stupid at times. Accidents happen, even to smart people. Accidental deaths are difficult to justify. They happen so fast, but regret is slow and excruciating.

"I told him not to go. But he laughed at me and went anyway. He and his dad. I told them, don't go. Stay and watch a movie with me."

This woman is on some kind of medication, I think. Her gaze is fixed over my left shoulder as if she is reading from a teleprompter. She is dressed all wrong. I should talk. I'm not even wearing a bra and I haven't changed my underwear in two days. To be fair, I don't have a washing machine and a trip into town to the laundromat is a pain. Still, my outfit is more in keeping with the weather and the surroundings. This woman looks like she is on her way to the theatre. Her sweater is low cut. Low enough to show off a delicate silver chain with an expensive handcrafted pendant dropping dangerously into the cave of her substantial cleavage. She is wearing heels. High spikey heels! They are muddy. I am not sure how she managed to get down the steep embankment to my studio without killing herself. The whole look says this is a woman who does not belong in cottage country. I have seen such women at the dump, trying to toss their scented garbage bags into the bins without stepping into the brown gumbo that eats delicate little shoes for breakfast. Impossible, and a bit comical.

"From what I understand," I tell her, "The accident was in the next bay. See the trail? Follow it to the far side of the point."

She looks at me like maybe I misunderstood. Like maybe I didn't hear about the tragic circumstances of her arrival on my property. I admit to some bias here. I did not want to learn the details of her story. Her grief. I have filled my life's quota of grief, thanks anyway.

"So," I tell her, "I have to get back to work."

I retreat into the studio and pick up the paintbrush. There is a drip of varnish where I was interrupted, and it is hardening. Yellowing. "Shit," I remark, louder than necessary, hoping she can hear. Hoping she will realize she messed up my nice little Zen buzz.

But apparently my subtleties are lost on her. She darkens

my door and steps into my sanctuary where even my neighbours know enough not to interrupt, and I give her the kind of warning glare I usually reserve for frozen seafood salesmen who come by trying to unload some crab legs from the back of a truck. Like, really? We have grocery stores in this town.

"Sheila," she says. "I should have told you. My name is Sheila."

I am mad about my varnish, so I dip a rag in the turpentine and try to fix it and, of course, it makes it worse. When I turn around again she is gone. Good. But my landscape painting has morphed into something new. The shoreline I was so pleased with earlier, now seems sinister. A purple shadow becomes an image of a boy's snowmobile suit filling with icy lake water. I set the canvas aside and climb the hill to the cottage.

I lose track of time in the studio, and I am surprised to see that it is already four o'clock. Ice pellets are tapping at the windows like typists in an old newspaper office. I add some maple logs to the wood stove and open a very nice bottle of red wine. On the radio, Ira Glass introduces an intriguing story about an abandoned house, and I cast 120 stitches onto my knitting needle.

Then a knock comes at the door.

Nobody knocks at the cottage door. They walk in and say, "Hey, Gloria. You home?"

I reluctantly rise out of my cozy chair and see Sheila blowing around in the wind on my porch. She has big hair, and it is whipping wildly toward the sky as if a UFO is trying to suck her into the mother ship. I open the door. A crack.

"Hi. Can I come in?"

"Of course," I say, stepping aside.

"Sheila. Remember me?"

"From this morning. Yes."

"Well, I could use your help."

I wait to hear what the help is. Her car broke down? She lost her designer purse? She stands in my cramped kitchen looking stunned. Or stoned. Not sure which. She gazes around, incredulous at the poverty, no doubt. She is thinking, So, this is where shabby chic comes from? Real life shacks, that's where. Finally, I can't stand it and blurt out, "What is it that you need?"

"I bought a memorial for Keith. It's in the car. Can you help me get it down to the site of his... death?"

"A memorial? I'm sorry. I don't understand what you mean by a memorial."

"Come," she says. "Come and see."

I can't believe I am pulling on my rubber boots and my coat and trudging outside in the sleet to look at a memorial, but alas. It is really happening. Sheila beeps her electronic key thingy and the hatchback door of her black Lincoln Navigator raises quietly and elegantly to reveal a huge metal cross with a plastic floral wreath.

"That thing must weigh, like, two hundred pounds," I say.

"Beautiful, isn't it?"

"Where were you thinking of putting it?"

"Down at the point. Can you help me? It's super heavy."

"Yes. I can see that. I can tell by looking at it that the two of us can't possibly carry it down a steep slope in freezing rain without the risk of injury. Anyway, Sheila. You can't place a memorial on somebody's property without their permission."

Sheila gives the waistband of her skinny jeans a tug to pull them up over the bare skin around her midriff. "I didn't think you'd mind."

"It isn't my property. The point belongs to the Barnards, and they are in Florida right now. But I can tell you, almost one hundred percent for sure that they won't want this… memorial… right at their waterfront. That's where their dock goes. And their boat and their chairs. You can ask them, of course. When they get back from down south. But I wouldn't get my hopes up if I were you."

Sheila starts to cry. She puts on quite a performance, unaware of my immunity to tears. In the glow of the interior car light, she looks puffy and orange. I realize it is make-up. Some foundation she probably thinks makes her appear younger, but instead it looks like she smeared Cheez Whiz on her face. I think of Eleanor Rigby. Wearing a face that she keeps in a jar by the door. Or the fridge, in this case.

"So, I'm going in now. Sorry I can't help you." I turn away from her, anxious to take a gulp of Chianti. A big gulp.

"May I come in for a minute? I don't have any friends up here in…"

"Hicktown?" Oh. Did that sound mean?

"What? Pardon?"

"Never mind. No. Sorry. Actually, I'm expecting company and I've got to get ready, so. Bye." I am pretty sure she says the "b" word as she mumbles her way to the driver's seat. The hatch door closes magically, and I watch her tires dig the shit out of my driveway as she pulls away.

I feel uncomfortable with my reaction to Sheila. I used to be a pretty nice person. If you knew me before I sabotaged my life with a really, really stupid infatuation, you would have said I was calm and helpful. The kind of person who would be patient with the Sheilas of the world. Always in control. But since the divorce, my moods are unreliable. I have made it my mission to free myself from anger. It is an aggressive and childish response to the things that annoy and frustrate me. So, I try to assess what it is about Sheila that got me acting so uncharacteristically cruel. She put me on the defensive, as if I had to protect myself from her.

The wine bottle makes a satisfying sound in the recycle bin. What possible harm could it have done to listen to the woman's story? Losing a child is awful, I know. I also know that some parents want to talk and talk and talk about their experience of loss. I never did. It is not a club.

I look out the kitchen window and squirt some dish soap into the sink. Something about immersing my hands in warm sudsy water is calming. I wash up a few bowls and cups and watch Mama raccoon waddle up to my new garbage hutch and fiddle with the critter-proof latch. HA! I knock on the window in triumph. I want her to know me. Her adversary in the trash wars.

She turns and her eyes flash in the reflected light. She pauses and stares for a minute and then casually starts digging at the base of the hutch.

"Oh no you don't!" I pull on my boots and step out into

the dark chill with a flashlight, but before I get down the steps, I see headlights going down the Barnard's lane. They have a chain across the driveway part way down and the vehicle stops there. Sheila! The inside light of her car glows as she pops her magic hatch.

My resolution to be nicer forgotten, I go back into the kitchen and call the police. The dispatch officer warns me to lock my doors and stay inside, but I cannot help myself. I put on my warm coat and go. It has stopped raining but there are no stars. The beam of my flashlight is dim, but I can make out a man helping Sheila bear her big cross. They are leaning against a tree. The man has a reflective vest on, and a hardhat. I know him.

"Stanley? It's me, Gloria." I turn the flashlight onto my face so he can see me.

"Oh, hi Gloria," says Stanley. Sheila steps in front of him as if to claim him. She has found some new footwear. A pair of suede boots that extend well above her knees. They make her look like a hooker.

"Stanley," I say. "Isn't it past your curfew?" Stanley looks at his watch. It is almost nine, and I happen to know that the curfew at the Community Living Home is eight o'clock. "Lorna will be worried about you."

"Oh my gosh, Gloria. You're right. I better go home. This lady needed help, though. But I better get home. Can I still get my hundred dollars? Sheila?"

"Hi Sheila," I say. Sheila has been pulling on the cross as if she hoped the situation would improve in her favour.

"It would be nice if someone would just help me! I am a

grieving mother!"

"Stanley," I tell him. "Go over to my place and use the kitchen phone and call Lorna and tell her where you are. Okay? So, she won't worry?"

"Okay, Gloria."

"And Stanley? Tell her the police are on their way."

"You! Fucking! Bitch!" Sheila says. I am hoping she doesn't have a gun or even a hatpin. I don't want to have to conk her out with my flashlight, but I will if need be.

"You shouldn't have kidnapped one of our vulnerable citizens, Sheila," I said.

"How was I supposed to know he was vulnerable? He looks like a construction worker with that helmet."

"He wears it because he has seizures," I say. "You're lucky he didn't have one while in your company. Where did you find him?"

"He was feeding the ducks near that bridge in town. Honestly, he's an adult, isn't he?"

"Yes. A very kind adult. And just as susceptible to women with big boobs as any man. Especially when lured with the promise of a hundred dollars. Perhaps you can give me the cash and I'll make sure Stanley's social worker gets it for his bank account."

"Of course, I don't carry money with me. I was planning on stopping at the ATM, on our way back to the village."

"Of course!"

The police cruiser is at the top of the hill, lights flashing. Sheila puts on quite a show for the officers, but when they find out she is driving with a suspended license, they arrange to have the car impounded and suggest she call someone to pick her up. The last we see of her; she is begging the tow truck driver for a ride.

"She says she has a cottage around here," I say as we watch the truck turn onto the main road.

Skip, the officer in charge, says yes. "A huge fortress of a place. All stone. With heated granite floors and surveillance cameras in every room. Me and Frank went over after the accident and yeah, that broad, Sheila was there. But I don't think she's the mom. Eh, Frank?"

"No. She isn't the kid's mother," Frank says. "She was crying and everything, but the dad told us not to pay any attention to her. She was drunk, is what he said. Like maybe we never seen a drunk before."

"Well, we better get you home, eh Stanley?" says Skip. "What did you learn about getting in a car with a stranger, Stanley?"

"Don't do it, sir."

The next day I call my friend Jack, the councillor in my ward. "Heard anything about Sheila?" I ask.

"Oh, sure. She was the dad's girlfriend and I guess she was quite distraught after the tragedy. Addiction issues and trauma is what she's claiming. Her boyfriend, or ex-boyfriend, is in Hawaii and she borrowed his car without his knowledge. She wanted to do something to impress him. The memorial was supposed to be a gesture of reconciliation. Like an apology, maybe, for being such a whack job that Keith and his dad went out for a snowmobile ride to get the hell away from her for a couple of hours. You see how that goes? How she was blamed for the whole thing?"

I do see how that goes. Somebody has to take the blame for catastrophic mistakes. That is why I am living alone. I am the one in my family who got the blame. Maybe that is why I didn't want to be Sheila's friend. I sensed that she was nothing more than a giant wakeboard wave of unfortunate fuckups and my instinct was to climb to higher ground.

A Stubborn Muscle

My mother lies in the fetal position, her hands, like the claws of a doomed baby bird are curled under her chin. Her feet are overlapping and blue. This is the end. There will be no recovery, like last winter when she surprised us all and rallied after a bout with pneumonia. I am staying at the house with her. She made us all promise that we wouldn't let them cart her away to die in the hospital.

I am not working, and I have no family of my own, so I made the commitment to be the main caregiver. And I am neutral in the sibling rivalries that have been spinning around this family for decades. Mom called me Switzerland.

I sit and listen to her breathing. The death rattle. It is subsiding somewhat now that we have stopped the fluids. There is a sponge to dampen her lips, but really, she does not seem to be in any discomfort. She is gone, gone, gone, my mother. Her eyes have sunken back into her head. The systems are shutting down like a factory that is moving operations to a far-off country, and the workers are reluctant to leave. They are not in any hurry. But closure is inevitable. I have little to do, other than go through the paperwork, watch a bit of TV. Knit. Even her diapers are not wet anymore.

Angela, my oldest sister, comes in the early morning and slumps into the chair by Mother's bed without looking at her. I lean in the doorway while she tells me all about her shitty life.

"You know I've been diagnosed with PTSD, right? The doctor has confirmed it. I get to the parking lot of the school, and I literally cannot make myself get out of the car. It's like there's ice water pouring through my veins."

Angela is the vice-principal. She got whacked in the head by a big grade eight kid. A kid who cannot take the blame for his actions because he is on the autism spectrum. She had a concussion. And she recovered. But I think she was humiliated because she had been a champion for this kid. Always excusing his behaviour to the teachers who complained that they were afraid of him. Including a pregnant kindergarten teacher. The kid was banned from the playground, so they let him take some fresh air time in the kindy-pen. Angela's reasoning was that he would not hurt the little kids. And he did not. He head-butted the teacher and she had to go to the hospital. She almost had a miscarriage. Angela thinks the teacher exaggerated because she has no empathy for special needs kids. Even after she read the medical report, she insisted that the teacher had escalated the boy's bad behaviour somehow.

"The teachers invite a power struggle," she told me once. "I never have any issues with him. He's a gentle soul under all that pent up frustration." She forced the teachers to take professional development sessions on the correct way to deflate situations with students on the spectrum. They hated her. So, when the kid shoved Angela's head against the cement block wall and knocked her out, she got very few get well cards.

Angela is a know-it-all. She thinks my life would be a whole lot better if I took her advice about men and careers and my wardrobe.

"Oh my god," she says this morning. "Is that Mom's sweater you're wearing? It's baggy as hell. You look like the cleaning lady."

Last week she told me that there is good money in house cleaning these days. "You can make a hundred dollars for five hours work." She doesn't realize how mean she is.

"And fucking Geoff!" Whenever she says the "f" word, Mother flinches. The only time I see any response from her is when Angela belches out the details of her desperate existence. "He is so fucking useless! I get in the car this morning and there is NO gas in it. The tank is below empty if that is even possible. I coast into the gas station on fucking fumes."

Mother's breathing stops.

"Fuck. Is she dead?"

"No. She just doesn't like the f-word."

Angela laughs. Then pauses and takes a close look at Mom for the first time since she arrived. "Well don't you have a mirror? To hold under her nose?"

Mom resumes her difficult chore. It seems unfair, this

last effort. But she has always been resolved to do the things required of her. It is impossible to accomplish this work graciously, but she chose it. She declined medical assistance.

"Does that include me holding a pillow over your head?" I asked only last week.

"You'll end up in Hell if you try it," she said. "Suit yourself." That was the last time she smiled.

Angela brushes past me. She stops at the kitchen counter and picks up the blister pack with Mom's prescriptions. "Which ones are the Diazepams?"

"The little yellow ones," I tell her. She pops a couple out and swallows them without water. I hope she enjoys a good bowel movement later. She has taken two stool softeners.

"What's that smirk on your face all about?"

"Nothing."

"She won't need the whole week's worth. And my anxiety's bad."

In fact, when the doctor was here yesterday, he checked her feet, noting the curling toes, and told me there was no need to administer any medications going forward except for a Fentanyl patch. He didn't say, don't let those Diazepams go to waste.

Angela moans as she bends to pull on her shoes. She really is suffering, I suppose. But I think of all the times she withheld big sister sympathy. Tough titty, said the kitty. The milk tastes shitty. That was about the limit of her response to my suffering.

Harley, second to the youngest, arrives mid-morning. He

manages to startle me, so soft does he tread on the carpet, so gently does he open the bedroom door. Harley moves through life like a ghost without a haunting permit. He hugs me and softly kisses the side of my head. We stand together for a minute, his arm around my shoulder.

The furnace comes on.

"This is hard," he says, simply. "You're doing great." Then he sits on the edge of the bed and covers Mom's hand with his own. "Hello Mom," he says. "I'm here, with you. I'm so glad to be here with you today," he says.

And he turns and tells me to go for a walk. "Take a break."

When I come back, Mom is clean and lying flat on her pillow. Harley has straightened her out, somehow, and brushed the wispy strands of her hair and crossed her hands over her sternum. She looks peaceful and ready to meet her maker with dignity. Harley is a lovely man. Alone, like me. His wife had an affair with the coach of their son's curling team and, although the affair did not last, Harley took advantage of her guilt and humiliation and left the misery of what had been a difficult marriage. Angela cannot bear to be around him. He is too nice, she says. Too kind. Too apologetic. He gives her the creeps.

Harley opens the window and tells Mother to let her spirit leave on the breeze. "Your work here is done, Mom," he says. "The dishes are all put away and the food is wrapped up and you've checked to make sure the oven is turned off. And one last thing you always do. Remember? You set the kitchen table for breakfast. Cereal bowls, spoons, juice glasses. All ready for a new day tomorrow. Go ahead and relax. Time for rest, my darling."

I hope Harley is around to see me out of the world.

Before he leaves, he washes his hands carefully in the bathroom and he hums softly to himself as he dries them on the towel. "She'll cross the river today," he tells me as he puts his jacket on. "I have a meeting at three, then I'll pop back around." He hugs me again. A generous hug. "That sweater is so soft," he says. Mom always loved it."

Later in the afternoon, Lloyd stops by, the middle child and self-assigned power of attorney. All business, he comes to pick up the papers for the funeral home. He glances at the DNR file on the kitchen counter. Do Not Resuscitate.

"Remember, Judy, don't call 911 when she passes." Then he rushes away without even looking at Mom.

I resume my task of cleaning out the basement. In the cupboard under the stairs, I find mouldy-smelling Christmas crap, old newspaper articles in faded green folders and a box of scraps from a long-forgotten sewing project. There are recipe books, pages stained with cooking oil and some kind of red sauce. And under a pile of textbooks, I come across Jane's thesis. Jane was the second oldest and she existed in Angela's shadow. A meek girl who did whatever her big sister demanded. She was never quite as confident as her excellent school grades would make you think. In university, she won scholarship after scholarship and then had a brilliant academic career in addiction research. But she died by suicide. Or maybe not. My mother always claimed that she took more sleeping pills than she thought and then slept so soundly that she suffocated in her pillow. And maybe that's true. But I doubt she could have accidentally taken fifteen sleeping pills. I doubt that.

I shove the thesis in the garbage bag. Then I take it out again to read the title page. It is some hypothesis about the effect of catastrophic ideation on the adolescent brain. Back in the bag it goes.

Albert also died. He was golfing with Dad when a thunderstorm came up out of nowhere. One of those violent weather events that blow in off Lake Erie. They were on the fifth hole, about as far from the clubhouse as you can get, and Dad yelled over to Albert to take cover under the big oak on the right side of the fairway, while he ducked under a stand of willows. That's where he watched the lightning bolt deliver its deadly blow to his favourite son. Well, he never said that. He never said Albert was his favourite. But he didn't really need to.

Dad never recovered because, of course, he blamed himself. Another father might have stepped up his vigilance to make sure nothing bad happened to the rest of his children, but he just quit. Like an athlete who finds he can no longer be competitive, he quit. He removed himself emotionally from the family and we tiptoed around his easy boy chair until one day he wasn't there anymore. And it took a while for us to notice.

Here is the family photo, taken in 1969. The cardboard matte is stained by water or humidity. Mother wears a sleeveless black sheath. Her lips are dark with lipstick. Her hair is dark with dye. But she is pale, and she does not smile. She looks like a suburban Jackie Onassis. Dad stands behind her with Harley and Albert on one side of him and Lloyd on the other. They all have hands on Mom's shoulders, as if they want to make sure she doesn't try to stand up. Jane and Angela are on a footstool to her right. Baby Judy (that's me) is sitting on Mom's lap in a frilly dress that is tight around my chubby belly. I look uncomfortable. Perhaps Mother is pinching me, which she did do on occasion.

She was never affectionate, our mother. But she was efficient. She had a system for housework that kept us all fed and clean. I remember thinking there was something humiliating in the way she got down on her hands and knees to scrub the kitchen floor, but she completed her tasks without comment, and we knew enough not to bother her as she moved across the floor like a dog on all fours. One Christmas, Dad bought her a Magic Mop. It disappeared, unused. There was a proper way to clean, and she would not compromise.

Over to the left side of the photo is Lorraine, sullen and slouching. Third eldest, she was always miserable. See how she stands apart, even though I'm sure the photographer encouraged her to move in. She had a baby when she was seventeen and ran away with the father, Dave Butcher, who was a football player in high school. They ended up in Ottawa and, I'm not sure, but I don't think they ever married. Dave went to jail many years ago, and the little girl, my niece, is a hairdresser, I think. Lloyd has called Lorraine to tell her that Mom is dying, but she has a lot of health problems related to her heavy smoking and doesn't think she'll be able to make it to Mom's funeral. The daughter might come. Lloyd says Dad sent Lorraine money every month and she was expecting the gravy train to continue after he died, but Lloyd refused to send money so she could buy cigarettes. Lorraine calls Angela once in a while, but she never calls me. I don't think she even knows my number.

Up the stairs I climb out of the cool cellar and force myself to check on Mother. It is hard to watch this process. The heart is a stubborn muscle. I open the window a little wider and put on some piano music. Apparently, hearing is the last of the senses to shut down. Then I go back to my task of disposing of Mother's memories. File folders with report cards and photographs and valentines. And a copy of a poem by Wordsworth.

"Sisters and brothers, little Maid,
How many may you be?"
"How many? Seven in all," she said,
And wondering looked at me.

"And where are they? I pray you tell."
She answered, "Seven are we;
And two of us at Conway dwell,
And two are gone to sea."

"Two of us in the church-yard lie,
My sister and my brother;
And, in the church-yard cottage, I
Dwell near them with my mother."

The poem is on parchment, thin and fragile as Mother's skin. It looks like she may have used a razor blade to cut it out of a library book. One corner is torn and fixed with yellowing scotch tape. It must have resonated with her, being the mother of seven, with two gone ahead of her to heaven. As the paper crumbles into my lap, I am suddenly very sure that her heart has stopped.

There is a rushing sound in my head as I enter her bedroom to check. No vital signs. I was worried that it wouldn't be apparent. Perhaps I read too many of those Victorian era stories about people waking up in their coffins. But there is no room for doubt here. My mother has successfully escaped from this corpse. She is with Albert and Jane.

Still, I am reluctant to act. There is no urgency. She can lie in peace for a while before her body is wrapped and removed for disposal. Outside, the world continues. A songbird trills sweetly. A lawnmower starts up in the next yard. I feel hungry. I make myself a tomato sandwich and take it to the chair in Mother's room.

She is still present somehow. More so than she has been in a long time. There is an energy I cannot explain, but I know for certain that Mother has not gone very far. She lingers. Watches. I imagine her testing the water of her afterlife with a tentative toe, cautiously casting off the crust of consciousness. My eyes are drawn to her housecoat hanging on the back of the bedroom door, pockets bulging with tissues, or perhaps regrets. I will not speak of this with the siblings. I cannot even think of the words I would use to describe the way the light is falling in prism-like drops around the deathbed. I know they would look at me strangely and believe me deranged.

An hour passes and I go down to the cellar. That is one thing I have in common with Mother. I hate to leave a task half completed. I drop the Wordsworth poem into the garbage bag and empty a box of birthday cards on top of it and tie it all up and push the contents down so that a waft of decomposing sentimentality escapes through the hole at the top. I carry the bag out to the curb and nod to Mother's neighbour who is getting into her car and then I go back inside to call Lloyd.

He'll be mad if he isn't the first to know.

The Downer

It was called The SunDowner Motor Lodge, but after a vehicle backed into the sign, Frankie refused to pay a thousand dollars for the repair. He painted a yellow circle where the word Sun used to be.

"Like hieroglyphics," he said. But the truth was, folks had been calling the motel The Downer for years.

Back in the sixties, The SunDowner's parking lot was jammed with station wagons. It had a four-star listing in the Canadian Automobile Association travel guide.
An ideal stopover for families travelling along the Trans-Canada Highway between Winnipeg and Thunder Bay. COLOUR TV in EVERY ROOM!

Frankie remembers seeing The SunDowner for the first time. He was twelve and the only one in his family who was not totally freaked out by his dad's craziness. For that vote of confidence, he got to sit in the front, in the co-pilot's seat, with the CAA strip map on his lap, reading out local historical and geographical landmarks as they passed.

"Did you hear that, girls?" his father yelled at the rear-view mirror in his booming voice. "Are you paying attention to Frankie? Read that part again, Frankie, about the dinosaur bones."

They had been driving for three days after Frank Sr.'s sudden announcement that his kids, goddammit, were not going to be the only ones in Moose Jaw to miss Expo 67 in Montreal, a World's Fair that would define the twentieth century. Mary, Frankie's mom, sat in the back seat with a little triangle of a scarf tied over her long blonde hair. The scarf had daisies on it that matched her dress, but the outfit wasn't daisy-fresh. She didn't have a change of clothes, or even a clean pair of underwear. She almost didn't come. Crying and threatening and trying to reason with her husband, she refused to pack a suitcase. The girls, fourteen-year-old twins who looked like their mother right down to the unhealthy blue smudges under their eyes, were begging her from the backseat. "Get in, Momma!" Frankie was avoiding conflict by studying the map. Finally, when it seemed apparent that Frank was going to take the kids to Expo with or without her, she hopped in as the car pulled out of the gravel laneway.

"God knows who will water my garden," she said.

The photos from the 1967 brochure did, indeed, make The SunDowner look like an ideal vacation destination. At the height of its popularity, the summer of Canada's Centennial, the No Vacancy sign was lit up by five o'clock every evening.

Frank Sr. turned in to inquire about the rates even though his intention had been to camp the entire way. Fed up listening to the whiny yeast-infected womenfolk in the backseat, he was starting to question the practicality of driving all the way to Montreal just to pay high prices for a bunch of stuff he could see on TV. An upside-down triangle for the Canadian Pavilion. Habitat. La Ronde.

A guy at the KOA campground just west of Kakabeka Falls, a tired looking sad sack of a dad on his way home from Expo, gave Frank a couple of beers and told him the whole thing was a giant rip-off. And the line-ups were killers.

Still, he didn't want to look like an ass and admit that Mary had been right all along. A night or two at The SunDowner might be just the thing. It would give him time to cook up a plan. The prices were a bit steep, but when they accepted his cancelled Diner's Club card, he upgraded to an efficiency unit with a little fridge. Room 6. Mary held a washcloth under cold water and lay down on the double bed farthest from the window. She put a quarter in the Magic Fingers machine and pretended to fall asleep with the washcloth over her eyes.

Frank Sr. could be a fun dad when he wanted to be. He organized a cannonball contest at the pool. Then they had a mini-putt tournament. On the eighteenth hole, where a giant clown head swallowed your ball to end the game, he showed the kids how to forfeit their last putt and play again, saving the seventy-five cents it would cost for a new round. Out behind the Motor Lodge, there was a tennis court, a shuffleboard court and a pond with a rowboat. Past the pond, there was a wall of black spruce that marked the end of the civilized world. All this was paradise for Frank Sr. who was sick of Saskatchewan.

When the kids met up with some foul-mouthed teenagers from Calgary, Frank went looking for a drink. He found the owner, Charlie Muir, who emigrated from Prestwick, Scotland after the war. Frank fell half in love listening to the guy's accent, especially when Charlie poured him three fingers of Scotch and invited him into his tidy apartment above the office. Seems Mr. Muir was a widower and planned to sell up and move back to the old country. He was just waiting for the right buyer to come along.

"There's a fair bit of maintenance involved," he said. "I'm getting too old to manage it."

Frank Sr. negotiated the best deal possible. Only an idiot would have passed on a deal like that. Back they went to Moose Jaw to liquidate their assets, and back again to Carlson, Ontario in time for the new school year. The girls, who were hoping to make the cheerleading squad at their high school, cried and threw up and cried some more. Mary chewed her nails down to the quick and watched the prairies disappear in the passenger side mirror through enlarged pupils. Young Frankie remembered only one thing about the migration east. It rained the whole way.

"Why pay a mortgage on a house and a business," Frank told anyone who would listen, "when your family can live quite comfortably in the apartment above the office?"

Lots of people lived above family businesses. The

undertaker's family lived above the funeral home and the Wongs had an apartment over the Golden Palace. Frankie's sisters learned how to change sheets and scrub bathtubs and lug the heavy vacuum from one room to the next. Frankie mowed the lawn and swept the tennis court. He cleaned frogs out of the swimming pool filter.

Northern Ontario, it turned out, was not ideal for cement swimming pools that are not winterized properly. Frost-heaved and forlorn, it never had another summer like '67. The slide became something of a hazard. The diving board snapped under the weight of a burly lumberjack from Blind River, and the surrounding hedge, the one that Mr. Muir trimmed by hand to look like undulating waves, crept out of control. By 1979, the pool was a pit of green algae with an unknown number of stained and waterlogged mattresses at the bottom, a breeding ground for mosquitos.

Mary didn't stick around to see The SunDowner drop below the horizon. After the girls got beaten up at Northview High School in the stairwell behind the gym, she moved back to the Mennonite community in Saskatchewan where she'd grown up. Frankie refused to go along. He knew what happened to boys in that community. They went weird. He stayed on and took his chances with the rough local crowd that started hanging out at the motel after his dad managed to get a liquor licence in '71. A big boozy year for teenagers. The Age of Majority and Accountability bill passed in the Ontario legislature and the legal drinking age dropped from 21 to 18. Frank Sr. painted the windows in the games room black and turned it into a bar called The Bomb Shelter. A tray of draft beer was $2.00. The place was packed every weekend until the RIDE program killed the buzz in 1977. Word got out that the cops were stopping impaired drivers as they pulled out of the SunDowner and business slowed down.

Frankie was twenty-two. Time to make something of himself. His sisters in Saskatchewan were both married. They sent photos of moon-faced nieces and nephews and tempted him with farm work and a spare bedroom. He got ready to leave a few times, but his dad had a way of making him delay his plans, one season at a time.

"Look at the books, Frankie," he'd say. "This place is making money again. A lotta potential here, son. Think of your future. Stick around! I got you on the books as co-owner. We're sitting on a goldmine here. Where do you think you're going? You go out west, your sisters already got a bride picked out for you. A frumpy Bible thumper with long skirts. Is that what you want? Go ahead, then. Suit yourself."

The guest rooms were rented to fishermen in the spring, golfers in the summer, hunters in the fall, snowmobilers in winter and divorced dads all year round. Frankie scraped the black paint off the windows of The Bomb Shelter and renamed it the Whiskeyjack Pub. Truckers occasionally pulled in if they missed the rest stop south of Hanlon and the weather was bad. Not many women stayed at The SunDowner. Women, if you wanted them, were up the road at the Bare Den where you could watch them writhe naked on a pole while you ate your all-day breakfast. The golden years.

On-line porn spelled the death knell for strip joints. By 2003, The Bare Den was empty except for a dozen or so regulars who knew the girls by name and kept their expectations low. A sad way to end up, for sure, Frankie thought, both for the strippers and the men who admired them. Not many places for local men to congregate these days. Pool hall was gone. The barbershop closed when Buck McLeod took his heart attack. Carlson Corners was suffering another slump and this time it was unlikely to recover.

Frank Sr. died in February of 2007. Frankie had been down in Panama City, Florida for a month with his girlfriend, Eileen, a retired dancer, so they didn't find him right away. The old man had taken matters into his own hands. He'd been gone for the better part of a week. Fortunately, the heat was turned off in Room 6. One final money-saving gesture, no doubt. The coroner raised his eyebrows, but he didn't put anything damning in the report. He'd seen a lot worse.

"Don't blame yourself," he said to Frankie as the body was being carried out.

No likelihood of that, Frankie thought, looking around Room 6. Nothing much had changed since he first saw it in 1967. Same geometric patterned drapes. Same paintings; swans in a green pond. He didn't have the energy to strip the beds or gather up the towels. He had wasted forty years of his life in this museum of despair. Time to sell it and get the hell out.

That's when he heard a crash and looked outside in time to see the hearse backing into the sign. The Sun was beyond repair. A bad omen. Then he discovered a hefty second mortgage on the property. A little kick in the pants from beyond the grave. Finally, the real estate agent told him he couldn't list the place until he made some major repairs. The place wouldn't pass a building inspection.

Frankie's girlfriend helps him through the rest of that grim winter. "Three bad things in a row, Frankie. That's how bad luck goes."

Eileen has crooked teeth and two adult children somewhere who never call, not even on her birthday, but she never lets herself get too far down in the dumps. On her bleakest days, she jokes that she is one bad day away from packing her bags and hopping a Greyhound back to Newfoundland. Frankie dreads that possibility. He knows he can't run The Downer without her. If she decides to leave, Frankie won't be able to stop her. Men are doomed.

"The world's up and changed and men just can't adapt," Eileen tells him. "Look around," she says. "All the losers who end up here, they have no idea how to get by since the factories shut down. What are they thinking? If they wait around long enough, General Motors will open up a plant down the street? Meanwhile their wives go back to school and get retrained and figure out the new economy. You and these local yokels still think you can find a woman to cook and clean and iron your underwear and keep you happy in bed."

When Eileen tells Frankie that he is an idiot in her Newfoundland dialect, it sounds playful and funny. He never takes offence because she has a big heart and besides, what she says is true. Without her he would fade into the netherworld of single men who drink alone in The Whiskeyjack and wander away into the wintery darkness after last call with tears in their eyes.

Not that he blames women. Frankie kind of understands how a woman might prefer to live with another woman. Someone who'll make her a cup of tea when she is tired instead of wanting to poke her in the middle of the night when she has to get up at six a.m. to get to Foodland in time for the early shift. There are lesbians all over the place these days. Cops and teachers. Lots of them were married once. To men. They had children the regular way. Then, snap.

He is uncomfortable around these ladies. He can chat with Ricky Anderson, the coach who spent time in jail for diddling five PeeWee hockey players. Him and Ricky can talk about the government and the impending death of Canadian football. Why is it he can have conversations with a pervert and not a couple of women? Women couples? Two wives? It's not that he doesn't like them, but he is pretty sure they do not like him. He can tell by the way they look at him. They think he is an asshole. At least with Ricky, he can feel good about himself. Someone is beneath him on the totem pole.

Lots of guys in this town went to work at the gyp plant right out of high school. Why go to university when you could make over twenty bucks an hour on the line? Double time and a half on statutory holidays. The union did all the thinking for you. It was a sweet deal until that last strike in '98 when the union turned down the company's final offer. Basically, told the management to go screw themselves. And they did. They screwed off to China and left the employees with no jobs. No pensions.

"Lucky you," they told Frankie as they ran up their tabs at The Whiskeyjack. "You have your own business."

"Lucky me," Frankie agreed.

They worked on and off, the men, plowing driveways and hauling gravel. Some of them tried logging, delivering face cords of shitty hemlock to people who still heat with wood. Some went to the tar sands, but didn't last long.

Things went along pretty much the same for a number of years. Frankie didn't have to go looking for friends. They came to him. But times got harder instead of easier. People moved to the city. The Rotarians, who had been meeting at The Downer every Thursday night for forty years, had to admit defeat when membership dropped to seven and the only new application came from Betty Waters, the dog groomer. The president made a motion to disband, and all were in favour.

One Monday night while they were watching football, Scotty Benson says, "Frankie? My wife is gone, my kids are gone, my house is dark and dreary. I'm ready to put it on the market and get what I can for it. How much would you charge me to rent Room 6 by the month?"

"That's my dad's old room."

"I know it. Empty. You might just as well make some money off it. And here's the thing. I want you to get some milk and Cheerios in here and maybe a toaster so I can fix my own breakfast. Peanut butter and jam. I'll help myself to lunch. But you fix dinner, you see?"

"I'm not running a charity here, Scotty."

"Well, wait a minute," says Walt. "Scotty's on to something. I read that the fastest growing business in the country is old people. Long term care."

"Now I got to change Scotty's diapers?"

"No, a course not. You hire a nurse to come around and tuck all the old fellers into bed. Somebody told me that dancer Candy at the Bare Den is a trained PSW."

"I think I know what the P stands for," says Scotty.

"Don't be an ass," says Walt. "It stands for Personal Support Worker. How long do you think those girls will keep dancing over there for your two-dollar tips?"

"Not sure that helping old guys into their diapers is a whole hell of a promotion."

"Whatever. There's subsidies for private care homes, Frankie. The government's got a whole army of old buggers to house, and they're willing to pay."

Frankie ran the idea by Eileen while she was filing her nails. "Go for it, Frankie," she says. "Those old coots practically live here anyways." She shook her bottle of nail polish. There was a little ball inside that clicked. Frankie mentioned Candy and her qualifications.

"If anybody's going to get paid for that job, Frankie, it'll be me. I was looking at the college brochure the other day for training programs. That Personal Care Worker career would suit me down to the ground."

The more the fellas talked about it, the better the idea seemed. They did a bit of research and learned the lingo.

"There's a big difference between a senior residence and assisted living and long-term care. It's a slippery slope and we don't want none of it," Ricky told them.

Frankie nearly gave up when he discovered that the Ministry required 57 regulations to meet the standards of a senior-friendly building. Safety bars alone won't cut it. Staff with first aid qualifications, shower stalls that can accommodate a walker or a wheelchair. Health inspections in the kitchen. Ramps everywhere.

"We might just as well forget about it, boys," he said.

But the idea festered. Bobby Gee kept a little journal of ideas that the Ministry didn't need to look at. "No need to call it anything," Bobby says. "No need to get the goddamned government mixed up in this. It's just shared accommodation, like the house me and Harold stayed in up in Fort McMurray. We took turns cooking dinner. Or ordering it. Whatever." He flipped open his little pad and read off some of his ideas about how they could divvy up the work like grass-cutting and snow-shovelling.

Brent MacArthur piped up and offered to start a vegetable garden out back and Sudsy McLeish wanted to restore the shuffleboard court. It was sounding good. Six of them signed on with cash up front to help pay for renovations. California shutters, hardwood floors, walk-in showers and bars to help get up off the toilets.

"We going to fix up the exterior, next, Frankie?" Walt asks.

"Hell, no," Frankie says. "We don't want to attract any attention. The property taxes would go up. We been screwed over enough."

The Emperor's Clothes

Jim came home from town feeling down. Not that he said anything, but I can always tell when something is troubling him. He said, "Annie? I'm going out to the garage." So, I threw in a load of towels and called Aunt Madge. She's in long term care over in Lindsay and she's lonely. I hear Jim start up the lawnmower, so I know it'll be a good half hour before he wants lunch. After twenty minutes of listening to Madge complain about the food and the nurses who stand out front and smoke, I wander over to the kitchen window and I look out and see Jim collapsed on his knees in the back garden. I tell Madge I got to run.

The lawnmower is clicking. Cooling down. And Jim's hunched over a nest of naked little creatures. Baby rabbits.

"Look at them, Annie," he said. "Look what I done." He was sobbing in a way I hadn't ever seen before. I handed him a tissue for his dripping nose.

"Mama rabbit picked the wrong place for a nest, is all," I tell him, rubbing his back. It is difficult to console a man like Jim who all his life has been the one to reassure people. "It's not your fault, Hon. Come on inside and I'll fix you a sandwich."

I am trying not to get alarmed. Jim was a police officer for almost forty years, and he saw some terrible things, so I was worried at his reaction. But then I pieced things together and I figured out what had him so upset. Gloria Powers.

Gloria walks up and down the aisles of Foodland with the regal posture of the newly transitioned. After 65 years of being male, this is her first public appearance as a woman. Since she retired from a career in education, she has had time to research her proclivities. Discovering that she is not some kind of a pervert, but a victim of gender dysphoria, she has been heartened and encouraged to correct the error that nature made at her birth. She reads all the evidence-based articles that support her self-loathing and plans accordingly.

Gloria has been scaling up her feminine attributes, growing her hair, shaving her legs and armpits, and experimenting with make-up. But the biggest breakthrough has been her communication with transgender people online. They are encouraging. They are supportive. They give her tips. They are all rooting for her big "hometown reveal".

Now, here she is, in the frozen food aisle of the local grocery store, a place she has been hundreds of times before. Her adrenaline is surging. She is infatuated with herself as a female grocery shopper. She takes a quick selfie in front of the dairy case and posts it to her Facebook page. Before she has finished checking out, she has 13 likes from her new trans friends.

As Gloria struts across the parking lot in her kitten heel pumps, she slips and falls on the ice. Murray Grayson comes to her rescue, grabbing her under the arm and hoisting her, with a grunt, to her feet. Why in hell, he wonders, would an old lady wear high heels in March? She must be on her way to a funeral, he guesses. Poor thing.

"You okay?" Murray says.

"Fine, thank you," Gloria says.

Murray recognizes the face. It takes a minute to sort things out in his head and then he asks, "Are you Gord Power's sister?"

Gloria hesitates. She has known Murray for years. A curmudgeonly Legionnaire who owns the bait shop.

"I'm Gloria Powers," she says. "How do you do."

"You didn't break a hip or nothing, did you, Gloria?"

"No. I'm fine," she says, brushing mud off her fur coat. She has a run in her new stockings and a bloody gash on her knee.

Murray is puzzled. There is something he cannot quite figure out, here. But he picks up the head of cabbage that has rolled halfway under her car and he hands it to her and wishes her a good day.

Gloria is shaking. She can hardly get her keys out of her purse. She takes a few deep breaths before heading home. Patty is sitting at the kitchen table when Gloria plops the bags of groceries on the counter and bursts into tears. They have been married for forty years.

"What did you expect?" Patty says.

I poured a cup of tea and made a few phone calls while Jim had a nap. What Gord, Gloria, Powers is doing has him all shook up. A man becoming a woman is not front-page news. The transgender population is burgeoning like autism and post-traumatic stress. But when the man is a guy who taught your kids at the high school, well that's another thing altogether. Gord and Jim flipped burgers side by side at the Lions Club fundraiser. Gord is one of the good guys, or at least, was one of the good guys.

This is not Hollywood. It's a little community with a history of logging and hard-scrabble farming and making do with less. Social change creeps along in agonizing increments, and we like it that way. Most local folks are not against change, but we do not jump on every bandwagon. We wait and see how things pan out. Lots of bandwagons pass right through and we never see them again.

Town folks don't give a hoot if Gord wants to wear women's clothing and call himself Gloria, although nobody thinks it improves his appearance. We are questioning the value of the thing. We are wondering how many taxpayer-funded healthcare dollars it takes to turn an old man into an old woman. Shit, we all look pretty much the same at seventy.

Who stands to benefit? Apparently, Gloria, who has experienced extreme discomfort and distress over her gender assignment. She has suicidal thoughts.

Who's getting screwed over? All the rest of us who have discomfort and distress and can't get specialist appointments in time to save our lives. Fred Peters died waiting for prostate surgery. Pia Grierson can't afford the medication for her rheumatoid arthritis. Roy Potts says he didn't like his assignment either, when he got born with cerebral palsy. We got a whole town full of stories about chronic pain and wait times in emergency rooms and cancer treatments gone wrong.

Down at the coffee shop, the retired men fire up Ralph Hicks' new iPad and check on the cost of gender reassignment. Hormone therapy. Facial feminization. Breast augmentation. Liposuction. Buttock augmentation. Vaginoplasty. It costs a lot. More than your house. More than the cost of sponsoring ten refugee families for a year. And, believe me, sponsoring one family has caused enough of an uproar around here. How bad did Gord want his penis hacked off?

Gord's wife, Patty will tell you.

Since his retirement he has been putting on women's clothes and make-up and watching Wheel of Fortune as a woman. Sometimes, after dark, he walks around the block in heels. Patty's close friends are supportive. Progressive thinkers. They know what all the letters in LGBTQ stand for. Patty tries her best to accept this modification in her marriage, but after four decades, and kids and grandkids, it feels like a punch in the stomach.

Patty and Gord go to counselling. Gord gets plenty of support. There is a whole world of support for gender issues. And the more support he gets, the more he hates being a man. He decides he's going to live out the rest of his days as a woman. So fine, Patty says. But before you start transitioning, think about how hard that is going to be. Think about the kids. Think about me.

Gord can only think about one thing. He signs up for reassignment surgery.

As Gord prepares to change into Gloria, Patty starts having suicidal thoughts. But nobody cares. She will have to suck it up, Buttercup. She will have to get on board the gender transition train and bear the humiliation of stares as her husband puts on women's clothing and heads uptown in heels with a cute purse over her arm. Let it be known that, in this town, women do not wear heels to Foodland. They wear boots. Rubber boots, work boots, warm winter boots. For a couple of months in the summer, they wear Crocs or maybe Birkenstocks. So, Gord is not dressing as a local woman. He is dressing as a city woman. Or maybe his idea of what a city woman might dress like.

When Gord, who was considered a fairly attractive man, reinvents himself as a woman with thin scraggly hair and a prominent bald spot, people take a second look. No one says a thing, but they blink and give their heads a shake and look again. He is like the Emperor in the Hans Christian Anderson tale, who paid a lot of money to have a fabulous suit designed by the most exclusive tailors in the realm. Gloria walks through the frozen food aisle thinking she looks fabulous. Inside people's heads are the unspoken dialogues.

Am I the only one who feels uncomfortable?

Am I intolerant about gender issues?

But Pete Louden thinks Gord is in a play. He has had several successful roles in local little theatre productions. Romantic leads, mostly. Male leads. "Hi Gord", he says, expecting a response like, *Hi! I'm just on my way to the community centre for rehearsal. Haha.* But Gord ignores him completely.

We admit, we have been wrong about sex stuff in the past. We were wrong about homosexuality forty, fifty years ago. Well in this town, maybe it was more recent. Maybe it was only ten years ago. But that tide turned, and we support gay relationships and gay marriage and gay parenting. Pretty near everybody's got a gay in the family, now. So, we know to shut up about stuff like that. Sexual preferences? Who cares? We're fine about that.

But we are having some difficulty with this sex reassignment thing. A million dollars? Lloyd Bain, whose prostate is so swollen that pissing is a slow and painful process, wants to be first in line to select a pecker from the discard pile. "I hope they don't just throw them away," he says.

Still. We keep our wicked thoughts to ourselves. We don't want to be politically incorrect. Well, we do, but we don't want to be judged over it. The young people are quick to congratulate Gloria's bravery. They think we old folks are being intolerant. My grandson shows me the section in the provincial Health and Physical Education curriculum to prove I am uneducated.

According to the Ontario Human Rights Commission,
"each person has an internal and individual experience of gender. It is their sense of being a woman, a man, both, neither, or anywhere along the gender spectrum. A person's gender identity

may be the same as or different from their birth-assigned sex. People may see their gender identity as fluid and moving between different genders at different times in their life. 'Trans' can mean transcending beyond, existing between, or crossing over the gender spectrum."

"You see, Nana? It's a human rights issue. You can't discriminate against Trans people."

I read the sections on sexual identity and orientation. There is stuff I never heard of before. When did all this get invented? Like pansexual. Yes. That is a thing the kids learn in school. Do you know what it is? Well, let me explain. It is a person who has emotional, physical, spiritual and/or sexual attraction to people regardless of their gender or sex. Pan means *all*. So fine. Anything goes. Pandemonium. Pandemic. Panic.

Patty supported Gord through bouts of depression over the years, and she does not believe her husband will be happier as a woman. I don't have one single woman friend who keeps her self-esteem in her vagina, she says. I doubt he'll like it as much as he, sorry She. I doubt she'll like it as much as she thinks she will.

In five years, when Gloria is seventy, she will have completed all the steps to leaving Gord behind. Remodelling herself will take most of her time and energy. Hormone treatments, plastic surgeries, hair implants, and chondrolaryngoplasty. That is a surgical procedure to have down the Adam's apple. That one costs about six grand.

My dad used to spout off about how the world is going to

hell in a hand basket. His favourite way to start a doomsday conversation was to say, "I never thought I'd see the day…" He considered himself a fair man. An ethical man. A man of principle. A community-minded man who kept his commitments, even when they were difficult. But in his declining years, he was bothered by the things he observed from his porch chair. Tattooed teenagers. Grown men humiliating themselves, picking up dog shit and carrying it around in little bags. Stuff like that. If he would've lived to see Gord Power going willingly under the knife to have his own penis and ball sac severed, it would have killed him.

Meanwhile, the guys meet for morning coffee like they always do. They crowd around Ralph's iPad to watch the YouTube video of male to female surgery. Jim says it started out kind of jokey, but then Dave Nesbitt made a weird sound. Jim thought Dave might be choking on his toast, so he reached over to pound him on the back, and that's when Jim realized that Dave was not choking. He was crying.

Jim tells me that he heard the same strangled cry before, back when he was a cop. It was one of those awful nights. A kid died in a car wreck. A good kid. A designated driver that got T-boned by a drunk. And Jim had to ring the doorbell at two in the morning to tell the parents. The dad, like a lot of men who are not accustomed to crying, let out a grief sound, raw and ugly. Jim claims he'll never forget it. Anyway, Dave is making that sound and Jim says to Ralph Hicks, he says, "Shut that fucking thing off."

Ralph turns it off. Then he clears his throat and pushes his chair back and goes up to the cash register and pays for the whole table and heads out to the parking lot. The rest of the fellows pull on their coats and pick up their newspapers without looking each other in the eye.

They felt ashamed, I think. Like they had been watching a genocide. One that they maybe could've stopped if they'd seen it coming. But the time to do something about it is long past. The future of men is nothing but a mass grave of severed dicks, pink and doomed like baby bunnies.

Something's Burning

The real estate agent didn't mention that a guy died in this house, a two-bedroom bungalow on a quiet street. It was a good deal. About twenty thousand dollars under market value. I mean, it only has one bathroom. That's an issue for some. Most people want an ensuite bathroom these days, but I'm single now, and I intend to stay that way. The place is in good shape. New kitchen cupboards. Fresh drywall in the living room. But apparently everyone in town knew something that I didn't. I was digging out the scraggly lilac bush in the front yard when a woman marched up the driveway with measured and deliberate steps.

"I'm Helen," she said. "Welcome to the neighbourhood. I've always liked this little house." And then she asked me if I knew a man had burnt to death in the living room.

"No," I said. "I did not know."

"Yes," she told me. Her cheeks were pink with the adrenaline rush of being the first one to relay bad news, and the story spilled out of her a bit too fast. "It was a shock, living around the corner and the emergency vehicles pulling up in the middle of the afternoon. They had to cordon off the street, so the school kids didn't walk by and see the blackened remains when they carried him out. Horace Bell was his name."

"What happened?" I asked her.

She got real close to me and lowered her voice.

"Oh," she said. "Anger. He had this condition. You could see it. You could smell it, even. If he got mad, which happened a lot, like if somebody let their dog shit on his lawn? He would short circuit like a robot. And you could see steam rising off him."

I stepped on the shovel, trying to divide the root ball. "Seriously? No."

"Seriously. Ask anybody. Ask Grace next door what happened when the wind blew some Halloween decorations over to Horace's side of the driveway. It was a crepe paper spider, and a cardboard pumpkin and Horace grabbed them and crumpled them up and shoved them in Grace's garbage can. Ask Grace what she found when she pulled them out. They were scorched. Just as if somebody had put a hot iron to 'em, in the shape of hands."

I shake my head a bit and wait to find out if she's pulling my leg. But I can see she's not the kind of person to make something up. Especially a whopper like this. People named Helen are generally pragmatic rather than imaginative. Her orthopedic shoes lend evidence to my assessment.

"The TV was still on when the emergency vehicles arrived," she said. "Something he was watching must have got his temperature rising. Could have been any number of things. He lost his job, and his wife left him and his son married a man, and he blames the government for all of it, so who knows what might have started him burning. He melted right into the upholstery. Fire retardant, the material is nowadays, but the black smoke poured out the window, and that's how the next-door neighbour, not Grace, but Wilma on the other side…over there, see? With the blue lawn chairs on the porch? That's Wilma's place. She called 911. Wilma was shaken, I'll tell you. She needed sleeping pills after that."

"Well, thanks for the information," I said. I stuffed the lilac branches in the compost bin and washed my hands under the hose and, I'm not going to lie, I was looking for excuses to stay outside. But eventually the sun was setting, and the mosquitoes started biting and I had to go in. There was no sign of smoke damage or anything. The flooring was new. A laminate that looked almost like real wood. I wondered if there was a burn mark underneath. Where the chair had been. So, I went down to the basement and looked at the ceiling and, sure enough, there was an entire new piece of plywood and a couple of beams that were obviously replacements. I had skipped the home inspection. I figured I didn't need a scam artist to tell me the roof needs re-shingling. But a fire? That might have been good to know about.

I tried not to let it bother me. People die in homes all the time. Usually, they go quietly in their beds, but still.

Then one afternoon, I smell smoke while I'm watching a

documentary about homeless army vets. Refugees and illegal immigrants are taking money away from these poor guys that have served their country and now they are living on skid row. The stench gets more intense when the journalist interviews a double amputee who spends his days begging in front of City Hall. Maybe some neighbour has fired up the barbecue, I think. I go and stand on the front step and sniff the air. Nothing but honeysuckle.

About 7:15 the next evening, I smell something burning again. I put Fox News on mute and take a few deep breaths. Singed hair, acrid and harsh. Times like this, I wish I didn't live alone. I could use a roommate to confirm or deny that I am going crazy.

Gradually, I pick up bits and pieces of information about Horace Bell from the neighbours. Grace is a single mom.

"I wouldn't let my kids go nowhere near that man's house," she told me. "He had a business in town. A garage. He was a decent mechanic, but no social skills. His customer base was a bunch of grumpy old men who didn't mind listening to his theories about the big car companies and the computers they install in every new vehicle. Designed to break down a hundred kilometres after the warranty expires."

I have suspected this conspiracy myself when the engine light comes on while I am hurtling down the highway at high speeds. Or the exclamation mark, which is alarming. But really? It just means you need some air in your tires.

"For a while after the garage went bankrupt, he worked from home," Grace says. "He always had a car jacked up in the driveway and two or three parked vehicles in front of the house. He did oil changes, mostly. Cash only. But the bylaw officer put a stop to that. Then he got caught rolling back odometers. More charges and a suspended sentence. Then, last October, he threw a Molotov cocktail through the GM Dealership window."

"Did anybody get hurt?"

"No. It was the middle of the night, and the wick fizzled out before it got to the gasoline. But the webcam was watching."

I nod and try to concentrate but I'm distracted by the food stuck in between Grace's front teeth. Is it spinach?

"Horace was sentenced to sweep the floors at the arena," she says. "But what kind of community service is it when a guy scares little kids who track in a bit of mud on their boots? His toque would stink like woollen mittens on a heat register whenever a hockey mom got careless tossing her cardboard coffee cup at the garbage can. Then some money went missing from the cash box in the skate sharpener's booth and Horace was blamed. He swore it was a set up, but the judge was tired of seeing him and put him on house arrest. He was wearing one of those ankle bracelets when he died."

I launched an investigation into home confinement products, thinking maybe they were fire hazards. Could they short out if you tampered with them? I even called the fire chief and asked if there was any indication of a burn around Horace Bell's ankle. He couldn't release that information to the public, but when I told him I was living with Horace's ghost, he was sympathetic

"He just combusted, Ma'am. There's nothing to indicate

foul play or a defective tracking device. My advice to you is to get out of that house. Pronto. I been chief here for twenty-one years, and you know what? Some places never recover from a fire where a death occurs. I don't know why. Same thing happens in a place where there's been violence. Murder. Or a fatal accident. You can expect unexplained disturbances for years to come. Once it's been opened up, the gate to hell is hard to close."

Now that I'm divorced, I figure I should be able to watch whatever I like on TV. For years I sat through hockey games when I would have preferred The Bachelor. "What are you watching that crap for?" my husband would ask if he came home and caught me sneaking a peek at a rose ceremony. But it turns out Horace Bell is sensitive to my program choices, too.

Women arguing on talk shows brings on a reek like fat sizzling in a deep fryer. Anything about unemployment or debt or politics can cause a chemical smell, like plastic melting. If I stick to game shows and home renovations, Horace stays happy. But I can't always control the media. One afternoon, right in the middle of Family Feud, the survey asks, "What are some bad jobs for people who are accident-prone?"

"Driver," one contestant shouts.

"Construction worker," is another guess.

All of a sudden, the program is interrupted to announce a terrorist attack in the nation's capital. The gunman has a foreign name.

And, what the hell! My ass is on fire. I jump off the couch and run outside and grab the hose and start spraying my butt.

It's smoking. Helen's head pops over the back fence. She's always on Neighbourhood Watch duty, that woman. "Hot day," I call out to her as pleasantly as possible considering my bum is scorched. The last thing I need is a rumour going around that there is paranormal activity in my house.

That night, I lie in bed and worry about immolation. I suspect that Horace Bell could burn me in my bed if he decided that was what he wanted to do. But I have never believed a person to be totally good, or totally evil. When All-Star Wrestling comes to the local arena, I root for the bad guy. The evil dude who gets all the boos. There's something vulnerable about a villain. Not that I want the job of curator for a dead man's reputation, but I hold out hope for the discovery of one redeeming quality in Horace Bell.

In answer to these ruminations comes a cry outside my window, like a baby left on the doorstep. I crawl out of bed and open the patio door to find a ginger tomcat. Now, I'm not really a cat person, but this guy has some manners. He sits on the mat, still and cautious, giving us both a chance to look the other one over. He sees a sour-faced woman in a faded flannel nightgown with a long grey braid running halfway down her back. I see a scruffy old stray with one ear split in half, a sore eye and some mange eating away his hind end.

The next day, Helen affirms my suspicions that the cat belonged to Horace Bell. "Yes," she says. "That cat was a stray around here for a long time, and Horace hated him. Sprayed him with the hose, threw tools at him. But Charlie stood his ground. He sat just out of range and watched Horace as he worked on cars. Eventually they adopted each other."

"Charlie?"

"He also called him *you goddamned orange bastard.*"

"Well," I say. "If I intended to keep him, I'd call him Charlie. That suits him. But unfortunately, I'm not fond of cats."

"You can drop him off at the Humane Society," Helen suggests. "Otherwise, he'll likely keep turning up. He's a stubborn creature."

So that is what I decide to do. Take him to the shelter. But when I go inside to get him, he has disappeared. I look everywhere, under beds, in cupboards, behind the furnace. I even open a can of tuna to tempt him. Nothing. He must have snuck out the door when I wasn't looking. Good. Problem solved.

After supper, two things happen. First, I smell something burning. "For crying out loud, Horace!" I say. Then Charlie propels himself from his hiding place behind the buffet and, shrieking like a banshee from the haunted swamp, he pounces on the exact place where Horace's chair went up in flames. Then he lies down, licks his paws and looks at me for a little acknowledgment.

"Good boy, Charlie," I tell him. "Well done."

It costs me three hundred dollars to pay for his shots, ointment for the mange, a litter box, a scratching post and a big bag of the good kind of cat food that veterinarians recommend. If I am going to have a cat guarding the gates of hell, I do not intend to be cheap about it.

We get along fine. And whenever Horace tries to escape from his eternal furnace, Charlie arches his back, dances around the perimeter of the living room, and launches himself at his invisible nemesis. When it's all clear, Charlie hops up in my lap and emits a deeply satisfying victory purr. He lifts his chin and I stroke him on the throat.

"Abandon all hope, ye who enter here," I tell Charlie. And then I turn on the TV and watch whatever I like.

Games Of Wrath

Atlanta won the bid to host the Olympics. Muhammad Ali himself was going to light the torch in the summer of 1996. The world was coming, and the IOC expected the city to be at its best before the athletes showed up. The venues were erected at staggering costs. Stadiums and coliseums and arenas. Olympic Village. An aquatic centre. A shooting complex and a velodrome. And there was some trash to take out. Namely, the unsightly homeless. Beggars and druggies and mental cases who wandered the streets, intimidating upstanding citizens and stinking up the joint. What was to be done with them? One city councillor came up with the idea to give them all a fresh start. A gift.

Indigent resettlement? No. Nothing like that. No pogroms. Just a special offer. A bus ticket anywhere in the U.S.A. Think about it! Pack up your shopping cart, Darlin' and hop on the bus to a new life.

If you are homeless, you are not accustomed to travel. You crouch in that lower echelon of Maslow's triangle, thinking about your immediate needs. Food. Shelter. A place to have a bowel movement.

And then an officer tells you to head over to the bus station.

"Special offer," he says. "Where do you want to go?" he asks.

You are not sure. Because poverty has been limiting your choices for a long time. You are out of the habit of making decisions. You just go along the path of least resistance like rain falling off a roof.

You know in your heart that this is no damn favour being offered here. They want you out. Gone. Away. You are dirt. They are sweeping up the streets to make way for prettier, more productive people.

Bye bye.

Still. A chance. An opportunity. What will it be? L.A.? Portland? Or Rock Lake, where your grandpa had that little cabin. He took you fishing there, once, when you were seven years old, and you can still recall the smell of pine trees and hear the frogs. You made a campfire on the rocky outcropping and fried up some trout. It was someplace in the Ozarks. You could find it again. You are sure of it.

You remember the story by Steinbeck about the Joad family who went west when their farm fell on hard times. They crawled out of the dust bowl with a truck full of pots and pans and bedsprings, headed for the golden land. California. Where the oranges hung heavy from low branches, begging to be picked. The thought of sucking on that sweet juice kept them going. They made it. Finally. But then they realized they weren't wanted. "Turn around," the sheriff said. "Go back where you came from, ya dirty Okies."

You are homeless, not naive. You understand that people in other towns, other cities, won't be pleased to see y'all stepping off the bus with your stinking sacks of shitty possessions. You know what you look like. So, you think, be wise for once. Pick a place where you can fly under the radar. Not California, with the models and movie stars and beauty queens. If California didn't want the Okies, they sure as hell won't want Atlanta's down and outs.

Rosa Newton was a journalist back in '96, newly graduated from the state college. Everyone was covering the Olympics, mad to get interviews with the runners and the swimmers and the gymnasts. But Rosa heard a rumour that there might be a story down at the Greyhound Station on Forsyth Street, SW. There was a fight out front when the cab pulled up. Screaming and hair pulling and a glass bottle smashing and a police officer intervening with a baton.

"This ain't no place for a girl like y'all," the cab driver told Rosa.

"It's okay," she said. "I'm a reporter."

She wished she had something to identify her as "media". Like a card to stick in the band of a grey fedora. Daily Planet. Nobody would mess with her. Instead, she wore her camera around her neck and held her notebook out ahead of her like a beacon to part the darkness. It didn't even get her close to the front door.

Rosa went back across the street and sat on the edge of a fountain. A cement tub that used to be a fountain. A once-upon-a-fountain, filled with garbage. Not garbage that you might see at the college, but nasty garbage, like soiled panties and needles and sticky Slurpee cups, the spoilage of lives gone wrong. An older woman sitting close by caught her trying to take a photograph. Her eyes, rimmed with something crusty and yellow, were knowing. I see what you are trying to capture here, they said. I see the part I play in your biased narrative.

Rosa asked her anyway. "Are you leaving the city? Did you get a ticket?"

"Yes," the woman said. "I'm going to Phoenix."

The woman's voice was clear and sure. Gwyneth was her name. Strands of greasy hair escaped from under her felt hat. A hat with a wide brim that would have suited Annie Oakley or Janis Joplin. It characterized her. You would remember her. That woman with the hat. Over her black t-shirt and black men's trousers she wore a green crocheted vest with a fringe that swept her knees. She might have been an artist or an eccentric English professor. From a distance.

"Your eyes look sore," Rosa said.

"Yes," Gwyneth admitted. "They are."

Rosa scrambled around in her backpack for the drops she kept there.

"Here. These will help."

Gwyneth took her hat off and placed it next to her. She tilted her head and squeezed the little plastic bottle until clear liquid dropped into her eyes. She cringed.

Rosa wished she had a warm washcloth to give the woman.

Instead, she handed over her own sunglasses. "Take these. The sun out in Arizona is strong. And Gwyneth? Can you drop me a postcard when you get settled? Tell me how it is. How it all works out for you."

Rosa had twenty stamped, self-addressed postcards in her backpack. The World is Coming to Atlanta, the postcards promised, above five interlocking circles. Gwyneth put the postcard in a zippered pocket on the side of her cargo pants before disappearing into the bus station where the cleansing was taking place, efficiently and without protest.

Gwyneth boards the bus behind Sally, a young mother who has LIFE SUCKS tattooed on her knuckles. The bus is full, so she knows she'll be sharing a seat with someone, and that doesn't bother her. Gwyneth is accustomed to making herself small and invisible. She is the fourth of nine children from a pecan plantation east of Gainesville, Florida. Her mother was always sick, and her dad was always tired. Her older brothers were angry boys who were either fighting or brooding.

Gwyneth keeps to the shadows and expects nothing more than to be left alone. When she quit going to school at fourteen, nobody came looking for her. When she left home and got work at the truck stop up Highway 75, just north of the Georgia border, nobody raised the alarm. If she had died in a ditch, Gwyneth knew for certain that nobody, except the coyotes, would care. So, when she sees that nobody wants to sit with the young mother and the squawking baby, she slides into the adjacent seat like a cipher, taking up space without requiring recognition. She might as well be a suitcase.

After the bus leaves the station and the baby settles down, sucking on a green Tootsie pop, Sally turns and looks Gwyneth up and down and starts talking about Niagara Falls.

"You can't even hear a person talk, even if they're standing right next to you," she says. "The sound of the falls is so loud. That's what I am looking forward to. I don't care if I ever hear another human voice. I been yelled at my entire life."

Gwyneth stays erect and still in her seat. She doesn't have a good sense of her own parameters, so she errs on the side of giving people more room than they might actually need wherever she settles. In church. At the mission table where they serve soup. In the hostel that she seeks out on cold nights. Here on the bus, she is right on the edge of her seat, as close to the aisle as she can get without falling off. Sally misinterprets. Thinks the woman is maybe racist. Doesn't like blacks. Until Sally hears the cadence of fear in the older woman's voice and recognizes her as somebody who's had the shit beat out of her.

"I'm going to Phoenix," Gwyneth whispers.

"It's okay. You can speak up," Sally tells her. "I didn't really mean what I said about human voices. What's your name, then? I'm Sally. And this here's Abigail."

"I'm called Gwyneth. You been to jail?" she asks, nodding to the knuckle tats.

"Juvie. You know, Juvenile Detention Centre. I ran with a bad crowd before she came along," Sally says, nodding toward the little girl who is crawling on the floor picking at a wad of old gum. "My Daddy told me and told me, if you run with the wolves, you die with the wolves. He was happy when they locked me up. Maybe he's right. It might have saved my life."

The baby crawls up onto Gwyneth's lap and she cringes a bit as the sticky fingers explore her vest, but eventually, she relaxes and melts into her new reality without protest. When Sally and the little girl nod off, Gwyneth closes her own eyes and thinks about Phoenix. She likes the idea of finding work on a ranch, mucking out the stalls, listening to the soft noises of horses. In her mind, Phoenix is a cowboy town, rural. With dirt roads.

Sally is a black, heterosexual Christian with borderline personality disorder. This is all according to her profile compiled at the correctional facility, where identity is everything. You got to know who you are. What your history is. What your skills are. And your failings. The psychologist at the facility was a fat German woman who helped her establish the pathology of her mental health issues, but it was the other inmates who insisted she nail down her identity. Are you black? How black? Somalian black? Jamaican black? Plantation black? What you know about your ancestors? Who you want to associate with? Pick a side and stick with your story if you 'spect to belong.

Sally knows that her grandmother on her Daddy's side was a housekeeper for a rich white family. That Granny raised her kids alone after her husband got killed in Vietnam. Granny had a sister, Sally's great aunt, who had a boy who played professional baseball and would have been super famous if he hadn't gotten murdered. There was a cousin's brother-in-law that did some civil rights work alongside Dr. King. Or at least he marched in Montgomery. Rode that bus to the protest or something. Granny showed her the newspaper clipping once, but all that was lost. All those memories died with the old woman. Sally hopes that her daughter, Abigail, will get educated. Be somebody. Somebody with a home on a nice street with a porch and a backyard. Somebody with a car. And a job. And a good coat. And high heeled leather boots.

Gwyneth is relieved when the time comes for her to transfer buses in Knoxville. Sally and her little girl will keep going up I-75 for a ways and then transfer northeast up to Niagara Falls. America is so big. She will never see them again. She wishes them luck and follows a young man with a guitar up the aisle. They are both headed west on a bus that is not so crowded. They sit far apart. They do not speak. But there is an invisible thread connecting them. Gwyneth is aware that he is quite possibly her last connection to Atlanta. His Braves cap is pulled low over his eyes in a protective way. When he stands to disembark in Nashville, she catches his eye and nods, and he nods back. Gwyneth senses that he is determined, like she is, to make a go of it. She digs in her pocket for the eye drops Rosa gave her and tilts her head back and Lord, how good that feels. How soothing.

Dink leaves Atlanta in the late afternoon on a bus headed southwest toward New Orleans. He served in Nam with a guy nicknamed Cannonball after some jazz musician. Cannonball told him to come visit. "Ask anybody in Lafitte where I'm at. Everybody knows me."

The sun is low in the sky when Dink notices a scraggly-looking old gal wander past his seat, on her way back to the toilet. Dink decides he better do the same, but ten minutes go by, and the woman does not emerge. He's been watching the door, trying not to think about pissing himself. He shouldn't have had that second coffee at the bus station. After twenty minutes, with his bladder bursting, he knocks on the door and gets no reply. So he begs her, letting her know how urgent the whole situation is. Nothing. The little occupied sign does not budge.

"Ma'am," he finally says in desperation. "I sure hope you're not in trouble in there. I feel like I might have to get the driver to stop the bus and check on you, but I don't want to interfere if you need privacy. Still and all, if you want to talk about your troubles, I'm a good listener. Just, please come on out of there. Let me relieve myself."

The little sign clicks to green. Vacant. Deanna peaks her head out. She is a wreck of a woman, that is plain to see. With ruined makeup and haunted eyes and missing teeth. Dink hugs her. Whatever made him do that, he could not have explained. It felt right.

Dink stands over that little tin toilet for at least four minutes of painful dribbling. Then he goes and sits beside Deanna and asks if she wants to talk first or listen first and she says listen. So Dink tells her the current version of his story. It lasts all the way to Panama City, Florida where they stop at an IHOP. Over pancakes, Deanna tells her story and Dink thinks she has made life rough on herself. Rougher than it needs to be. The peeling pink polish on her manly ridged fingernails makes him think that turning into a woman can't be easy. But he offers no advice.

Neither one of them feel better after all the sour milk is spilled, but it eases the bad ache somewhat. At Biloxi,

Deanna is desperate to get off the bus and she collects herself, puts her purse over her arm, wishes Dink well and disappears into the mist of a Mississippi morning. She likes the look of the gulf waters as the sun breaks through. Otherwise, there is no reasonable explanation as to why she does not stick it out to New Orleans. But it turns out to be a good place for her to land. On her feet. In a scuffed-up pair of ballet flats that are much too tight.

Dink is alone for the last stretch of his journey, and he does not mind. He is social enough when he needs to be, but he likes his own thoughts and Deanna has given him a lot to think about. Why, for instance, did he spin out the myth of his hard-scrabble childhood? Because, truth be told, he had quite a pleasant growing up experience. It just seems easier, sometimes, to present an excuse as to why he ended up the way he did. A mean old Daddy and a drunk of a mother elicit sympathy. He'd had good luck with it in the past, even had a few dinners bought for him. It was like acting in a movie. The fact that it may be dishonest, and that honesty might be a worthy characteristic, is only just occurring to him. His parents were hard-working, honest people. They taught him right from wrong. But, through no fault of their own, they raised up a liar and a cheat and a coward and an addict. A goddamn calamity. Deanna's truth made Dink feel guilty. His pretense of childhood suffering, shameful. Not that he hasn't suffered. He has. But that story is deep in the muck at the bottom of the Mekong River.

Gwyneth stepped off the bus into the 100-degree heat of

a Phoenix afternoon. She sought out some shade under a concrete canopy and put on Rosa's sunglasses and gathered her thoughts. She was not in a foreign country. This was still the United States of America. Back in fifth grade, she coloured in the geographic features of Arizona. Yellow desert. Purple mountains. Blue for the Colorado River. Orange for the Grand Canyon. It seemed that all the grandeur possible in the world came together in Arizona. And yet here she was, in a bus station that looked and smelled no different than the bus station back in Atlanta.

Sally heard the falls before she saw them. She felt the vibrations coming up through the ground. It was like standing next to train tracks. No. The hum went deeper than that. She walked along Niagara Street and followed the path to Prospect Point and stood at the brink of the falls with Abigail in her arms, until the fine spray cleansed them.

After a time, they walked back toward the city. It was not a prosperous place, downtown Niagara Falls, New York. Empty buildings. Rusty fences. Garbage that had wintered under drifts of snow. And something else, under the shabbiness. Barely perceptible. A shift in the way the planet was turning. A difference in the slant of the rays of the sun.

Sally stopped in front of a shop window to check her own reflection, and someone tapped on the glass from the inside, beckoning her. Sally let herself be led along a long hallway by a woman with sleeve tattoos and bangled wrists. She accepted sandwiches and apples from another woman whose hands had been burned in some terrible accident. She let herself be driven to a women's shelter by a woman with painted on eyebrows.

It was as if she had jumped into the Niagara River and given herself and her child up to the current with utmost trust.

The woman at the shelter looked too old to be still working, but she made it clear she wouldn't take any shit. Not from Sally or Abigail or some pissed off boyfriend or a cop or the Lord himself. She laid out the rules. Sally agreed to them and then the woman softened up and gave Abigail a colouring book and let her dig through a box of shoes to find a pair that fit. Abby picked some pink ones with purple laces. That night, Sally and Abigail slept in a room with two single beds and a real door with a lock on it.

It didn't take long for Jeremy to come up against the hard side of Nashville, Tennessee. He was not stupid. And he had a talent for reading people. So, he saw right away that most of the tourists were not all that discerning in their appreciation of music. The cover bands that had a big repertoire of country favourites, the ones who would take requests and joke around with the drunks, they were the headliners. If you wanted to hear some real talent, a singer-songwriter in survival mode, you had to seek out the mid-afternoon shift. A guy would walk in, carrying his own amp and plug it in and do a sound check and then he'd set up on a stool and look around at the three or four people who were still finishing their fries from a late lunch, or maybe waiting for a girlfriend to get off her shift. No big tippers, that's for sure. That's how it works in Nashville. The musicians survive on tips. Those bands in the big honky-tonks on the main strip, they have a whole schtick, passing the bucket and jollying the crowd out of their five-dollar bills. But

Jeremy could see right off he would never make a living here in Nashville. He was ready to leave. Suck it up and admit it was a stupid idea. Go on back to his mother's apartment and hope she had broken up with Wilfred, the guy whose guitar he stole. Not that Wilf could play worth a shit, but he was probably wondering where it was so he could pawn it. By now, Wilf and his mom had put two and two together, thinking it was no coincidence that Jeremy and the guitar had both disappeared around about the same time.

Jeremy wandered the streets. Checked out the cowboy stores where the smell of leather hit you as soon as you walked in the door. He sat by the river and wished he knew the name of it. He asked a guy who was sweeping up garbage and the guy didn't know either. A fellow in a suit overheard and told them. It's the Cumberland River, he said. Jeremy repeated the name to himself a few times softly, so to remember it. Then he walked up to the Ryman Theatre and read the plaque and stepped into the foyer, hoping to slip into the concert hall, see the stage.

The guy at the ticket window said, "Can I help you, son?"

Jeremy got choked up. Nobody in his whole life had ever called him son. And as he hesitated, the fellow said, "The musician's entrance is around the side, if that's what you're looking for." Jeremy nodded and thanked the man. He looked like a musician! Back outside, he wandered around the corner and saw the steps leading up to a steel door, propped open with a chair. The musician's entrance. A girl in western attire was leaning on the iron banister, having a cigarette. He walked past and nodded to her, and she nodded back.

Deanna liked Biloxi. The impermanence of the place appealed to her. Like an illegal craps game in a back alley that could pack up and disappear if the cops came around the corner. The casinos were all on barges. So, technically, they were afloat in the gulf and not part of the city. They could be launched anytime. Just unhook the gangplanks and give 'em a good kick and the flotilla of slot machines would sail away, leaving Biloxi pure and free of the scourge that was gambling. An addiction that led people to drink and drugs and sexual perversions. Deanna's kind of people. Not because she was an addict herself. But because she was good with addicts. She recognized the seven symptoms of mania, from fun to 911. She had experienced a range of depressions from feeling blue to suicidal despair, so she knew it was useless to try to solve other people's problems or probe into childhood traumas. Didn't even try. "Looks like you're having a bad day," was about the extent of her counselling strategy. No social worker degree needed. Just a nudge to push a guy through to the far side of his rough patch.

Deanna finds a room at the Seashore Mission on Division Street. The pastor has a friend who is hiring dealers over at Boomtown. The job comes with a uniform, and the manager forwards her a couple days pay so she can "do something" with her hair. She'd once been a pretty man, but with thinning hair and a prominent Adam's apple, she is homely as a hedge fence. One of the waitresses, Lonnie, offers to sell her two wigs for a hundred bucks. Her mother's, who died recently of ovarian cancer. They are good quality. This is the reason Deanna took the drastic step of transitioning from male to female. She longs for the intimacy between girlfriends. Her big sister used to slam the door in her face when she begged to sit and watch as she applied lipstick and chatted on the phone about Butterick sewing patterns and the cheerleader who got pregnant and the boy who everyone thought was the father. Guys didn't have an equivalent for that kind of relationship.

Deanna buys the wigs, a blonde layered chin length, perfect for work, and a shoulder length platinum for dates. She plans to get back on the hormones and have the feminization operations. She will take care of herself.

Dink made it to New Orleans. He didn't hold out much hope for Deanna. Biloxi was a hard town. A low place. New Orleans wasn't a whole heck of a lot better. There was no sign of Cannonball, but he liked the vibe. Music for the soul, Lake Ponchartrain for fishing, and Jackson Square for telling fortunes. He had a talent for clairvoyance, and no one questioned him when he offered to share his psychic powers for five dollars. It was a good gig if he could manage to change his habit of getting drawn into peoples' schemes like some kind of an idiot. That is how he got into the damn army. That is how he got himself kicked out of the damn army, too. That is how he hijacked a truck full of frozen seafood and got thrown in jail before he could sell the stuff. He had a long history of failure, but he was surprised, nonetheless, to hit rock bottom. New Orleans was likely his last kick at the can. He was over fifty, now, and not in the best of health. Some kind of open sore on his leg was giving him grief.

Rosa lost her job in 2015. Newspapers were history. She started teaching a journalism course at the state college. She wrote a blog about women and business that met with some success and had a series of articles published in Atlantic Magazine. They helped her land an interview with NPR, and she found herself writing human interest stories for an afternoon show. When she got an email from Deanna, one of her Atlanta homeless people, she pitched the story to her producer and got a green light.

Of the twenty postcards Rosa handed out that day back in 1996, she got four back. Gwyneth's came first, arriving within a week. "Thank you," it said, "for the eye drops. They help a lot."

She also received a reply from Sally B., who boarded the bus to Niagara Falls with a three-year-old on her hip and a canvas pack on her back. And one from Jeremy who carried a guitar with all the tender attachment of a lover. The biggest surprise was the postcard and ongoing letters from Dink, the army vet whose shoes were bound to his feet with duct tape. She almost didn't waste a postcard on him, he was so filthy and messed up. His ravings included flashes of brilliance about science and history and social justice. So many did not respond. Of course not. It was a dumb idea. Or was it?

A week after Trump was sworn in, some twenty years after the Atlanta Olympics, Rosa received an email from Deanna.

I found your postcard in an old handbag, she said. *Sorry to take so long to reply.*

Rosa remembered Deanna clearly. A delicate trans woman with wispy shoulder length hair that she tucked behind her ears continuously, like a teenage girl.

May I come for a visit? Rosa typed back.

Of course, Deanna agreed.

Rosa pitched the story to her producer. The story of her emigrants. How they fared when Atlanta cast them out.

Funny. When she covered the story at the bus terminal in 1996, she considered it a total failure. Her submission, earnest with idealism, was turned down by the editor at the Journal-Constitution. Too controversial. There was no proof that the City Council supported the mass exodus of homeless people to points unknown. Who paid the bus lines? The IOC? The Russians? Nobody knew. Or if they did know, they weren't saying anything. Somebody, Rosa was sure, knew something. And she was quite certain that the crowd of indigent people at the bus depot that day was more than an urban myth. She was young, but she saw it all with her own eyes, and she was willing to give voice to the voiceless, but at what cost? Lesson one in journalism school -You don't get to pick the headlines. If you want a paycheck, you do what you're told and shut up about the rest.

Deanna gave a candid and emotional interview about her experience. It motivated Rosa to update her investigation. Injustice and political cover ups are hot topics. If some aging millionaires think they got away with relocating Atlanta's ragged people, she tells her producer, well they have another thing coming.

Dink was easy to find through Veterans Affairs. And his memory was intact. He was that rare storyteller, a genius who understood humanity, but struggled to maintain his own basic needs. He bounced around, from one brilliant idea to the next, making a living for a while and then sabotaging it for himself. Learning a trade, then trading it for an ill-advised scam. He admitted that he was often the master of his own disasters.

"I'm a survivor," he told Rosa. "But most of the folks at the bus station that day were not. I fear they did not have the strength to start over. All those postcards you didn't get back? They likely ended up in a gutter somewhere."

Sally, in Niagara Falls, had met with moderate success. She worked at a Long-Term Care home for the elderly and raised her daughter, Abigail, to set goals and achieve them. Abby was a graduate student of African American Studies at SUNY Buffalo State. And she was more than willing to do a radio interview with Rosa on the disposability of poor people. Poor black people in particular.

Jeremy had done okay for a while, working at the new arena in Nashville. He had been only 17 years old when he left Atlanta. His postcard, written in childish scrawl, asked Rosa to check on his mother. Rosa went to the address he gave her and knocked on the door.

"Are you Jeremy's mother?"

"That depends."

"He asked me to look in on you."

"Where the hell is he? He owes me some money."

Rosa found Jeremy at the Bridgestone Arena. He is a zamboni driver for the Nashville Predators. She interviewed him at The Full Moon Saloon, where he plays afternoon gigs. He has a girlfriend who tends bar and a golden retriever named Georgia.

Gwyneth didn't stay in Phoenix long. She hitchhiked up to Sedona and camped with some hippies near the Cathedral vortex until she heard about work at a candle factory in Flagstaff. That didn't work out, but it led her to the Grand Canyon where she got a job cleaning rooms in the Maswik Lodge. Room and board were deducted from her pay. She met a man named Willie, a mule hack. Willy cared for the poor creatures that slave away carrying tourists down into the canyon and back up again. In 2006, they had their fill of tourists and bought a trailer in Wickenburg, a cowboy town. That is where Rosa interviewed them. They had a lot to say about respect and how the lack of it erases a person. It was one of the "most listened to" interviews of the series.

Rosa kept digging. The interviews would be more authentic with evidence of intention. She wanted to know how many were rounded up that spring. How many boarded buses. Who went willingly? Were any coerced? What percentage were black? Mentally ill? There had to be at least three or four hundred. A conservative estimate. There could have been a thousand or more. Rosa made phone calls. She visited the bus depot and the mayor's office. She made connections with police officers at precincts in rough downtown neighbourhoods. It was frustrating work, but she talked to enough people who remembered, vaguely perhaps, but yes, it did happen.

"There was a round up," says the nurse in the meth clinic. "Hell, yes, you can use my name. I was right here. I watched them line up for tickets like they were offered a free Caribbean cruise. They cooperated, mostly. And why wouldn't they? Those Greyhound buses were luxurious, with reclining seats.

Air conditioning. Tinted windows. It all seemed perfectly civilized except for a few tussles over what they were allowed to take with them and what had to go in the dumpsters. I had a vague sense that it wasn't right, but I didn't do anything. It wasn't until years later I wished I'd spoken up. But there was no denying that this area was instantly prettier without the sleeping bags and cardboard mattresses and shopping carts full of crap."

"I often wonder what happened to them," says the guy who owns a cigarette and newspaper kiosk. "One fellow had no legs, Danny. He motored around on a skateboard. He did okay begging over by the convenience store. And there was a woman with a funny little ferret that she kept in her apron pocket. And a guy who thought he was The Boss. He knew all the words to I'm on Fire. You know, *Someone took a knife baby, edgy and dull and cut a six-inch valley through the middle of my skull.* Freaky. He scared people who didn't know he was just quoting Springsteen lyrics. And there were lots more like him. They just disappeared. Like they walked off the earth."

"Did they make out okay, do you think?"

"Probably not," he said. "They had a community here. People knew their names. If one of them took a heart attack or OD'd, someone had their back. You get dropped off in a town where nobody knows you? You die in an alleyway like a dog."
Rosa finally gets a break, following a tip from a guy who knows a guy who has a cousin who used to work at City Hall. The cousin, it turns out, is an eighty-year-old retired clerk named Constance Bain who worked for three different mayors. In the months leading up to the Summer Olympics, her office was

tasked with resolving some mistakes, misunderstandings and outright crimes committed by high-ranking politicians and dignitaries.

The Olympic Games represent unshakable core values. Friendship, respect, excellence, equality, inspiration and courage. Constance Bain's parents gifted her with a name that stands for steadfastness and honesty. So it chaffed her, like a pea under her mattress, to cover up the dirty deeds of those who triumphed, not on the athletic field, but in the arena of wealth and power. Until the day Rosa knocked on her door, no one was interested in looking at the incriminating documents, receipts, bank statements.

It takes a certain kind of vigilance to guard the burden of an unpopular truth. And enough resolve to survive cautions and insults and even threats. Rosa recognizes the reticence in Constance Bain's voice when she calls to request an interview. She herself is protective of this story, and wary of those who would prefer to subvert it.

Rosa parks her car in front of a tired bungalow on Highland Avenue. A whiff of fried onions escapes as Constance Bain opens the door. Rosa respectfully takes her shoes off and follows Constance down a narrow wallpapered hallway. They sit at the kitchen table and Rosa turns down a slice of lemon cake as politely as possible before describing her research. She shows Constance photographs and describes the trajectory of her podcast.

"I think you'll agree that it might be of interest to listeners if we had some evidence to prove that the resettlement scheme was intentional."

"Come," Constance says, simply. "Watch your step," she says as they descend into the basement. Past the washer and dryer is a desk with a brass study lamp, a stapler, a hole puncher and a mason jar full of pens. It looks like a war room in a secret bunker.

Constance reaches up on tip toes and pulls the string on a bare overhead light bulb. She points at a locked metal cabinet in the corner.

"It's all there. And it's all yours," she says.

Rosa feels the weight of the burden as it transfers to her shoulders.

"May I?" she asks.

Constance nods.

Rosa opens the top drawer and her heart leaps to see the carefully labelled file folders. Names and dates pour forth, like the product of a vineyard where the games of wrath are stored.

"Glory, glory, Hallelujah!" she whispers.

Acknowledgments

I want to acknowledge my enduring love and appreciation for friends and family members who contributed the tinder that sparked the stories in *Something's Burning*. How could you know that the experience you shared with me would smoulder in my memory and provide precious fuel for fiction. Like logs on a fire, all our joys and sorrows are piled together, connecting us and keeping us warm in the gloaming. Thank you from the bottom of my charred heart.

Also, it has been a pleasure to work with the At Bay Press team who combine Canadian literature and book design with stunning results. Special recognition goes to editor Nina McIntyre with her fresh and insightful perspectives, and to the eternally encouraging publisher, Matt Joudrey (the guy with the match).

Photo: Merron Vermeer

Janet Trull's debut collection of fiction, *Hot Town and Other Stories*, was hailed as fearless and perceptive by reviewers, and received a nomination for a Manitoba Book Award. With characters as lonely and isolated as rural Canadian backroads, Trull's stories continue to examine the shifting landscape of identity.